THE DARK FIGHTS

ALEXANDRA VINAROV

THE DARK FIGHTS

BLACK STONE
PUBLISHING

Copyright © 2020 by Alexandra Vinarov
Published in 2020 by Blackstone Publishing
Cover and book design by Sean M. Thomas

Printed in the United States of America

First edition: 2020
ISBN 978-1-982682-44-6
Fiction / Action & Adventure

1 3 5 7 9 10 8 6 4 2

CIP data for this book is available
from the Library of Congress

Blackstone Publishing
31 Mistletoe Rd.
Ashland, OR 97520

www.BlackstonePublishing.com

For my parents and for my brother

CHAPTER 1

There are no more than ten people in the ER waiting room. It is past eleven at night and rather quiet, NY1 News humming drowsily somewhere in the background. Danilo is sitting with his eyes closed, taking careful, measured breaths. I suspect he has broken ribs, and I hope he doesn't have any internal bleeding. He cannot move his right arm—the shoulder must have been dislocated or separated. I look at his face and have to blink rapidly to control the tears. A broken nose with crusts of dried blood, huge bruises, cuts. His beautiful face is now almost unrecognizable.

"It's all right," Danilo says with difficulty. It hurts him to move his lips. He is not the type of man to withstand pain. I am not sure if it's true that some people have naturally high pain thresholds, but I do know that you can train yourself to raise your tolerance. You acknowledge the pain, take it in, and deal with it. Danny cannot do that. He feels the pain acutely and does not know how to cope with it, how to process it, and so he is suffering now. I can see it, and I wish it was I who felt the pain instead.

"It's all right," he says. Damn it. Nothing is all right. I clench my fists and breathe deeply, in and out, trying to calm down. I feel so bad for Danny. I can't remember the last time I cried, and now it's all I can do to hold back the tears—but I'm also angry with him. He promised he would stay away from 2 Gild Street.

When the bartender from Wolf Flannigan's pub called saying Danilo had been dropped off there in rather bad shape and I'd better come get him, I got a cold spasm in my stomach. Wolf Flannigan's is right around the corner from 2 Gild Street. I do not believe in coincidences.

Ah, damn it! He promised. He looked me in the eye and promised. But then again, Danilo is not the type of man who can keep his word. He never could. I have a few questions to ask him, but now is not the time.

In an effort to divert my thoughts I look around the room, take in the silent figures sitting here at this late hour. One man in particular catches my attention. He is perhaps in his thirties, has a muscular build and cropped hair. He's wearing old jeans and a fisherman's sweater. He frowns and glances at his watch every few minutes. He looks very tired and you can tell he hates this waiting. I wonder what brought him here. Must be his hand, which looks very swollen. I bet one of the bones is broken. He glances at me several times and smiles—a weary, barely perceptible sort of smile. He then shifts his gaze to Danilo's face, frowns again, and shakes his head slightly.

I lean back in the chair, close my eyes, and go back to my breathing exercises. Breathe in deeply, imagine the air moving to the back of my head, then swallow, bring it down to a point just below the navel, hold it, and then breathe out very slowly. This helps me to relax, and I probably doze off for a minute or so.

The next moment the room seems to explode with deafening shouts and chaotic movement.

I am not sure if the person causing this has just come in from the street or from the inside of the hospital. He was definitely not one of the people in the waiting room. He's a big guy in his twenties, now moving around in a frenzy, kicking chairs, and screaming. He then turns toward an older woman who is sitting by herself on a cushioned bench positioned somewhat away from the other seats. He removes a switchblade from his jeans pocket and goes straight for the woman, all the while shouting a mixture of threats and obscenities. Panicked, the woman jumps up and steps back until she is backed into a corner.

Fixing my eyes on the knife, I have gotten up and moved in close, and I'm now standing barely a few feet away, not letting the hand with the knife out of my sight. But my interference is not needed.

The following sequence of events occurs within a span of no more than two or three seconds. It all goes so quickly that, for an untrained eye, it is hard to grasp what has just happened. One moment the aggressor is standing up wielding the knife, next he is flat on the ground, and the man in the fisherman's sweater has him in a choke hold. In slow motion it would look like this—

"Hey asshole," the man in the sweater shouts to divert the attacker's attention. The latter jerks his head and freezes for a moment but doesn't change his course.

The man in the sweater rushes over and positions himself between the attacker and the woman in the corner.

Next, he intercepts the hand with the knife and twists the wrist until the knife falls out of it.

In the finale of this perfectly executed sequence, he throws his opponent down, landing on top of him, and puts him in a choke hold.

The security guards are at the scene already, and soon thereafter NYPD officers arrive. They talk to the man in the sweater and thank him for neutralizing the attacker. When the man replies, I can hear he has some kind of an Eastern European accent, but it does not sound Russian.

His hands handcuffed behind him, muttering something unintelligible under his breath, the aggressor is led away. After this, things quiet down surprisingly fast. I look around, and except for the old lady, nobody seems all that rattled—not the patients, nor the hospital personnel, who return to their work almost right away. Maybe the danger of the incident has not quite sunk in yet, or perhaps we have been New Yorkers too long, for better or for worse.

The situation does bring us closer for a time. All of us perfect strangers only a few minutes ago, there is now a sense of almost-camaraderie in the waiting room. Someone opens a box of granola bars and passes them around, someone else comments on the increased number of knife attacks in the city and in the world, and other people pick up the topic, talking in hushed, knowing voices, nodding at each other's statements. The man in the fisherman's sweater, however, is standing apart, still engaged in conversation with the remaining police officers, holding his swollen hand at a conspicuous, unnatural angle. I notice how tall he is, must be around 6'2", and how very straight his posture is, his broad shoulders even turned backward slightly.

A nurse calls Danilo's name and we follow her into the triage area. I cast one last glance at the man in the fisherman's sweater. He does not look back at me, and I catch myself wishing he would.

*****

After a speedy drive through nighttime streets, the cab stops at the corner of 82nd and 1st and the driver thanks me for paying cash. I help Danny out of the car and then up the four flights of stairs to the top floor of the old walk-up. The brownstone was built in 1910 and the ceilings are very high. I am counting the number of stairs we have to climb as I feel the first big wave of tiredness roll over me.

Danny is pumped full of painkillers and it seems as though he could fall asleep at any moment, and I practically carry him up the last flight. While I fumble with the keys, I have to lean him against the wall and then steady him when he starts sliding down. Finally inside, I lay him on the bed, take his shoes off, and make sure his head is comfortable on the pillow.

The heat is on, and the air is hot and stale in this tiny one-bedroom apartment. It is a hole of a place but it is rent-stabilized, and, with the recent rent hikes on the Upper East Side because of the new Q train, perhaps the last affordable place in the neighborhood. When I lived here with Danilo, I worked two jobs—teaching kids' martial arts classes during the day and bartending at night. I was saving money for the future, in the hopes my dream would come true—that Sensei would accept me to be his *uchi-deshi*, I would be allowed to move into the dojo and practice martial arts full-time.

Back then Danilo would only spend an occasional night at the apartment, coming in half-starved, with huge dark circles around his eyes, unwilling or unable to speak from exhaustion. I let him sleep for fifteen to twenty hours and fed him oatmeal. And then he would disappear again, for months on end, into his own life. If I questioned him, he would give evasive answers, saying he stayed here and there, at hotels or with friends and such, but I highly suspected he was more or less homeless. It's true that on his good days, after an especially well-paid modeling gig, he had money to stay at the Carlyle, party with models, and eat in the best restaurants, but on his bad days . . . well, I once found him sleeping on a bench at Pier 16. When my dream came true and Sensei allowed me to move into the dojo, I made Danilo promise he would live at the apartment more permanently. The rent here is very reasonable, yet on some months he does not have enough, and I have to pay, out of my savings.

I open the window to let the fresh cold air cut through the heavy atmosphere inside. I stand for a few minutes looking out into the dark courtyard. I am tired. The heavy pressure that originated somewhere behind my eyes is spreading all over my body. Up since five in the morning, training the usual long hours . . . and now I am starting to feel a bit like a zombie, staring at a single, indistinct point somewhere outside the window, not thinking anything, unable to turn away. I tell myself to focus and get it together.

I go to the kitchen and open the fridge. Just as I thought, it is absolutely empty except for a carton of expired almond milk. I pass my finger on the table surface and there is a visible trace left in the coat of dust. By the overall look of the place I can tell no one's been staying here the last couple of weeks at the least. The bathroom has heavy mildew on the sink and stains from the dripping water in the toilet bowl—a clear indication. Ah, Danilo, didn't he promise? Well, I should not be surprised.

I go down to the twenty-four-hour corner store and get some almond milk, cereal, orange juice, and a few other things for Danilo. I bring everything up to the apartment, moving my legs slowly, counting the stairs at each flight again. I consider for a moment cleaning the place up, but I am exhausted. I only have enough energy to clear empty chip bags off the couch, put the dirty liquor glasses with solidified dark substance on the bottom into the kitchen sink, and pick a pair of jeans and a sweater off the floor and hang them in the closet.

I check on Danilo. He is sleeping, breathing heavily out of his mouth, his broken nose stuffed with plastic inserts and gauze. I cover him with a blanket and sit at the foot of the bed for a while.

The already habitual sadness about my brother has intensified to the point of squeezing my stomach and making me almost nauseous. His injuries turned out not as dangerous as I had feared—no internal bleeding, no damage to internal organs—but that does not cheer me up a whole lot. Two broken ribs, a dislocated shoulder, and a messed-up face are bad enough.

He turns on his side, moans, and then opens his eyes.

"You all right, Danny? You in pain? You need anything?"

"What time is it?" he asks, slurring words and struggling with pronunciation.

"Quarter to five."

"Evening?"

"Morning."

"You should go back to the dojo, Sash. You'll get kicked out for breaking the rules. You are an uchi-deshi. Dojo is important to you. That's your home now."

"*You* are important to me"

He mutters something under his breath. I can make out "*I don't want you to have problems because of me*," but the rest of the phrase is unintelligible. He then remains quiet for a while and I think he might have fallen asleep again.

"You must go," he says all of sudden. "Please, Sash," he adds in such a gentle supplicating voice.

"All right, I am going," I say but just keep sitting there. Then I finally get up. "How much do you owe him this time?" I ask on my way to the door. I pause, waiting for an answer.

"Danilo?"

"Ten grand."

I close the door carefully behind me.

CHAPTER 2

It's not yet 6 a.m. and it's both very cold and still dark outside. Coming out of the subway on Union Square West, a chilly gust of wind hits me in the face. The slush from the last snowfall is still on the ground, and my boots alternately sink into the boggy mess of the dirty snow and slip on the icy patches that have frozen overnight. There is not a soul in sight and the square is really quiet. Lights are on inside some businesses on the ground floors of the buildings encircling the square, but the upper floors are almost all dark.

Soon the morning rush hour will start and throngs of New Yorkers will emerge from the numerous subway exits at Union Square, jostled by the opposing crowds of those wanting to dive in. Right now however the square is as empty as can be, the only person in sight is a homeless guy in a sleeping bag huddled against a building wall.

At six the Pret A Manger on the northwest corner opens. I walk in quickly and ask for a cup of their freshly brewed dark roast. "Nah, you're good," the guy at the counter says when I'm about to pay. "First customer of the day—coffee's on the house."

The coffee warms me up somewhat as I walk west on 16th street, cross 5th and 6th Avenues, and approach a three-story brick building. The first floor is rented out to a parking garage. A tiny plaque above the front door reads Dojo. The plaque and the door itself are quite overshadowed by two huge PARK signs of the adjacent business.

By the building wall, my friend, Amadeus the Homeless Guy, stirs under his numerous blankets. He is a prominent fixture of the neighborhood and has been around for as long as anybody can remember. Sometimes he sits on the corner asking passersby for an exact sum of ninety-nine dollars. He says his calculation is that people would pause to wonder why precisely that number and would give him something anyway. Other times he stands by the local café opening the door for the customers and wishing them a good day. But most often he just lies down reading paperbacks. Even in the winter, when most other homeless are spending nights at Penn Station or elsewhere, he sticks around, saying he is impervious to the cold and that he even likes the snow.

Amadeus sticks his hand from under the blankets, pointing at my coffee. I realize he is reminding me not to take it inside the dojo, a clue that can reveal my outing. I give him the cup, and he wants to chat a bit, but I apologize that I really must hurry now.

I punch in the code to unlock the front door and then go up the narrow creaking stairs. The lights are still out on the second floor, where the training area, the reception, and the changing rooms are. Good. It means neither Liam nor Hiroji have come down yet. I go right up to the third floor. Everything is quiet here. The door to Sensei's rooms is still closed. I tiptoe along the hallway and get to the common area of the uchi-deshi quarters. Here I walk with even greater care—Liam is sleeping on the couch. He has his own room of course, but he always prefers to sleep on this red couch.

I take one careful step after the other maneuvering in the narrow area between the back of the couch, from which Liam's measured breathing issues, and the antique armoire. I am almost past the tricky zone when I glance around to check the surroundings, and suddenly I freeze, barely able to contain a gasp. A white silhouette is suspended in the air in the corner of the room. For a moment I am glued in one spot peering into the darkness.

I exhale slowly as I realize that the white shape is not a ghost or a flying burglar. I know exactly what it is. Liam's gi. The top part of it, that is. I can't see the pants. After the last class of the day, Liam didn't put his uniform in the laundry but decided to just hang it up on the bathroom door to air-dry the sweat out of it. He does this sometimes, the lazy pigeon. According to the dojo etiquette, we are supposed to wear clean training gis for each practice and wash the dirty ones every day. Liam insists with great firmness that lower ranks like me should follow the rules and etiquette to the dot. Due to his own high rank and position of power, he cuts himself some slack, especially when Sensei is not watching.

I am already in the hallway and thinking that perhaps it might be all right and my absence has not been noticed, when Liam's morning voice greets me from behind, "Pack up your shit right now and get the hell out of here."

"Liam, come on," I start saying as I turn around and face him. He has gotten up from his couch and is standing there looking pretty livid. He is wearing his gi pants and I am guessing he was not asleep at all—just lying down quietly, waiting for me to come in. He doesn't have anything else on other than his gi pants, which sit extremely low on his hips. In the past, this habit of male uchi-deshi walking around in nothing but their gi pants without even any underwear underneath made me a bit uncomfortable. I guess I got used to it during my time here at the dojo, but I still cannot help but be aware of it.

"No!" Liam interrupts me. "Don't try to talk your way out of this. Uchi-deshi are not allowed outside the dojo without permission. Spending a night out is strictly forbidden. You broke the rules. You don't give a damn about being an uchi-deshi. Dojo means nothing to you. So just get the hell out."

Yes, I know the rules are very important here. The dojo, being a highly traditional martial arts school founded by a renowned Japanese martial artist, follows the strict procedures and decorum of the centuries-old dojos in Japan. It has none of those lax manners of the modern-day training places that pop up on every corner in New York. Here, there are numerous rules and etiquette regulations to be followed by all students, such as bow to higher ranks after receiving instructions from them, treat lower ranks with courteousness, keep your appearance and your gi neat, always trim your toe and fingernails, don't slouch when sitting in *seiza* or let your back touch the wall, and many, many others.

Unlike the regular students, who come in and train when they like, we the uchi-deshi must adhere to an even stricter set of rules and principles. We are Sensei's direct disciples, hand-chosen by him as worthy to follow the path of the ancient Japanese martial art. We are completely dedicated to the training, serving Sensei and the dojo. We live inside the dojo, rarely stepping outside, and train on a full-time basis, which means six or seven hours a day. The only excuse for missing a practice is a serious illness or a bad injury. A sprained ankle or a pulled muscle doesn't constitute a valid reason for not being on the mat. If we cannot take a class, we must sit on a bench in front of the training area and learn through observation.

When there are beginners present, our duty is to instruct them. Outside of training, we are to serve Sensei and to do numerous chores around the dojo. The head uchi-deshi assigns the chores to us. Most interactions with Sensei are carried out through the head uchi-deshi. There is a strict chain of command here at the dojo. It's not often if ever that Sensei would talk directly to a junior uchi-deshi.

Having been an uchi-deshi for two years now, I am well aware that one of the strictest rules is not to step outside the dojo without an expressed permission, and never to spend a night out. Yet I also know that from time to time even this rule is bent, sometimes by Liam himself, who is our head uchi-deshi.

I can guess, though, why he is so furious now. He thinks I spent the night with a man and is angry or jealous or, most likely, both. His volatile attitude toward me has often made me wonder if perhaps he has never gotten over what happened between us last year. I can tell him of course that he has no reason to be jealous, that I was not on a romantic tryst of any kind but was in the ER with my brother. I don't feel like giving excuses though. Let him think what he wants. I look him straight in the eye and don't say anything. I can tell that my silence irritates Liam to no end. He desperately wants to interrogate me about my night and to find out where—and with whom—I was, but he is making a huge effort to contain himself. For a few long moments we are both very still and quiet, staring into each other's eyes, neither of us wanting to look away first.

Hiroji walks past us, gives us a quick glance and a good morning. He surely grasps the situation right away but does not interfere. Even if he wanted to help me, there is nothing he can do. Being the head uchi-deshi, Liam outranks Hiroji, and at the dojo rank is everything. Only Sensei can rein him in now, if Liam really wants to throw me out. But something tells me he doesn't. He probably won't even tell Sensei about my breaking the rules. So I just keep standing here, without proffering an explanation, waiting to see what he does or says next. Then it occurs to me that he has gotten himself into a difficult position and is not sure how to get out of it. He has given an order and now cannot contradict himself just like that. It would make him look bad. I realize I need to help him.

"I am sorry, Liam. I am really sorry. You know how much the dojo means to me. You know that right? Please, let me stay," I say. This should be enough.

"The class will start in a few. Get changed," he grumbles, then turns away and walks to the bathroom, shutting the door behind him with a loud bang. He is still very angry. That's not good. It's never good to have Liam angry at you. He'll find a way to make me pay for this, that's for sure.

*****

In my room I undress as quickly as I can, catching in the mirror a glimpse of a very fit body and a vague oval of a face with big eyes, exaggerated by the play of shadows. As always, it occurs to me that I don't really know what my face looks like. People say that Danilo and I look very much alike, so I guess I only know my face through my brother's. I put on a sports bra and underwear, then my gi and my black belt. On my way downstairs I put my long hair up in a high bun. I have been considering cutting it short for a while now, but so far have not had the guts to do it.

On the main floor Hiroji is standing by the side of the mat smiling and chatting with some students who have just arrived. His seemingly perpetual good mood never ceases to amaze me. He always has a smile on the ready, for anyone. Even when he trains, throwing someone really hard or being thrown down himself, he smiles. Yet in those instances that I observed him when he thought he was alone, his face assumed such a tough expression and there was such a cold look in his eyes that I almost felt a bit scared.

Puzzling guy, Hiroji. I've lived and trained side by side with him for a while now, but I can't say I know anything about him. He is always happy to chat with you, but after the conversations you realize that he has not actually said much. Mysterious. Very good-looking too. Tall, with lean muscles, elegant face, long hair, which he puts up in a high bun while training. Girls are always after him. Girls who do not even train at the dojo come in and watch a class, just to see Hiroji training. On the mat he is spectacular. Powerful and graceful. No matter how hard he is thrown, he flips in the air like a cat and lands softly without a sound. He is famous for that.

I am not even sure how old Hiroji is. Never occurred to me to ask. I guess he is a bit older than me, probably around twenty-five and already a third-degree black belt Liam must be at least a few years older and a fourth-degree black belt. He is rather good-looking, too, but so very different. Medium height, stocky, broad shoulders, buzzed haircut, strong facial features, often a two-day stubble. Tough, powerful, and explosive on the mat. And you would definitely not call Liam friendly or cheerful. A frown or a smirk is what you most often see on his face. There he is now, walking down the stairs in his usual off-the-mat lazy fashion, looking displeased at the whole world. He notices me standing about, knits his eyebrows, and looks away.

Despite the early hour, there's already quite a number of people at the dojo. The first class today is taught by Sensei. There are six or seven classes daily, and Sensei teaches at least one every day, sometimes more, with the rest of the classes taught by other high-ranked instructors. When Sensei is teaching, students flock to the dojo in droves. Sometimes there are fifty or more people on the mat.

Sensei comes downstairs a few minutes after Liam. The commanding presence of this seventy-year-old man always amazes me. When he walks into a room, no, actually, even before he does, as soon as we see him approach from the distance, all conversations stop, people get up from their seats, and everybody turns in his direction. The dojo etiquette requires that we do so, but I believe it goes deeper than that. There is something about this legendary martial artist that fills us with deep awe, respect, and admiration.

Now, Liam, Hiroji, and I bow to him, and Sensei mutters a dispirited good morning to us. Looks like he did not sleep well. With another bow, I offer Sensei some green tea, but he does not want any. His shoulder aches and Hiroji massages it for him, but a minute later Sensei motions for him to stop. By looking at Sensei's face, we can tell he is not in a very good mood—the corners of his mouth are drawn down. He closes his eyes and sits motionless on the wooden bench, and we remain nearby, in case he wants something, but we know better than to approach him uncalled for at this moment.

*****

At the beginning of class it is very cold. For some reason the heat never comes on at this early morning hour. There is a heat pipe right by the entrance to the training area, and in the wintertime it is almost a ritual for the students to touch the pipe upon stepping onto the mat. I guess we are always hoping for a little miracle, but it never happens. I touch the pipe now and, as expected, it is perfectly cold.

My joints and muscles are very stiff. When it's this cold, the mats are hard as a rock and every time I am thrown down I feel as if I were hitting asphalt. Still, I shouldn't be complaining, I guess. I remind myself that I'd take training in the winter any day over training in the summer. In July and August when it's ninety-something degrees outside and really humid, it is over one hundred degrees on the mat. Even with all the windows open and the fans buzzing loudly, the heat and moisture just keep accumulating and there is not enough oxygen in the air. The dojo has no air conditioning. We often joke that having air conditioning must go against the samurai spirit. During infamous NYC heat waves, even the highest-ranking black belts look like zombies on the mat, moving slowly, rationing every breath of air. A few years ago a visiting martial artist actually passed out from heat stroke.

This chilly morning there is plenty of energy on the mat. I glance around and see everybody is working on their technique intensely. Everybody except for me. I must look as sluggish and slow as a snail on painkillers. Training on no sleep and no food will do this to you. When was the last time I actually put food in my body? Oh yes, that granola bar at the hospital. Nothing since then.

We are practicing a takedown followed by an arm bar. Hiroji and Liam, who are training just a few feet away, are throwing each other as hard as they can and cranking each other's elbows with all their might. There is a blissful smile on Hiroji's face, and that inscrutable smirk on Liam's.

Liam catches my eye and gives me such a stern look that it definitely unnerves me.

As we move on to a new technique, I am starting to feel very physically weak. Mentally I am in an even worse shape, I guess. I just can't seem to focus. My mind keeps wandering. Danilo's beaten face appears before my eyes and his words, "ten grand," ring in my ears. He'd owed money before, but never this much.

Pow! My head jerks back violently.

I have just caught a punch under the jaw from my training partner. Completely my fault. You must never get distracted on the mat, and right when I was supposed to be fully concentrated on blocking an attack, my thoughts were entirely elsewhere.

Suddenly, I hear Sensei's loud voice, and for a moment my foggy brain thinks that he is yelling at me. But no, he is scolding another student, telling him to correct a mistake in his footwork. The student keeps making the same mistake and finally Sensei loses patience altogether. "Get off the mat," he orders, "you are not worthy of a black belt!"

For a few moments there is complete silence. It's not often that Sensei loses his cool, and it shakes us up. Such a presence this formidable man commands, such charisma and influence he possesses, that his one word of praise makes you feel you've achieved the ultimate success, and his one disapproving look makes your legs tremble.

As the training resumes, everybody's faces are gloomy and extra focused. I am partnered with a guy of the same rank as me, but he is almost twice my size and probably weighs some 180 pounds against my

110. Good thing the size and strength of the attacker do not matter as much. It is more about unbalancing your opponent, positioning your body at precise angles, and reversing the attacker's power and strength to work against him. A properly executed combination of a joint lock, a take down, and a pin has my partner on the ground and tapping out vigorously within a split second. Out of the corner of my eye I see Sensei watching and smiling his approval. He likes to see girls make big guys hit the mat hard.

Sensei's mood improves visibly and the ambience on the mat picks up.

*****

Sensei demonstrates a new technique, a variation of a hip throw combined with a joint lock. Because of the large number of people on the mat we are to practice it in groups, one person executing the technique on several attackers who come at him in a rapid succession. I am in a group with four people, Liam being the highest ranked among us, so he gets to throw first. I notice him glance at me again, his eyes narrowing and his smirk turning almost villainous. Damn, I feel so very tired and the earlier punch on the jaw has debilitated me even further and made me somewhat dizzy, but seeing Liam's ominous facial expression I know I really need to focus now and pull together the last bits of energy for what might be coming next.

One by one people attack Liam, and he throws everyone down in his precise and powerful way. Now it's my turn. I am actually a bit scared and so tense up. Breathe, I tell myself, breathe. For a second it seems to me that everything slows down, almost stands still—me, Liam's figure right in front of me, people in the background, the whole dojo—then the motion speeds up to its utmost and I feel myself being lifted off the mat, high— too high. I am not going over Liam's hips. No! In a flash I realize he's hoisted me higher and I am going over his shoulders. He even jumps up and throws me down with incredible power.

Surely this will kill me.

Landing on my side, I hit the mat with such force that I feel the violent shock in my whole body. It does not kill me, but it does certainly put me in a bit of a stupor and I stay glued to the floor for a while.

As I get up, people are exchanging wondering looks. They are not sure what has happened, but of course no one will dare to question Liam. Hiroji is shaking his head. Strange. It seems he is expressing his disapproval of me, not of Liam. But why? What have I done? It was Liam. He was not supposed to do the shoulder throw. And he did it while Sensei was not watching. That sneaky Liam.

Again and again he throws me down in the most vicious manner, coming up with new tricks. I try to land smoothly, try to soften the impact, but it is of no use. My body hits the mat with terrible intensity every time.

What is Liam's objective? Is he really aiming to harm me, or just to teach me some sort of a lesson? I try to convince myself that it is the latter. The good thing is that his technique being so highly skillful and accurate he can be fully trusted not to make a single awkward move, which less experienced martial artists often make and which can cause an accidental injury to their training partner. Liam will slam me into the ground but will make sure I don't fall on my head and break my neck. I'll be OK, I keep telling myself, I just need to stay focused and brace for the brutal collision with the mat again and again.

As the exhaustion takes over however, I find it harder and harder to keep focused. I steal a glance at the clock. Only a few minutes left till the end of the class now. Oh, good. That's not enough time for Liam's turn to come around again. A white-belt student is up next and his throws seem as soft as a touch of a squirrel's tail. I relax and let my mind wander once more.

I think about a nice hot shower. I can almost feel the soothing effect of the water running down my body. And then some food. Oh, yes, definitely food. And if I do the chores quickly, I might be able to get in a nap before the next class, if Liam allows it. I probably will not be able to sneak out of the dojo today to check on Danny, but maybe tomorrow. With that, my thinking reverts back to my brother's broken face and his feeble voice saying, "ten grand." I am pretty sure he does not have a hundred bucks to his name.

My thoughts are still entirely outside the mat, when I find myself being thrown by the white belt and realize his position is not well-grounded, too unstable. He doesn't know what the hell he's doing, and the throw turns awkward, at a bad and dangerous angle for me. And I was too distracted to have noticed in time. Now it's too late. Damn it. Haven't I seen just such awkward throws result in serious neck injuries and broken vertebrae?

At the last moment I desperately try to readjust the angle of my fall and not let my neck go straight into the mat.

It seems I might have pulled it off. My arm and my shoulder have the first contact with the mat, which is a good safe way to land.

Then there is an audible cracking sound.

CHAPTER 3

I don't feel the pain right away. The adrenaline is still kicking in. For a few moments I think everything is fine. I am in one piece. No blood or anything. Then I glance at my left foot. Two of the toes are bent almost ninety degrees to the side. They slammed into the heating pipe and broke on the spot.

Sensei motions for someone to escort me off the mat. But the toes need to be put back into place, so why delay it. I'll do it myself right now. I take a deep breath in, then exhale slowly, and in two brusque motions set the toes straight, one after the other. Oh, that hurt! That hurt like hell. You train yourself to deal with this kind of pain. You know that most often it is the anticipation of the pain coming that makes it worse. You tell your brain to accept it, to take it in and not fight it. Knowing all this, I am prepared, but still there is this brief moment of acute pain, as if all the nerves in my body are suddenly located in those two damaged toes. I can't help but utter the F word and blink rapidly to make the tears disappear. I hope no one's heard the curse. Swearing on the mat is strictly against the dojo rules. I continue breathing in and out slowly, trying to take control of the pain.

Damn it, how could I be so stupid and let myself lose all focus? Don't I know that injuries happen exactly then? Well, I try to console myself, at least it's just the toes. I am lucky my vertebrae are intact.

I glance at Liam and expect to see his mean smirk again, but instead there is a concerned, perhaps even caring expression on his face. Could it be just a trick of my imagination? I am really not sure. His eyes are locked on mine for a mere moment and, as always, there is something uncomfortably strong in his gaze, as if those very dark pupils of his were trying to drill into me. I don't know what the hell he is thinking, and, as I limp away, I try to get Liam and his unsettling and perplexing attitude out of my head.

*****

I am sitting on a bench in the women's locker room. I have taken a shower but have not dressed yet. The heat has come on and it is nice and warm in the room, and I have only my towel wrapped around me. The toes now look pretty swollen and have turned a bright purple color.

Martine, the only other girl who was in the early-morning class, comes out of the shower. She is a good friend of mine and we've known each other for years training at the same dojo. I don't think I sought her friendship—I guess it was she who always tried to get close to me, chatting me up, telling me secrets about her life and love adventures, and partnering with me as often as possible on the mat. Over time I started enjoying our training together and our conversations and opened up to her a bit more. Her exuberant outgoingness weighs down on me somewhat, but I do appreciate how caring, strong, and resilient she is and how optimistic she always seems. Martine is French and does not have a work permit here but always manages to find work in bars and such.

She wraps a towel around her hair, puts on her panties, sits next to me on the bench, and helps me tape up my toes. The idea is to tape them up to the next toe pretty tight so as to immobilize them. We really should be binding them to a piece of wood or something so that they definitely heal straight, but I guess I don't care too much about the perfect straightness of my toes. Just taping them up tight should do it.

"The examinations are only a few days away," Martine says.

I know what she means by that and her words irritate me, and I don't reply anything.

"With this injury you'll have to stay off the mat for a while, huh?"

"Nah, couple days at the most."

"But your toes won't heal that quickly!"

I shrug and again don't say anything.

"Wow! You uchi-deshi definitely lead a strange life!" she exclaims. "Training six hours a day, all the endless chores around the dojo, not being able to go outside when you want to, and on top of everything, to train through injuries. You think it's worth it?"

I ponder my answer for a few moments. Martine has described quite accurately the life of an uchi-deshi, and yet her words do not capture its true sense. It is not just about living inside the dojo, training full time, and cleaning toilets—it is being Sensei's direct disciple, knowing that you have been personally chosen as worthy of his close instruction both on and off the mat.

Uchi-deshi live and breathe their martial art twenty-four seven—it becomes their life and permeates every aspect of their existence. Their skills on the mat improve at a rate that regular martial arts practitioners could only dream of.

And then there is more.

Being an uchi-deshi is also about learning to understand the true essence of the martial art, what it really means to be a martial artist, how to perceive the world and your position in it, and to learn to control and avoid the aggression and violence in yourself and around you.

Before I came to this dojo, I'd trained in different martial arts—judo, sambo, and Russian hand-to-hand fighting. I competed quite a bit in my teen years and was making a name for myself on the junior tournament circuit. Winning felt good, but it wasn't fully satisfying. Something was lacking from my martial arts training, and I didn't know what it was. I was so young, of course, I couldn't possibly be aware of what I was searching for. When I stepped into this dojo, as a regular student at first, I immediately sensed that this was not an ordinary place.

The true tradition of the ancient martial art lives on here, and Sensei carries on the code of honor and wisdom passed through generations. Somehow, I felt right away that this was what I wanted to be a part of, that I belonged here. And when, later on, Sensei chose me to be one of his uchi-deshi, I realized that he understood me better that I did myself, that he knew exactly what it was I searching for.

Sensei rarely has a direct conversation with a student, so the words he said to me on the day that I became uchi-deshi are etched in my brain. I was invited into Sensei's quarters for the first time. I hadn't had time to change out of my sweaty gi after the practice and it was cold in the room and I started shivering. Or maybe it was the solemnity of the moment that made me so tense. As soon as Sensei spoke, the shivering stopped and instead I felt hot all over.

"The true martial art is not just about winning. The most important part is attaining balance, harmony in all aspects of life, inner strength, and discipline. The true martial art teaches us to be strong and empathetic and to treat others, on and off the mat, with respect and honor."

That was what he told me on that day, and I hope never to forget a single of those words.

Sensei's uchi-deshi learn the physical aspect of their martial art and participate in tournaments and often take first places, which is of course good for the name of the school, but their path leads much deeper than just competing. We are to carry on the code of honor, the very principles of the true martial art. And the more skilled you get at a technical level, the more in control of your body and mind you grow to be. I know it will take me many, many years to get there, and who knows I might perhaps never reach those levels, but it makes me feel good to know that I am at least heading in the right direction.

I don't explain any of it to Martine though. It's too early in the morning for such a deep conversation.

"I think it's worth it," is all I say.

"Well, as long as you're happy," she makes a face showing that she highly doubts my happiness.

"Didn't you want to be an uchi-deshi too?" I ask, and I immediately regret the question. I am pretty sure she did, but Sensei did not choose her, and Martine and I never discuss the topic.

She gives me a strange look and then laughs. "Nah. It's much easier being just a regular student here—come in and train when I feel like it and then leave, no chores, no responsibilities, no strict rules."

We finish taping up my toes and I make a huge effort, unglue my exhausted body off the bench, get up, take a couple steps, and wince. Putting the full weight on the left foot is not an option for now. Oh well, I will just have to work around it somehow for a few days.

"You'd better take a few ibuprofens," Martine suggests.

"Nah, I don't like that stuff."

"Or I can bring you some pot for the pain."

"Nah, thank you though."

I take off the towel and start getting dressed.

"You are becoming too skinny," Martine says. I can see in the mirror she is staring at me. "You have very nice shape, but you are losing muscle weight."

She might be right. I have been training so much and probably not getting enough calories in. I examine my pale face, shadows under my eyes, protruding cheekbones. I need food and a bit of rest, that's for sure.

"Want some help with the chores? I can clean the shower or wash dirty gis or something."

"Thanks, Martine, I appreciate it, really, but it's not allowed. Hey, I don't mean to rush you, but . . ."

"Yeah, yeah, I know. I'll just blow-dry my hair real quick and I'll go." Still she keeps sitting on the bench and looking at me while I am putting on my clothes. "Hey," she says, "I always meant to ask you—do you think Sensei will pick one more uchi-deshi? That's a lot of work for just three people to do around here. Was easier when it was four of you, wasn't it?"

I've recently overheard Sensei mention to the head uchi-deshi that he has no intention of taking on another in the foreseeable future, if ever, and that all the chores will have to be handled by Liam, Hiroji, and me. I don't relay this information to Martine, however. I don't feel it is my place to do so.

"But what actually happened to that fourth uchi-deshi?" she asks. "He just disappeared last year. People say he got horribly injured on the mat."

"Well, yeah, that is exactly what happened. He got injured and had to leave the dojo."

"Hmm, but did you actually see it happen?"

"I did not."

"That's the thing. Nobody did. Nobody! You don't think it's very strange? Kind of mysterious, no?"

Why is she pressing with these questions? I know she likes to gossip and it seems she wants to tell me something. She is just waiting for me to ask. But I don't.

As Martine finally starts blow-drying her hair, I debate whether to tell her again she needs to hurry up and leave soon. She is my friend and I don't want to be rude to her, but according to the rules I cannot start cleaning the locker room if there is someone still using it. And I only have that much time to do all the cleaning and my other chores and get everything ready before the two midday classes, after which there is a short break, followed by the evening classes.

Suddenly the blow dryer stops and I hear Martine's voice. "Hey, Sasha, have you ever heard about the Dark Fights?"

*****

I still haven't had time for a decent breakfast. I quickly ate two bananas and then had to get on with the chores. Now I'm in the laundry room, taking a load of gis out of the washer. The gis are double weave, 100 percent cotton, and the damp heap weighs quite a lot. It's my job to get them as clean and white as possible, leaving no traces of blood, dirt, or other stains. I inspect them one more time before putting them in the dryer, all the while thinking that it would be nice to somehow sneak out to the café across the street and have a hot ham-and-cheese croissant or maybe a mushroom-and-goat-cheese omelet and some home fries. Ah, but that's pure fantasy. All I have upstairs is oatmeal. I guess that will have to do.

Hiroji sticks his head in.

"There is somebody to see you at the front desk."

"What? Who?"

"Says he's your uncle."

"Is Liam around?"

"Upstairs having coffee."

I shut the dryer door, set the timer, and then limp to the front desk, wondering what the hell is going on and who the visitor might be. I don't have any uncles. In fact, after our grandfather passed away, it is just Danilo and I—no other relatives at all.

The man standing here is probably in his mid or late fifties and is tall and well built. He has short salt-and-pepper hair, a short beard, and very dark eyes.

I have an unpleasant pang in my stomach when I see him. "What are you doing here, Sergey?"

He winces and I know why. He prefers that people address him by his first name and patronymic, Sergey Petrovich, but I'll be damned if I give him that respect.

"Hello, Sasha. So good to see you. I would say you are looking well, but I would be lying. You look exhausted and too thin. Still beautiful of course, but far too thin. And what's with the limp?" His heavy Russian accent grates on my nerves.

"What do you want, Sergey?"

"No need to be rude, is there? Just stopped by to see my friend."

"You gotta be kidding."

"Well, the sister of my friend."

"Again, you gotta be fucking kidding."

"Language, Sasha. You picked up such bad manners living in this place among boys. You've been here for too long. How old are you these days, beauty?"

I do not answer.

"Let's see. Your brother is twenty-seven and he is four years older than you, correct? Perfect, you are just the right age."

"The right age for what?"

This time he does not answer, just stands there looking at me in an evaluating manner.

"Did you come for the money, Sergey? I don't have it here. But I will get it to you in a couple days. And then leave Danilo alone. You hear me?"

"Ha-ha-ha. Now it is my turn to ask if you are kidding. Do you really think I ever personally come to collect debts? I am a proponent of division of labor, ha-ha-ha."

He thinks he is being funny.

"Whatever. I will get you the money, and Danilo will not set foot at 2 Gild Street ever again, and we will have nothing to do with you, ever."

"Why talk about money?" He makes a face. "It absolutely goes against my upbringing to discuss money with a woman. I am a perfect gentleman. There are some things a gentleman just does not do."

"Oh, don't give me that shit," I say and start walking away. Sergey grabs my arm to stop me. I turn brusquely and apply a classical rotational wristlock. During practice on the mat, my partner would flip over his own arm to prevent his wrist from breaking. Sergey instead starts sinking down on his knees sort of sideways, grimacing in pain. I was being careful and did not do it hard enough to cause any serious damage, but I know it still hurt a lot and a muscle or a tendon could have been pulled.

I release the wristlock and Sergey straightens up and, looking quite angry, actually tries to punch me with his uninjured hand. So much for his being a gentleman. I intercept the punch, rotate his arm so that his shoulder is down and his wrist is up, and put him in an elbow-hyperextending arm bar. He attempts to get out of it, but I apply more pressure on his elbow and with each move he just causes himself more pain. The elbow is such a delicate joint and it takes precision and self-restraint on my part not to dislocate it now.

"Hey, is everything okay?" Hiroji calls out from the door of the laundry room.

"Fine," I reply and keep pinning Sergey down.

Finally Sergey taps out. I let go and he emits a few colorful Russian expletives under his breath while bending and straightening his arm several times to make sure the elbow is intact and is working all right. Then quite unexpectedly he smiles and nods his head in approval. "Hey, this is what I am talking about. You are good. You are very good. I'll go now, but I will be seeing you. We have a lot to discuss."

"No, we do not."

"Indeed, we do. I will definitely be seeing you again, beauty. I hear you're taking your examinations in a few days. Relatives and friends are invited to watch, correct? I will be sure to stop by."

How the hell does he know about the black-belt examinations? Damn, the upcoming event is a rather sensitive topic for me.

In order to be promoted to the next rank, which for me would be Nidan, second-degree black belt, you must win a certain number of competitions, which I already have. Afterward however come the examinations. They are the most important, difficult, and spectacular part of the passage to the next rank. There have been a few occurrences when a martial artist who competed successfully in tournaments, then performed poorly at the examinations and was not promoted.

Only Sensei determines if you are qualified to test for the next rank. I did have high hopes that I would be allowed to participate in the examinations this year. I felt I was ready. I was waiting that any day now Sensei would let me know. In fact, most everybody at the dojo already took it for granted that I was testing and were wishing me good luck. But the stupid accident in today's morning class has ruined everything. And it's not about the broken toes not healing in time—I could not care less about that, I can deal with the pain all right. But Sensei saw my failure on the mat. A martial artist worthy to try for a Nidan does not lose focus on the mat, no matter what. None of it is Sergey's business though.

He goes away waving goodbye as he walks, then turns around and blows me a kiss. He smiles, then almost instantaneously the smile disappears, and his face gains a serious and focused expression, and he looks at me attentively for a few moments, as if appraising me. I feel uncomfortable under that heavy stare, but I do not turn away and I hold his gaze. Sergey smiles again and disappears down the stairs.

In less than an hour, while I am still busy with the chores, a delivery guy brings a bag for me. In it there is a variety of freshly prepared breakfast items, enough food for several people. I know Sergey has sent it, and my first impulse is to throw everything out, but I am just too hungry and the food smells so good. I unwrap a ham-and-cheese croissant and bite into it.

CHAPTER 4

The noise from the old industrial-size vacuum cleaner is deafening, and its cord has a tendency to snake around on the floor and try to trip me. I kick the infernal machine in desperation. Well, at least we only bring it out on special occasions. But damn it, why do I have to be the one vacuuming? Oh, of course neither Liam nor Hiroji can be bothered with this chore. Being the lowest in rank among the uchi-deshi, it's me who has to do it. I do miss the days when we had the fourth uchi-deshi, who was the same rank as me. He was a quiet and hard-working guy who, in rare moments of free time, liked to make sketches of martial artists performing various techniques. Said it helped him understand the dynamics of the movement. Someone once called him "Leonardo da Vinci," then it was shortened to Da Vinci, then to Dav and that was what everybody called him.

So strange that nobody talks about him. Last week in the locker room when Martine was asking questions about his disappearance was the first time in a long while somebody had brought him up.

The vacuum cleaner is so loud it's shutting out my own thoughts and the whole world around. For a while I'm working almost on autopilot, my head filled to the brim with the noise. Suddenly, as I look up, I see Liam's figure towering over me and his lips moving emphatically, but I can't hear a word he is saying. The cringe on his face reflects an infinite irritation, and I can guess that the owner of the cringing face has been taking a nap upstairs and been woken by the roar of the vacuum cleaner.

Liam gestures for me to shut it off.

"What the fuck are you doing?" he asks, clearly a rhetorical question. "Sensei is taking a nap."

Sensei. Yeah right. There is a very visible pillow mark on Liam's cheek.

"I thought Sensei went out for an early dinner with his guests?" As is customary every year, some of Sensei's friends, very high-ranked martial artists from Japan, came to NYC a few days ahead of the Winter Assembly. "Didn't he cancel the evening classes because of the upcoming snowstorm?"

Liam's eyes narrow and he gives me an evil look. "Go clean the toilets now," he orders.

"Already did that."

"Then wash the towels and make sure there's enough for all the visitors tomorrow."

"Done."

"Refill the medicine cabinet. Last year there was not enough sports tape and some of the visitors complained."

I open the medicine cabinet to show Liam that it has been fully stocked.

Liam then starts walking around the dojo checking if everything is ready for the big event. Surely he expects me to follow his every step so as to give immediate instructions on what still needs to be done, but, even though I know it will annoy him, I remain standing in one place leaning onto the vacuum cleaner. I can't quite explain why I have these urges to push his buttons. I know better than to do that, yet somehow I just can't help myself.

He comes back grumbling under his breath, and I can't tell if he is mad at me or is in a bad mood because of tomorrow. Probably both.

We uchi-deshi all share the same contradictory feelings about the Winter Assembly, which is the biggest event of the year on the dojo's calendar. On that day there are classes from early morning on, attended by hundreds of martial artists from all over the world. The black belt examinations presided over by Sensei follow right afterward, and our famous dojo party is later in the evening.

Martial artists from as far as Japan and Argentina, not to mention various parts of the US and Europe, come to the Winter Assembly, drawn by the fame of the Sensei and by the level of martial arts taught at the dojo. Many of course come specifically to test for various degrees of Black Belt. You can always tell them by how nervous and eager they look and how hard they train in the hours leading up to the examinations. Often times they get themselves pretty exhausted on the mat before the tests even start. The preparations for the event, the big day itself, and the cleaning up afterward increase the uchi-deshi's regular amount of work tenfold and put a lot of pressure on us. Also, many of the visitors specifically seek out the uchi-deshi to train with. I suppose it gives them certain gratification to be able to take down one of Sensei's disciples. And, because of hospitality, we are not encouraged to retaliate. Despite all that, we do feel rather proud that our dojo is so famous and attracts such a great number of martial arts practitioners.

For a few moments Liam and I stand quiet, understanding each other's thoughts perfectly and united in our sentiments. Then Liam remembers he is angry with me and pulls himself up.

"Well, don't just be standing here like an ice sculpture. Get back to your vacuuming," he says and suddenly starts blinking rapidly and rubbing his right eye. A dust particle must have flown into it. "Also clean the swords and daggers. Sensei said he might use weapons during the examinations tomorrow." He rubs his right eye again. "And then pick up a shovel and help Hiroji up on the roof. Looks like this goddamn storm is going to be pretty big. There's like a whole foot of snow on the roof already."

"Hmm, maybe because of the snowstorm the Winter Assembly will be canceled."

"Ha!" Liam exclaims and smirks. He clearly finds the idea very intriguing. "Well, anyway, hurry up and finish here and then help Hiroji shovel. Ah, damn it!" He kicks the vacuum cleaner. "Does this fucking machine even work? There's more dust around than ever before." He opens and closes his eye vigorously and rubs it hard. It looks pretty red now.

"Stop rubbing it, Liam! Don't move. Open your eyes as wide as you can." I come up very close to him and hold him by his arms to make him stay still.

"What are you doing?"

"Just stand still, can you?"

Then I blow into his right eye with all my might.

Liam sort of gasps, unsure of what I have just done, blinks, and senses the relief, the dust particle having been blown out.

"Oh, thanks, Sasha," he mutters.

I let go of his arms but immediately he takes hold of mine and pulls me into him, gently but firmly. I do not resist and for a moment his lips are almost touching mine, but then I turn my head slightly, avoiding the kiss. Still he keeps holding me against him, and I feel his breath on my cheek and his two-day stubble against my skin. I tense up and pull back. He holds me for a moment longer and then releases me, glaring at me silently from underneath his knitted eyebrows. He then turns around and starts walking away but trips on the cord from the vacuum cleaner and almost falls down. He curses out loud with great intensity, and somehow I feel that the cursing is not directed at the cord but at me.

*****

Up on the roof, it is very cold at first, but as I start shoveling, I warm up quickly and feel the sweat trickle down my back. I realize I am working too intensely and need to slow down. It is the incident with Liam that has gotten me so agitated.

Liam.

I try not to think about him and our complicated history. I can't let myself dwell on it now—I have more pressing issues to worry about. My brother sitting alone in the apartment on the UES, all beaten up and moneyless, is surely more important than my unsolvable problems with Liam. Yet the almost-kiss has stirred up something in me, and now I cannot help but picture Liam's frowning face and his dark eyes glaring at me.

He was the first person who greeted me when I walked into the dojo years ago. I was sixteen then, barely old enough to be allowed into adult classes. Liam was an uchi-deshi already and helped me a lot with my initial training. Sure, it was his duty to train a newcomer, but I could tell he really enjoyed working with me. I was quite fascinated with him and thought him an extraordinarily talented martial artist with such a precise and power-ful technique. I also thought him a handsome and attractive guy, and I must say I really liked our training together. There was something really exhilarating and exciting about those classes. Training with him was most exhausting physically, because he always moved with great speed and power and never gave me a moment to even catch my breath. Ten minutes in and we would already be covered in sweat, and by the end of the practice, our gis would be soaking through. Difficult and strenuous, yes, but how enor-mously satisfying those classes were. Our fellow students often commented that we both had huge smiles on our faces when we trained together.

Under Liam's tutelage I made quick progress and Sensei noticed me. So, in a way, I owe a lot of my success at the dojo to Liam.

When, two years ago, Sensei chose me to be his uchi-deshi, I was so happy and excited and thought Liam would be happy for me too. I was caught completely off guard when it turned out he was not. He was in fact heavily opposed to my being an uchi-deshi. His reasoning was that he did not want a girl living upstairs, in what had previously been an all-male environment. He went as far as expressing his thoughts on the issue to Sensei directly. By then he'd already been made the head uchi-deshi and his opinion mattered.

Sensei did not change his mind.

After I moved in, Liam made my life very difficult at first, trying to prove that a girl would not be able to endure the tough uchi-deshi life. At several moments I indeed was close to giving up, especially when I was injured or sick. As time went on, however, Liam let up. I guess he respected my perse-verance and hard work. And then . . . what happened then was probably my fault, or it was nobody's fault, it just happened, but things got so messed up between Liam and me after that. I wonder if they can ever be fixed.

Quite unexpectedly, Liam comes out to the roof to help Hiroji and me shovel. This is most unusual. Liam the head uchi-deshi rarely if ever stoops to doing any sort of menial work around here. The only instances I can think of is when he puts on a show for Sensei. Liam is sneaky that way. Under normal circumstances he is . . . well, he thinks himself above such chores. What he likes to do is supervise and order people around and

give them hard time if his commands are not carried out with prompt-
ness and precision. That's the Liam we know. So naturally Hiroji and I
exchange quick surprised glances upon seeing our head uchi-deshi with a
shovel in his hands.

The three of us work together for some time. Liam shares a few obser-
vations and a couple jokes with Hiroji but does not direct a single word
to me. He is altogether actively ignoring my presence. I try to tell myself
that I could not care less about his attitude, but it does make me feel rather
uncomfortable. Soon, he declares he needs his gloves, goes inside, and
does not come back out. Yep, that's more like him. Lazy pigeon. Sure, he'd
much rather sprawl on his red couch than shovel the snow up here. It's all
right though. Hiroji and I manage on our own just fine. There's quite a bit
of snow, but not nearly as much as on some previous occasions, definitely
not a "whole foot" that Liam talked about.

*****

As it often happens, against the meteorologists' predictions the "big snowstorm" does not really materialize and at some point they downgrade
the Winter Storm Warning to a Winter Weather Advisory. At JFK and
LaGuardia a bunch of flights are delayed, but only a few canceled.

Sensei announces that the Winter Assembly will go as scheduled and
that we should be ready to open the dojo at 6 a.m. tomorrow.

In the evening, having finished all the preparations for the big day
ahead, Liam, Hiroji, and I are sitting upstairs in the living room. The guys
are having warm sake and I'm drinking ginger-lemon tea. We are watching
the new installment of *John Wick* for the hundredth time, mostly fast-for-
warding to the fight scenes. Liam and Hiroji are playing the "if you spot
John Wick do a joint-lock or a throw, empty your sake cup" game. After
every such technique, they refill each other's cups. Hiroji is very particular about the ritual of serving and drinking sake and would not be caught
dead filling his own cup. After yet another of John Wick's throws, Liam
says to count him out of the game because he must be in top shape later
tonight. The movie keeps playing, but soon Hiroji is the only one really

paying attention to the screen. Liam is checking his phone every few minutes, and I am keeping a watchful eye on Liam, quite anxious about why he is still here and whether he is going to leave at all.

About once a month Liam gives himself permission to go out for a few hours to bounce at a bar on Irving Street, when they have a big party or a formal event or such. These gigs pay well and with the money he is able to finance his stay at the dojo. At one time he invited Hiroji to join him, but Hiroji declined. He is the only one of us who does not have financial constraints. I've heard rumors that he comes from a very rich family in Japan. It's been also mentioned that he is actually a member of a Yakuza clan. I don't know if there is any truth in that. If he is a Yakuza, then why would he be living here, shut voluntarily inside the dojo? In any case, while Liam and I are always extremely careful about spending any money, Hiroji does not have such problems.

As uchi-deshi we stay at the dojo rent free, but we still have to pay for our food. Liam and I mostly subsist on cheap nutritious things, like oatmeal, pasta, eggs, and bananas. Hiroji often orders in expensive restaurant meals. He treats us sometimes, stating expressly that on such and such evening he is ordering delivery for all of us. I've noticed that Liam has certain qualms about eating these meals paid for by Hiroji. He acts as if it were not a big deal, but I know him well and can tell that when he is being a bit too nonchalant, it means he is quite uncomfortable.

Every once in a while Sensei invites us to dinners with his high-ranked guests. These are great feasts in Sensei's quarters at the other end of the long hallway. There are several courses and various drinks to go with each course. Sensei and his friends mostly converse in Japanese, and sometimes Hiroji is asked a question and says a few words. The deference with which these guests treat our Hiroji makes me think that the rumors about him must be true.

Other than these occasional lavish meals, Liam and I eat the simplest stuff and regard food as just necessary fuel for our bodies. We each cook for ourselves, there are no rules stating that the junior uchi-deshi must cook for the senior ones, but I don't see it as a problem or a bother to cook an occasional pasta dish or oatmeal porridge for everyone. The boys don't take it for granted and always thank me. A prepared bowl of porridge doesn't seem like a big deal or anything special to be thankful for, but when you train six–seven hours a day and somewhere in the middle start to feel that your energy level is plummeting and you are running on empty, this bowl really makes a big difference before the next class.

"Yesss!" Liam exclaims after checking his phone for the hundredth time. He immediately gets up and goes into his room. I guess because of the "snowstorm" he was not sure if the event on Irving Street was going to take place or not, but now has gotten a confirmation that it was. He emerges from his room some ten minutes later wearing a suit and a tie. It is the only suit he owns and he takes really good care of it, sending it to the cleaners after each outing. He looks cool all dressed up, his buzzed haircut and facial stubble relieving the overly formal effect of the black suit. He knows he looks good and he pauses in front of the couch, pretending to be giving Hiroji some necessary instructions, all the while glancing at me, making sure I see and appreciate the dressed-up version of Liam.

"Well, I think I'll go to bed early tonight," I announce as soon as Liam disappears down the stairs.

Hiroji shows a thumbs up without turning his head from the screen. He is positioned very comfortably on the red couch, sunk into the old, partially discolored cushions, his legs spread onto the huge coffee table.

Already in the hallway I suddenly remember something I've been wanting to ask Hiroji all day. I pause, hesitate whether to ask or not, but then go for it.

"Hey Hiroji, do you know what actually happened to our fourth uchideshi?"

"What do you mean?" Hiroji turns with a brusque movement and sits up so as to see me. He gives me such a strange and unnerving look that I think twice before continuing.

"Well, we trained in all the same classes and if Dav had gotten injured on the mat, I would have seen it happen. But I did not. All of a sudden he was gone—just not here anymore."

Hiroji is silent for a few moments.

"Weren't you going to go to bed?" he says. "Good night." And he turns back toward the screen.

Well, so much for my asking. Strange, though.

In my room, I change into jeans, a sweater, and boots and wait, listening at the door. It should not be too long. Hiroji has had quite a lot to drink. Yep, I am right. A few minutes later I hear the bathroom door open and close. I grab my coat and get out as quietly as I can. Earlier today I applied some liquid coconut oil to the old squeaky hinges of my door. I didn't have anything like WD-40, but the coconut oil did the trick. Now the hinges don't make a noise.

CHAPTER 5

"Ah, you came, in the snowstorm!" Danilo hugs me with his left arm, the right one still in the sling. "Here, sit, let me pour you a drink. Ah, it's so good you came!"

His overly good mood and broad smile make me suspicious right away. On the coffee table there is a big open bottle of whiskey, and two bottles of oxycodone, one empty.

"Where did you get the second one, Danilo?"

"Don't start in with the interrogation, please. Let's just have a nice quiet drink together." He pours whiskey in two glasses. "What shall we drink to?"

I push my glass away.

"Fine. I'll drink alone. To you, Sasha!" He swallows his whiskey in two big gulps, then picks up my glass and wants to finish it off too, but I take it away from him.

"How are you feeling? How are the ribs and the shoulder? The pain should have gotten better by now, no? Do you even need to be taking painkillers anymore?"

"Sure I do. Thanks for reminding me." He shakes two pills out of the bottle, puts them in his mouth quickly, tries to swallow, chokes, and, with a tortured grimace and unintelligible sounds indicating the urgency of the moment, grabs my glass and washes the pills down with the whiskey.

I just gasp, unsure of what to say to that.

"Did you at least have anything to eat?"

He shakes his head, putting on that stupid drunken smile again. How I hate to see my brother like this. I cannot quite control my irritation.

"Damn it, Danilo! Popping pills and drinking whiskey on an empty stomach! What the fuck are you thinking?!"

He turns away.

"I'll order some food. Will you eat Japanese?"

No response.

"Kani salad, seafood spring rolls, and broiled eel over rice. Sounds good?" I know broiled eel over rice is his favorite.

Still nothing.

"Danilo?"

He nods without looking at me.

"I am sorry, Danny. I didn't mean to be yelling before."

"Sash," he pronounces gently and strokes my arm with his knuckles several times—his very own gesture that I know so well. When we were kids and one time I was sick with something contagious—don't remember what it was—and was put in a separate room with strict instruction to Danilo to stay away, he snuck in anyway to bring me some sweets and to cheer me up. Somehow he got the idea that if he stroked my skin with his knuckles only he would not get infected. Since that time the gesture stuck.

"I am worried about my face," he says. "My nose especially. Does it seem like it's healing right?"

They have already taken out the plastic inserts that keep the nose straight while the bone is healing, and it looks like they did a very good job of repositioning the bone in the first place. Still, a broken nose is a broken nose, and in most cases you can always tell.

"It's fine. It's still a bit swollen, that's all. There is nothing to worry about. Your nose will be as beautiful as before," I say putting as much confidence into my voice as I can.

"I had a modeling gig all arranged this week. My agent had been slacking off for a while, or rather blaming me and my work ethics, ha! for not being able to find me anything, but he finally came through. I was to do a great commercial shoot. And now it's all ruined." He sniffles with his nose, but the tiniest motion still hurts him. He opens his mouth and breathes through it, tiny drops of saliva appearing in the crusted corners of his lips.

"Don't think about it, there'll be other gigs."

He sighs deeply. "I want to show you something. I was watching this movie. Here, look, there is a scene in Amsterdam. What do you think?"

"About what?"

"About Amsterdam. Look, look at the screen, Sash. Don't you think it's a beautiful town? Look at all the old buildings."

"There's plenty of old buildings in New York."

"But Amsterdam has all these canals."

"There is the East River couple blocks away."

"Not the same thing. Look, you can even live on a boat in Amsterdam. And there is a casino right in downtown. Isn't it cool? That's one thing New York does not have—a conveniently located, real casino."

"And yet you still manage to find spots to gamble here, don't you? Isn't 2 Gild Street where all the action takes place?"

He ignores my snarky remark.

"I think I might want to chuck everything and move to Amsterdam."

Here we go. He gets these ideas into his head every once in a while. They never amount to anything. Last time it was Lucerne. Now it's Amsterdam. Always a town with a casino.

Danny, Danny. There was a time when he was truly passionate about martial arts. He was very good, so limber and so strong on the mat. He trained in judo, sambo, and Russian hand-to-hand fighting. But then one day, he came home all excited saying he would not go to the next day competition because instead he had a modeling gig. That first shoot went really well. I wasn't surprised at all. My brother being so handsome and fit—of course he was going to be a great model.

I suppose somebody with more internal discipline and strength could have balanced martial arts and modeling, but Danny could not. Very soon the scale started tipping. There was more and more after-the-shoot partying and drinking all night with his new friends and less and less training. And when he did show up for training, he was too hungover and sluggish and couldn't do much. Strangely enough, he didn't give up competing, but in competitions you are only as good as your training.

And then Sergey appeared, or rather reappeared, because I am pretty certain I remember his face from long ago, from when I was very little, and our parents were alive. Danilo says he just chanced upon him one night at some party or such. Hmm, I am not so sure how accidental that was. I don't trust this Sergey person at all. He got his talons into my brother pretty hard, although I could not understand what he wanted from him. But he introduced him to gambling and got him really hooked on it, taking him often to his illegal gambling dens and to all the "best parties." The gambling, the drinking, the vertiginous heights and rock-bottom lows with money—this has been my Danny's existence, and for a while now I've had such a heavy feeling about him, always half-expecting that something really bad will happen to him and hoping so much that it will not. This feeling doesn't leave me, even when I am very busy, training—it's always inside me, weighing down on me.

Just before Grandpa passed away several years ago, he told me that even though Danny is older than me, I'm the stronger sibling, and I should take care of my brother. I don't think I have been doing a very good job. "Danilo, can you shut this off," I say pointing to the screen, "I need to talk to you. Can we talk, please?"

He turns the movie off, leans back, and puts his head on the cushion. His eyes are cloudy and his mouth is slightly opened in that unnatural smile. I don't think he is in a condition to have a serious conversation now, but I don't know when I will have another opportunity.

"It was Sergey who had you beaten up, wasn't it?"

"Hmm, well, not exactly. It wasn't like that."

"What do you mean? I thought you owed him money and wouldn't pay and he had his people beat you up."

"You've seen too many Guy Ritchie movies."

"Danilo!"

"All right, well, I do owe him money, but . . ."

"But what? Damn it, Danny. Talk to me."

"Well, he had me do a Dark Fight."

Dark Fights. Didn't Martine mention these words in the locker room? But she didn't explain what they meant.

I look at Danilo questioningly. "A Dark Fight," he repeats, his voice rising and becoming almost shrill. "Yes. And I did it. And if I had won, it would have erased the whole debt." He is talking very fast now. Agitated he leans forward, beads of perspiration appearing on his forehead. "But I lost, damn it, I lost."

"What's a Dark Fight?"

He does not hear me. His previous outburst seems to have exhausted him and he slumps back into the cushions and closes his eyes.

"Danny?"

"What?"

"Tell me about the Dark Fight."

He sighs. "I don't want to talk about it anymore. I am tired."

"Please."

He shakes his head and starts the movie again. "Let's just watch this together. And I'm going to have another drink."

I get up from the couch and put on my coat.

"Where are you going?"

"I am going." I feel pretty frustrated. I wish I could get more information out of him about these Dark Fights, but it would be useless to try now.

"What about the food?" he asks.

"Not hungry."

As I walk out of the apartment, I remember to leave some money on the shelf near the door—for Danny to pay when the Japanese food arrives.

*****

Outside it is quiet and lovely, the streets blanketed with a fresh white layer that has not yet had time to turn into a dirty slush. The snowfall has dwindled to a few large snowflakes, each one very visible when caught in the brightness of a streetlight. There are few cars and only a handful of people out. All the sounds are muffled, the dirty smells masked, the garbage and the rats invisible. The city looks its most beautiful—a fairytale-like, but short-lived and deceitful beauty. I breathe in deeply, filling my lungs with the fresh frosty air as I walk around the neighborhood, trying to dissipate the heavy, ominous feeling inside me, but not quite succeeding. Danilo's oxycodoned and whiskeyed voice pursues me and cuts through the enchantment of the night.

The Dark Fights. I just can't get these words out of my head. In the locker room, all Martine told me was that she had overheard Liam and Hiroji mention them at some point and was very curious herself. Strange. Well, one thing's for sure, if Sergey is behind these Dark Fights, they must be a nefarious and dangerous thing, and I need to get my brother out of all that.

Having walked west, I find myself standing in front of the Met, gazing absentmindedly at this impressive building. I walk up Fifth Avenue alongside Central Park for a bit and then turn back into the streets. On ninety-something they're filming a movie. There are several vans parked, many lights, and a large crew. I pause on the south side of the street to watch. Quite a few people have gathered and the crew members ask us to stay on this side, as they are filming a scene on the other. We all stand and watch as the director explains something to the actors, moving his arms emphatically, and a car involved in the scene backs up and moves forward innumerable times, and a girl in tight black leather pants gets in and out of the car. We discuss which movie it might be and someone says that it's actually an episode of a series that is currently airing. A crew member signals to us to be quiet each time they start shooting.

They shoot and reshoot the scene at least ten times and I never knew it took so long to get one tiny scene. I am getting tired of watching the car drive up to the curb and the girl in tight leather get out of it again and again. I am about to walk away when there is finally new development. A guy comes out of a building and pulls out a gun and another guy throws him down in what is a rather awkward hip throw.

"Nah, that does not look right," a loud voice to my right comments.

A crew member overhears and is visibly irritated. "What does not look right?"

"That throw. Not realistic at all." The voice has a familiar accent.

"And who are you?" the crew member asks.

"Me? Nobody. Just a passerby."

"Well, then keep passing by."

The man smiles a sort of a condescending smile, starts walking away, but then pauses, turns around, and looks directly at me. I come up to him.

"He at least should have tried to get the *kuzushi* and the footwork right, no?" I ask the man in the fisherman's sweater. Without the *kuzushi*—unbalancing the opponent—the throw looked really artificial. You cannot throw somebody who is so firmly planted on his feet unless he is basically letting you do it or is just jumping over you.

"So you know martial arts?" The man smiles, this time a nice, genuine smile.

I smile back at him.

"And is your boyfriend also a martial artist?"

"My boyfriend?"

"The guy in the ER, with the broken face."

"My brother. And . . . well, he is sort of a martial artist, or used to be. He doesn't train much these days." I look away, lost in my thoughts for a moment. Then I glance back at the man in the fisherman's sweater.

"Why are you looking at me so suspiciously," he asks.

"No, it's just . . . it seems a bit strange that we should run into each other again."

"Why strange? We probably live in the same neighborhood is all. Now that the snow has stopped, everybody's out for a walk. Don't you ever run into the same people around here?"

I don't answer. I know life is full of coincidences, but for some reason it's always hard for me to write them off as such.

"You're too suspicious." He wrinkles up the corners of his eyes. "You don't think I have been tracking you, now do you? I'm not nearly as romantic or crazy to be tracking a girl, even if she is as beautiful as you are. Besides, it was you who approached me now. And I am glad that you did."

I am still just looking at him without saying anything.

"You been living around here long?"

I am not sure how to answer this simple question. I am not technically living in this neighborhood now, but yeah, Danny and I were very little when we came to live here with our grandfather in his rent-stabilized one-bedroom on 82nd street after our parents died. And when Grandpa passed away, the friendly super didn't let the landlord know, and we were able to keep the apartment. I sum this all up with an affirmative nod. The man in the fisherman's sweater returns my nod and smiles.

"Are you hungry, neighbor? I am hungry and I don't want to eat alone," he declares all of a sudden. "Let's go have dinner."

It does not sound as a question but as a definite statement. I notice that all his sentences have a very convinced, confident ring to them. In other people it would have annoyed me, but in this man somehow I find it very appealing.

"I'd like to . . ."

"But?"

"Well . . ."

He thinks I live around here. I can come up with an excuse, some lie, of why I don't have much time for dinner. But for some reason I don't want to lie to him. And then, without giving it another thought, I just tell this unknown man the truth about my training in an ancient Japanese martial art, being an uchi-deshi and living in a traditional dojo with very strict rules, sneaking out tonight to see my convalescing brother, and having to be back before the head uchi-deshi gets in. I am amazed at my sudden openness. I never tell people about myself.

"An uchi-deshi, huh? Did not know a thing like that existed in the modern-day New York. Definitely sounds like something out of the past centuries Japan. Well, tell you what, uchi-deshi girl, we go and have a bite to eat now and then I drive you the dojo myself. Yes?"

"You have a car?"

"Yup, parked a few blocks up."

"And I'll be back at the dojo by midnight?"

"Guaranteed, Cinderella. Any more questions? 'Cause we can certainly stand on this corner and talk some more or we can go, say, into that restaurant over there and continue the conversation inside. You know, where it's warm and there's food."

As we walk toward the bistro, he notices me limp slightly and nods questioningly at my foot.

"Nothing. A couple of broken toes."

He gives me a long and attentive look. "Tough girl."

*****

In the French place, over a meal of *duck a l'orange*, I learn that the man in the fisherman's sweater is called Drago and that I was wrong about his accent. He is not from Eastern Europe but from the Balkans and has lived in New York for ten years. He is a fifth *dan* in judo and a two-time national champion—and besides judo he has had other martial arts training, something to do with his previous work in Europe. That part—about his other martial arts training and his previous work in Europe—he is not very, if at all, willing to talk about.

I listen to his every word with great attention. Everything about this man seems exceptionally interesting to me. Noting the manner of his speech and his body motions I get an impression that he would behave the same self-assured and confident way in any situation, that there is nothing in this world that might make him lose his cool. As first impressions go, it might be wrong of course.

At the very beginning of the meal the waiter comes over and asks, "How's everything." A standard question, to which I give an expected reply, "everything looks great, thanks."

"We'll see," is what the man in the fisherman's sweater answers instead.

A small detail, but it makes me think that perhaps this man does not like to follow social rules and conventions. He must have his own set of rules according to which he lives. I wonder what they are.

"Do you want dessert?" he asks after we are done with the duck.

It's been a long time since I had a dessert. Sugar is bad for your muscles and makes you feel sluggish on the mat.

He notices my hesitation. "You should get one. Find something good."

I choose a *Tarte Tatin*. When the waiter brings it, Drago asks for the check, pays it right away, and gets up.

"Stay, don't rush," he answers my silent question. "Eat your tarte and come outside in fifteen minutes."

I can't say that I have a vast dating experience, but I went on a number of dates before I moved into the dojo, and so I'm pretty sure it is not a standard procedure to leave your date at the table alone and give her precise instructions as when to leave. But I have already realized that I am dealing with a rather extraordinary man here, one who has his own way of doing things.

When I step out of the restaurant, he smiles to me from inside his car. "Your carriage is served, your ladyship. It will get you to your castle by midnight, as promised. Hope it won't turn into a pumpkin afterward."

Driving on the streets of New York is a special skill and getting into a car you tend to wonder whether your driver has truly mastered it. Could be a hit or a miss. You never know. You might get someone who blends in seamlessly with the chaotic picture made up of other vehicles, streetlights, bicyclists, and pedestrians. Or you get a driver who proceeds with jerky motions and erratic changes of speed and is unnerved by such a common thing as one or two persons crossing an empty avenue on red light late at night. Even cabbies, who are supposed to be professionals, often times make me quite tense. But with Drago at the wheel, I relax completely. I have never seen such mastery of driving, such confidence and smoothness on the road. Perhaps this man does everything with great skill and this same calm assuredness. It's as if his inner strength shines through in all of his actions. I find it amazingly attractive.

Drago turns into 16th Street and finds a parking spot. We sit and talk for a few minutes. I know I must go very soon because I absolutely cannot risk Liam returning home before me and settling on his red couch for the night, but I really don't want to get out of this car, to say goodbye to Drago. It seems almost impossible that I should open the door and walk away from him. I don't think I have ever felt this attracted to anybody before. Such attraction cannot be one-sided. I don't have a logical explanation for why, but it strikes me as absolutely inconceivable that he should not be feeling the same as I am at this moment. It is as if there are invisible threads pulling us together, and if I can feel their pull, so can he, I am certain of it.

I reach over and touch Drago's arm. His sleeves are rolled and I move my fingers up along his arm, from the wrist to the elbow. The feel of his skin is intoxicating, and the sensation goes through my whole body. I am not sure I know what I am doing. Never before have I initiated physical contact with a man, not like this. He leans in and kisses me with intensity and strength. I pull back and look him in the eyes for a few moments. I touch his face with my fingers, tracing a line from a cheekbone to the chin. Then I bring my face closer to his, past that point where you can look at the eyes, closer still, and then feel his lips with mine gently and softly. When he tries to kiss me, I pull back slightly, and then move in again. I brush my lips against his lower lip, touch his upper lip lightly with my tongue, and bite it a little bit. At that he starts kissing me again, with even greater intensity than before, putting his hand behind my head and pulling me toward him.

At first, I am very aware of his tongue and his teeth, but then everything gets rather hazy and the lines are blurred, our mouths are so melted together. I don't know how long it lasts and who breaks it off. Suddenly we are just looking at each other.

"Wow," he whispers.

"What?" I ask. My voice sounds strange and unknown to me.

He does not reply and takes my hand and puts his lips to it

"I have to go, Drago."

He nods and yet keeps holding my hand. "Kiss me just one more time."

*****

Unlocking the front door, I walk up carefully. I know exactly which of the stairs squeak and don't step on them. As I pass the second floor landing I see a dim strip of light under the door. What the hell? I remember perfectly well all the lights were off when I was sneaking out a few hours ago. Hmm, unsure of what is going on, I open the door slightly and peek in. At the farther end of the training area one ceiling lamp is on and I see Hiroji practicing cuts with a wooden samurai sword. His moves are strong and precise and he seems fully absorbed in his activity. I was certain he would be in his room sleeping by now, yet it doesn't surprise me too much that he should be on the mat training alone at this hour. It somehow goes hand in hand with his whole mystery-shrouded image.

He raises the sword for a sideways cut, pauses for a split second before finishing the full-body-turn, and at that moment it seems to me that our eyes meet. No, it must be just a trick of my imagination. I am sure it's impossible for him to see me from where he is. I close the door carefully and continue up the stairs.

Back in my room safely, not having encountered anything but an empty red couch in the common quarters, I sit on the bed for a while staring at nothing and smiling. The scene in the car with Drago is playing in my head, in all its details. I am perfectly aware of the smile on my own face. I don't know how much time has passed, when suddenly I am awakened from my entranced state by a knock on the door. What the hell? I was so sure I got back in unnoticed. I open the door and there is Hiroji standing there looking at me in a strange manner.

"I heard you leave earlier and I heard you come back," he says.

As I am about to give some explanation, he interrupts. "Why were you asking about the fourth uchi-deshi's disappearance all of a sudden?"

"No reason. Just curious."

"Well, don't be. It's better you should stay out of all that, trust me."

"Stay out of what?"

He does not answer.

"Hiroji, what are Dark Fights?"

A momentary shudder runs across his face and his lips tighten into a narrow line.

"You really should get some sleep. How are you going to test on no sleep? Don't you think you are taking your examination too lightly? A Nidan test is kind of a huge thing. You should be prepared and well rested, hundreds of people are going to be watching. It's a big responsibility."

"Hiroji, what are you talking about? I'm not testing."

"Yes, you are. I just saw the list with the names. Yours is on it." His voice sounds tired, but there is this focused, almost tough expression on his face.

"What? Sensei did not tell me."

"Sensei did not have to tell you directly. He told the head uchi-deshi, and he was to relay Sensei's words to you. The chain of command, you know."

Yes, I most certainly do know how the chain of command works here. Sensei gave the message to Liam, fully trusting his head uchi-deshi, not doubting that the message would be passed on.

I don't have any words for a reply. I just stand there staring at Hiroji in utter dismay.

The head uchi-deshi did not tell me anything. He just didn't.

How could he do that to me?

CHAPTER 6

Sitting at the top of the stairs in the dark and waiting, I catch myself biting the inside of my lip. A bad habit I tried hard to train out of myself. I don't know when I started doing it again, most likely just now. It is almost one o'clock at in the morning, and he should be coming back any moment. I hear the front door open and slow laborious steps going up the stairs.

He stops a few stairs below.

"Why didn't you tell me?" I ask him.

He is silent for a while.

"Move! I'm tired," he then says.

The staircase being so narrow, he can't go around me.

"When were you going to tell me?"

He shrugs. "In the morning. Or right before the tests. Or maybe you would have found out hearing your name called to the mat during the examinations."

"That's fucked up, Liam. Really fucked up."

"Don't know what you mean. What difference does it make when you find out?"

"I could have had a chance to prepare, to practice the techniques, to work on stuff!"

"Bullshit. You prepare for a black-belt examination over many years of training. Now you are either ready or not. We'll soon find out. Move! I want to go to bed, and I suggest you do the same. Oh, and next time you talk to a higher rank, watch your language." With that Liam advances toward me and there is nothing for me to do but get up and let him pass.

Back in my room, I can't sleep. I am lying in bed absolutely awake, my thoughts racing. I am so angry at Liam and anxious about the examinations. I am trying to go over the list of the most difficult techniques Sensei might call out, and to devise a strategy for the second part of the test, when you are attacked by multiple fighters simultaneously. How I wish I had had time to prepare. I have half a mind to go downstairs and practice weapons, as there is a big chance Sensei might call *boken*s and *tanto*s during the test. But I know it would be of no use now. What I need is to get a few hours of sleep. But I can't fall asleep, damn it, I just can't.

I focus on some of my favorite techniques, the ones I have found to be the most effective, and review the movements in my head, again and again. The footwork, the timing, the positioning of my body at precise angles. Suddenly, as it seems to me right in the middle of a technique, I hear loud knocking on the door and a voice calling, "It's past six. You overslept. Hurry up." For a few moments I keep lying down uncertain of what is going on. My heart is pounding, which happens when you are in deep sleep and are brusquely woken up. I breathe in and out slowly to adjust myself to a sudden change in reality. Then I get up, get ready as fast as I can, and go downstairs. The first person I see is Liam. He looks at me, opens his mouth, most likely to scold me for being late, but changes his mind and just turns away.

*****

Hours of training at the Winter Assembly go by in sort of a haze. I practice with different people, we work on various techniques, but moments later I cannot recall who I have just trained with or which technique we did. As each class starts and ends, the only thing I am intensely aware of is that the examination time is getting nearer. In the intervals between classes people talk to me, and I suppose I reply, but the topics of the conversations elude me. There are tons of people, familiar faces and ones I have never seen before, talking to each other in various languages. I hear English, Spanish,

French, Russian, Japanese, German. After a while the faces and the voices all melt into a big blurred mass.

As always at such a grand event, when in each class there are over a hundred of martial artists practicing throws, takedowns, various joint locks, holds, and chokes, all in a limited amount of space of no more than a thousand hundred square feet of mat area, injuries are unavoidable, and I find myself helping someone tape up an ankle, giving someone else an icepack for a shoulder. I do other uchi-deshi duties as well—wiping down the mats, disinfecting the bloody spots, cleaning up the women's locker room, restocking toilet paper and towels. And then I am on the mat again, training, training. At one point, while working on a shoulder throw with a big and heavy visitor from Turkey, I hear someone tell me "hey, you need to slow down, save some energy for the examination." I am not sure whose voice it is. Is it Liam's? Or Hiroji's? Or someone else's?

At various moments throughout the day Liam's face stands out against the background of innumerable blurred faces, his ambiguous smirk and his bright dark eyes looking at me with severity.

According to the dojo rule, we are not allowed to drink water on the mat. Some people step out to get a drink from the water fountain, but being an uchi-deshi, I would never get off the mat for such a reason. In the middle of one of the afternoon classes I feel pretty dehydrated. I realize that my body has stopped sweating, which is a clear sign of dehydration. Still, I won't step out. I am training near the entrance to the mat area. It is as packed outside as it is on the mat. Spectators watching, martial artists taking a break and waiting for the next class to start—a massive crowd. An arm reaches in and places a water bottle up to my lips. I take a few hurried sips and then turn to glance at who the kind person is. But the arm has already withdrawn and disappeared behind the innumerable bodies. I go back to training right away.

*****

At five o'clock all the practitioners sit in *seiza*—a kneeling position. There are so many people, we are squeezed in tight, occupying two thirds of the mat, row upon row, shoulder to shoulder, knees almost touching the toes of those in the next row.

I sit with my fellow martial artists from the dojo, who at this important moment feel like a true family to me. Everybody—the over-ly-energetic gentleman who likes to give unsolicited advice and to correct everyone on the mat and gets on people's nerves a bit, the tough woman who treats every technique during class as if it were done for a competition and scares most of her training partners, the young silent guy who never says a word beyond what's required by the training etiquette, the hard-of-hearing man of completely unidentifiable age who has been training here since the beginning of time but decided not to test and to remain a white belt forever—now they are all family. We never feel as close as during the examinations, supporting and cheering for each other. There is something about these events that unites us and gives us a sense of home and belonging and of being amongst people who truly care. When we nod our heads encouragingly or bump our fists, or pat each other on the shoulder, there is an unmistakable feeling of perfect mutual understanding.

The front portion of the mat has been left clear and a low table for the presiding committee has been brought and placed in the front left corner. Besides Sensei there are two other high-ranked martial arts masters at the table, but their presence is mostly symbolic. It is Sensei's word only that counts during the examinations.

A huge number of friends, relatives, and other spectators crowd the area to the back of the mat. A bunch of people have climbed onto the benches, some even onto the windowsills to get the best vantage point. There is a continuous loud clamor of voices, but it subsides and dies down as soon as Sensei takes up his position at the low table. The examinations start with those testing for a Shodan—first degree black belt.

According to the tradition of classical Japanese martial arts, prac-titioners advance to the next level upon mastering a certain group of techniques, which include throws, takedowns, joint manipulations, chokes, as well as strikes, both openhanded and closed fist, to vital points. With each level, the number of techniques and their complexity grows.

Testing for Shodan, one must demonstrate an excellent ability to do all the techniques as well as to fight off several opponents at a time.

It is often said that the real martial arts training only starts when you achieve the rank of Shodan. Everything before that is just a preparation. Having been awarded a black belt, a student then spends years working on perfecting the execution of the techniques, striving to achieve true mastery. A martial artist testing for Nidan—a second degree black belt—must really impress Sensei not only with the perfect execution of the techniques, but also with the speed, the force, and that hard-to-define quality that shows the techniques have truly become an intrinsic part of the martial artist's body and mind.

Sitting in the first row I wait and bite the inside of my lip. I get more and more nervous as I realize that Sensei is not very happy with the way the black belt examinations are going this year. He is failing quite a number of visiting examinees and telling them to come back and try next time. So far, only one person from our dojo has failed. I know how hard he worked for this and that he was well prepared, but the nerves got the better of him and he started messing up technique after technique.

The Shodan examinations go on for over two hours, and then those testing for Nidan are called to the mat. There are only a small number of martial artists up for a Nidan, and one by one their names are called out, but mine is not. Today, they go in the alphabetical order and I should have been called some time ago.

What is going on?

Have Liam and Hiroji played some sort of very mean joke on me?

Perhaps Sensei never intended to have me test after all.

I bite the inside of my lip to the point of being able to taste blood. I wish I could clarify the matter with one of my fellow uchi-deshi right this minute. That is, of course, impossible. Both Hiroji and Liam are now at the front of the mat attacking one of the examinees with bokkens— long wooden swords that samurai used for training purposes. After this student's test is finished, a committee member announces that it was the last examination for this year.

So that's it, then? I'm not testing? Oh, well, maybe it is for the better.

Perhaps Sensei will tell me to test next year and I will not be caught unawares and will have more time to prepare. Still, it was a vicious thing my fellow uchi-deshi pulled, messing with my head like this. And surely Liam was behind it.

"Last but one," a committee member says.

Then my name is called.

*****

The dojo becomes extraordinarily quiet. Everybody knows that I am Sensei's uchi-deshi, and to watch an uchi-deshi test is rather a special occurrence. With so many visitors from around the world watching, I certainly feel the pressure of the moment. They are all waiting with bated breath to witness something extraordinary. It is well known that Sensei puts his uchi-deshi through the most difficult examinations, expecting much more from them than from regular students. People from the Dojo, with whom I have been training side by side for many years, and beginners whom I've personally trained, they are all genuinely rooting for me to do well. And the visitors, well, I suspect it does not matter much to them if I succeed or fail, they just want to see a thrilling spectacle.

During the first part of my examination, Sensei has Hiroji and Liam alternate in attacking me. They are to attack with strikes to the head and torso, and various grabs. I am to fight off the attacks using a variety of techniques. And Sensei does not want to see any basic ones. He's looking forward to something of high-level of difficulty, such as throws that require joint manipulations, sacrifice throws, arm bars, and chokes.

Right from the start I can feel that something is off. I don't seem to have the full command of my body. I am able to execute the techniques, but my motions are stiff and lacking in power and energy. At one moment, when I am locking Liam's shoulder out and am about to throw him, our heads touch and I hear him hiss into my ear, "*Too slow. Sensei is not happy. You're too slow.*" I take a quick glance at Sensei and indeed see that the corners of his mouth are very visibly down.

Liam attacks me with a strike to the center of the head, I change the angle of my body, intercept the strike and go in for a throw, but Liam manages to get a hold of my sleeve and is able to reverse my failed technique into a throw of his own, after which we engage in a ground fight, which is stopped by Sensei's order. We get up and both stand there panting for a few moments. Sensei is looking at me displeased, frowning and shaking his head. Damn it, I am letting Sensei down, betraying his expectations. Nothing could be worse than that.

"Too slow," Liam mutters under his breath again.

What is going on with me? This does not look like me at all. At one time, not so long ago, Sensei commended the "lightning speed" of my reactions and the "clean precision" of my technique. He didn't say that to me directly—that's not something he would normally do—but I overheard him talking about me to one of the high-ranked visiting martial artists. Now I'm showing neither the lightning speed nor the clean precision. What is wrong? My body just feels so strange.

It must be the nerves. Can't be any other explanation . . . or can there?

For the briefest moment a strange suspicious thought shoots through my mind, but I dismiss it immediately. I don't have such enemies capable of slipping me something that would slow me down on the mat. That's just not done among martial artists. No, I bet it is nothing but the stupid nerves. Being so anxious, I must have been overthinking every tiny move, every angle, trying to make it as perfect as possible. And it has had the reversed result, slowing me down and making my technique ineffective. I need to just shut off my mind and rely on the knowledge and skills that my body has absorbed during the years of training. Suddenly I remember something Liam told me on the stairs in the dark. "You are either ready or not." He was right. It dawns on me now that Liam was right—after so many years of training a true martial artist should just be ready, warning or no warning, prep time or no prep time at all.

But I am ready. I am! I have the technical skill, the power—which is amplified by positioning my body at precise angles and using the opponents' power against them—and I know that I can have the speed. I can be so damn fast that the attacker won't stand a chance against my technique and will hit the ground before realizing how or what I did. I just need to get over my nerves and demonstrate all that I have in me, right now, right at this moment, when Sensei and so many people are watching. I *am* ready.

With this something changes. I relax, I breathe deeper. I make a huge effort and am able to compel this strangely unwilling body of mine to cooperate. When Hiroji attacks next, I counteract immediately, unbalance him, and, his head now positioned rather low to the ground, I grab his head tight and do a *head throw*. The audience gasps. It is a very dangerous throw that can snap the opponent's neck in an instant. And yes, I execute it strongly but with great precision and caution. I hear voices of approbation. After a few more well-executed techniques Sensei announces that the first part of the examination is over.

*****

For the second part, Liam and Hiroji are called off and six fresh fighters are invited to the mat. All six of them are to come at me simultaneously, using any attack they want.

We are sitting in *seiza*, me facing the line of the opponents, some fifteen feet separating us. Upon a sign from Sensei I initiate the bow. According to the tradition, I look into the eyes of each of my opponents for a brief moment and then make one bow directed to all of them. They respond with a bow of their own, and then . . . I don't wait for them to attack first. My strategy is not to let them surround me. So, while they are still straightening up after the bow, I have already sprung to my feet and am running toward them.

Fifteen feet, ten, five—I have singled out one of the opponents and locked my eyes on him. He is charging for an attack. At the very last moment before the collision, I drop down, hitting with my body against his legs. With all the force of the forward motion he goes tumbling in the air over me and falls down hard. Ha! He will be out of the fight for a few moments. I am back on my feet immediately, dodge a punch to the stomach from another attacker, grab his arm, lock the wrist joint, and throw him into a breakfall.

Another attacker is now trying to choke me from behind. I tense the neck muscles, take a quick step hooking his leg and then drop on my knee unbalancing and throwing him. Right away I dodge an incoming punch to the head and move in, wrapping the guy's body round my shoulders, one arm cupping his thigh, and throw him in a precisely executed drop *kata guruma*—a fireman's carry throw—one of the most difficult but extremely effective techniques. At that the audience just cannot keep quiet anymore and erupts in applauses. I keep going, using the attackers' energy and force against them—the harder they come at me, the harder they hit the mat.

At some point Sensei signals for two of my opponents to get *tantos*—samurai daggers—and incorporate them into the fight. The weapons have been laid out at the side of the mat and it takes the guys a split second to pick them up and get back into action. So now it is four people coming at me barehanded and two with weapons.

I don't realize it right away, but when I chance to take a closer look, I am taken aback. To my utter amazement, one of the attackers is not holding a wooden tanto that we always use during training and examinations.

No, it's a real steel weapon.

*****

The attacker with the real knife makes a few tentative and careful moves, and I fight them off easily. Then, however, he picks up speed, and the combat becomes much more dangerous for me.

Out of the corner of my eye I notice Sensei rise slightly from his sitting position and his face tense up. Yet he doesn't give a command to stop the fight. I instinctively know why Sensei remains silent. He is worried that an abrupt order would make me freeze and thus become exposed and vulnerable to the knife, in case the attacker, for some reason, does not honor the command.

The audience is quiet too. Certainly they must have noticed, but perhaps they think that all is going according to a plan and that a real weapon was meant to be used during this uchi-deshi's examination, as a special test of her skills.

The following actions take place within a span of only few seconds.

Executing a shoulder throw, I manage to land one of the bare-handed attackers right in the way of the other two. They trip over him and for a few moments are busy disentangling themselves.

The next instant there is the real tanto coming right at me.

Damn, it is one thing to fight against a wooden tanto. But it is a completely different thing to have sharp steel pointed at your stomach.

I shift my body, just missing the weapon. I grab the attacker's wrist as hard as I can and get him into an arm bar, applying pressure until the knife falls down. I kick it with my foot sending it flying off to the side of the mat.

One of the bare-handed fighters has in the meanwhile disentangled himself and is coming at me again. I do a *sweeping hip throw*. The audience gasps and a murmur starts to build up until voices grow loud.

At this point, it seems to me that the lightning speed of the events slows down, as if to give an opportunity for all the sounds and visuals to really sink in. I look, and the guy I have just thrown is all bloody, a huge streak of red all across his *gi*. I don't understand what is going on. I haven't injured him in any way. He fell down safely. There cannot be any wound. Where is all the blood coming from?

The audience is pointing at me, people's faces rather horror stricken. I look down and on my right side, right above the black belt, there is a gash. With all the adrenaline pumping I didn't even notice when I got cut. The tanto must have been so sharp it slashed right through the heavy double-weave fabric of the *gi*, like sliding through butter, and cut into my flesh. The blood is coming out profusely.

CHAPTER 7

The black belt examinations end in a much less formal manner than they're supposed to. There's quite a commotion on the mat—people have surrounded me and are talking loudly, asking a million questions. The crowd opens up when Sensei approaches. From all directions voices suggest with insistence that I should be taken to the ER. Sensei pays them no attention and looks straight at me, studying alternately my bloody *gi* and my face.

"I'm all right, Sensei. I'll be fine here," I say trying to add weight and significance to my every word.

Sensei beckons to the attacker who had the real tanto, and who now looks completely confused. He is talking fast and is trying to explain that he picked up one of the weapons laid out at the side of the mat and, yes, it did seem strange to him that the dagger was real, but he thought everything had been sanctioned by Sensei. It was not his place to ask questions in middle of the fight. He doesn't know where the weapon is now. After he dropped it, someone must have picked it up.

It all seems very odd and mysterious to me, but the guy's face portrays such honest confusion and dismay, and besides, I've known him for a while, and he is a good and diligent martial artist, so now I rather believe that he doesn't know anything about the provenance and the purpose of the real tanto. Someone else must be behind it. The guy was just a tool in that person's dirty game.

Sensei stands, deliberating for a few moments and then gives me a brief nod of the head, which I construe as a permission to get off the mat. I bow to Sensei and make a dash for the changing room across the narrow hallway, and then I lock myself in the bathroom. Martine has followed me and asks to be let in. I need her help so I send her for some medical supplies and when she returns I let her in and shut the door quickly again, in the noses of the innumerable inquisitive well-wishers.

In the tranquility of the bathroom we take off my *gi*, disinfect our hands, wash the wound on my side with copious amount of hydrogen peroxide, and discover that the cut is several inches long, but not deep at all, even though it is bleeding a lot. Perhaps at the ER they would have given me stitches despite the wound being so superficial, but I don't think it's necessary.

I pick the shreds of the gi from the wound, then hold the edges tightly together and spray almost half a bottle of medical glue into it. It burns like hell, but I breathe in and out deeply to control the pain.

"You sure it will hold?" Martine asks.

"It should. At one time Hiroji had a bad cut and had Liam use a stapler on him. I don't think I want to do that."

"Nah, those boys are crazy."

When the glue dries, we put sterile gauze on top and a large plaster.

"Ah, damn it," I exclaim. You know what I forgot to do?"

"What?"

"To take a shower first. I am covered in sweat from the whole day of training and the examination. And now, how am I going to take a shower?"

But Martine is pretty inventive. "Don't worry. We can use this." She holds up a bottle of medical alcohol. I take the rest of my clothes off and she helps rub me down with cotton wool drenched in the alcohol.

By the time we get out of the bathroom, the changing room has filled to the brim, and outside it is even worse. Martial artists, friends, relatives—all crowd the hallway and the reception area, discussing the eventful examinations they have just witnessed, and waiting for the party to start. There is such a multitude of bodies that it feels the walls of the old building are going to burst at the seams. Martine helps me get through, fending off people's questions.

On our way, amongst the mass of all the faces, for a brief moment one familiar bearded face catches my attention. What the hell is he doing here, I wonder feeling a sudden and unpleasant tightness in my throat, as if I wanted to swallow and could not. Hmm, maybe I am just thirsty. I drink from the water fountain and when I look up again, the bearded face is not there. Martine leads me to the foot of the stairs, where we part, as only uchi-deshi are allowed to go up.

*****

The adrenaline rush over, I am lying in my bed, drained off all energy. I am supposed to be downstairs for cleaning up and setting up for the party, but I am too exhausted right now and too overwhelmed. The cut is not bothering me much, I just need a few minutes to be on my own, away from everybody. In my mind I go over the examination. There was a pause before my name was called to the mat, it must have been at that moment that the wooden *tanto* was switched for the real one. Of course I was too anxious and was not paying attention, but I think . . . yes, I am pretty sure I saw Liam go up to the weapons shelf. He knew my name was going to be called next and he laid out the weapons that would be used during my test, and somehow he must have managed to make the switch.

Damn it. First he conceals from me that I am taking the examination. Then he replaces a wooden *tanto* with the steel one, and an extremely sharp one at that. He truly wanted to sabotage my test, *didn't he?* Oh, he must really hate me. I don't believe he wished for me to get seriously injured, but he definitely wanted me to fail. He must be holding such a grudge about what happened between us last year.

Sensei would no doubt investigate the incident, but Liam is too sneaky. He will find a way to stay beyond any suspicion and will lead Sensei to believe that it was just someone's mistake, made in the tumult of the crowded examinations.

Hiroji knocks on the door. "Sensei wants to see you in his office."

Immediately I get up, pull on sweatpants and a hoodie, and go out into the hallway.

"You ok?" Hiroji asks.

"Yep."

He points at my side and looks at me questioningly.

"All good now," I reply. "Just a superficial cut. Could have been much worse."

He shows a thumbs up.

"Hiroji, about the cleaning up and setting up for the party?"

"Don't worry about it. I got it. Go see Sensei."

Sensei's office is on the other side of the stairs at the end of a hallway. Its door is almost always closed. Now it is wide open. Inside, Sensei is entertaining a few high-ranked guests. On several tables there are trays with Japanese food and a number of *tokkuri*, porcelain flasks for serving sake. There are also bottles of French wine and cognac. Sensei is sitting behind a huge desk. He has exchanged his gi jacket for a striped sailor's shirt, the one he wears for the dojo party every year. I am not sure if it is the exact same shirt or he has several identical ones, but in all my years at the dojo I have seen him in a striped sailor's shirt at every party.

The walls are hung with old black-and-white photographs and weapons—samurai swords and daggers. It occurs to me that Liam might have sneaked into Sensei's office and got the *tanto* here. As the head uchi-deshi he knows the combination to the lock on the door. I have half a mind to ask Sensei if maybe one of the weapons is missing, but I decide against it. It might very well be that Liam has already had a chance to put the *tanto* back.

I hover at the door and Sensei waves me in. I come in and bow.

"You did good." Sensei nods his head several times. "It was the best test I have seen in a long time. The beginning was not so good, but the rest was very, very good. Congratulations on your Nidan."

Sensei does not give out praises often, if ever, and his present words have such a great impact on me. Oh, he must really have liked my test and truly thinks me worthy of a Nidan. I suddenly feel so very happy. Sensei's few words of approval have made me forget all my tribulations. What matters most to me right now is that I have passed the examination and am a second-degree black belt. I try to adhere to the solemnity of the moment and keep a serene face, but I can't help but smile broadly.

"Thank you, Sensei." I bow again.

"And are you feeling okay?" Sensei asks.

"Yes, Sensei, thank you."

"Then go change! Just look at what you are wearing. You are a pretty girl. Put on a nice dress and go downstairs and party."

*****

I put on a short, sleeveless off-white dress and let my hair down, but quickly realize it's not particularly clean and so gather it up in a loose bun instead. I get the envelope from under my mattress and go downstairs. The party has already started. On top of the reception desk, which serves as a bar counter now, there are trays with all sorts of food items—sushi, guacamole and chips, dim sum, chicken wings, and mini spring rolls. Hiroji stands behind the counter playing bartender. At his disposal there are numerous bottles of white and red wine, sake, whiskey, rum, and cachaça. There are also two coolers filled with beer. When I ask for a ginger ale, Hiroji shrugs, searches everywhere, and finds one lonely can of Sprite. At the dojo parties, nonalcoholic beverages are a rare commodity.

The crowd gets thicker by the minute, people now standing several rows deep around the counter reaching over heads to get to the food and the drinks. As the last of the martial artists finish taking showers and getting dressed and emerge from the locker rooms, they are immediately absorbed into the party and the reception area gets even more packed. From all directions people talk to me, offer me drinks and congratulations. Everybody is commenting on how exceptional my examination was and discussing the sudden appearance of a real weapon. Of course no one has any definite ideas, but the general consensus is that the *tanto* was meant as an extra test of skill, specifically for an uchi-deshi. I don't enter into discussions and just give out brief *thank you, thank you very much* and an occasional *oh careful,* when someone gives me an extra zealous hug pressing against the spot of the wound.

Holding the envelope tight in my hand I make my way through the crowd looking for the bearded face. It must still be somewhere here, I am sure of it. I caught a glimpse of it earlier by the water fountain, so I head in that direction, maneuvering amongst the eating, drinking, and loudly talking groups of people that stop me at each moment. I also seem to be going against the current of those that are moving toward the counter, which slows down my advance. With many pauses I finally reach my destination, but the bearded face is not here. Well, at least there is something non-alcoholic for my thirst. For a few minutes I lean down over the water fountain and drink the wonderfully cold water. I straighten up, as I feel a hand touch my bare shoulder.

"Congratulations, beauty. That was an exceptional examination. You showed such great skill. I especially enjoyed your *kata guruma* throw. You know, I watched carefully and the way you executed it is now considered illegal in many competitions. You did it old-style. I liked what I saw. I bow to you." Sergey inclines his body slightly. "I trust your wound is not dangerous?"

I hand him the envelope but he pretends to ignore it.

"And look at how beautiful you are tonight. Such a rare pleasure to see you in a dress."

"Take this and leave me alone. And leave my brother alone," I say as I press the envelope into his hand.

"What's this?"

The party is so loud that we have to converse standing very close to each other.

"The ten thousand. Now Danilo does not owe you anything."

Sergey pushes the envelope away.

"It is not your obligation to pay your brother's debts. I will not take money from you, my beauty."

"Yes, you will." I quickly glance around and place the envelope in his pocket. I am pretty sure no one has noticed the little maneuver. Everybody is fully immersed in the festive ambience, a natural effect of the copious amounts of alcohol .

Sergey does not remove the money from his pocket and so I consider the matter settled and want to walk away. He grabs my elbow, but probably remembers what happened the last time he did that, and so retrieves his hand quickly.

"Wait, wait, beauty. Don't rush away. A few words, if you will."

"What?"

"Do you know what Dark Fights are?"

He notices my uncertainty and moves his mouth in an unpleasant smirk.

"You had my brother do a Dark Fight and he was badly injured," I say quickly.

"Ah." Sergey waves his hand in a deprecating gesture. "Your brother is no fighter. I knew that. He has some skills, maybe even some talent, but no discipline at all. I understand he stopped training a while ago. All he does is drink, gamble, and party."

"He gambles in *your* gambling dens. And he drinks at *your* parties."

"I give to people what they want." Sergey shrugs and puts on an innocent expression that I itch to erase with a good punch.

"You get people into debt and then enslave them."

Another shrug. "Difference in terminology."

"Why the fuck did you make Danilo fight?" I feel the anger building inside me and try to control myself. "If you knew he was not a fighter and would definitely lose, then why make him fight?"

"I gave him a chance to make some money. And it was not such a bad fight either. The audience quite liked him. They called him a *pretty boy*. And he did put up an earnest defense . . . until he got destroyed. People enjoyed seeing the *pretty boy* get destroyed. There was this beautiful aura of the doomed about him, right from the start."

He says this to me, Danilo's sister, so casually, so matter-of-factly. What a bastard. Standing in such close proximity to him, I can clearly see the neatly trimmed hairs in his nostrils, the pores on his face, the clusters of small moles on his neck where his beard ends, and the exact location of carotid arteries, and somehow I can't help but visualize my arm around his neck in a choke hold, tightening against those carotid arteries for a few seconds, restricting the blood flow to the brain and putting that smug face into a sudden sleep.

"I am just being honest with you, beauty. That's one thing you can always expect from me, honesty. So, hear me out. I invite you into the Dark Fights. No-gloves, no-rules bouts attended by select public paying high dollars. Everything done in complete secret. Fighters do not know each other and only see their opponent when they step into the cage. No real names ever. No word gets out. It will not affect your training at the dojo. I strongly believe you will be a great success. With your superb martial arts skills and your looks, you will shine. Unlike your no-good brother, you have strong discipline. You train hard and are a real martial artist. You will win and make a lot of money. What do you say?"

"I say go to hell. Your Dark Fights are fucking illegal bloodbaths," I shout into Sergey's ear. The music has just been turned up, making a conversation in normal voices impossible.

"I strongly prefer the term 'underground matches.'"

"Difference in terminology."

"Ha-ha-ha, I like your spirit. I believe we will work very well together."

"I believe you should get the fuck out of here."

"You are refusing my invitation? And in such a rude manner! I might even get offended. You know, it is not my habit to recruit fighters personally. I usually prefer to stay in the deep shadows, so to speak. No fighter gets to know that I run the show. But I've made an exception for you! I came for you myself. And you treat me this way. Wait, we are not finished . . ."

He wants to say something else, but at that moment we are interrupted.

"Come, Sasha! They are making caipirinhas!" Martine grabs my arm and pulls me in the direction of the bar. "Come on! They are delicious. We must drink to your success. Everybody is talking about how awesome you were on the mat."

Sergey looks Martine over from head to toe, his eyes narrowing in that unpleasant evaluating manner that I have seen before. His gaze rests on her muscular arms, broad shoulders, and strong neck. Then he turns to me again, lifts his hands up, and makes an applauding gesture.

"Your friend is right. Indeed you were magnificent on the mat. It does warrant a drink and a celebration. Enjoy!"

As I walk away with Martine, I turn my head and see Sergey's hands up above the crowd, applauding. A cold shudder runs through me, leaving behind a bitter taste, as if a premonition of something terrible to come. He is a dangerous man, that Sergey. Oh, I do hope that after the horrors of the Dark Fight my brother has finally realized it too and will now stay away from him.

*****

A visitor from Brazil has found all the necessary ingredients—cachaça, lime, sugar, and ice—and is mixing caipirinhas at the improvised bar. He makes a huge pitcher and Martine takes a sip from it and declares the drink is not strong enough. The Brazilian looks a bit offended that his mixology skills have been put to doubt, and he and Martine argue for a while. Then the party spirit prevails and he pours more cachaça into the pitcher.

I rarely, if ever, drink alcohol. I cannot say I don't enjoy how light, cheerful, and carefree it makes me feel, but the effects the next day cancel all that out. It's really difficult to train when your head weighs a ton and your whole body is sluggish and weak. Right now, however, being so worked up and angry after the conversation with Sergey, I decide to have a drink. I need to drown the unpleasantly dark and ominous sensation that has been building up inside me for a while, which increased tenfold just now. The caipirinha tastes smooth and sweet and goes down very easy. Cheered on by Martine, I finish my whole glass.

I don't know how many drinks Martine has already had tonight. That girl can really drink. She often brags that she can drink like a man. I think she can actually outdrink any man, and the alcohol does not have any significant effect on her except that she gets very flirtatious and goes with great assertiveness after her chosen targets. For a moment Hiroji gets scared that he might be her objective for the night and escapes from her behind the counter. She then focuses her attention on the young Brazilian mixologist, who welcomes her advances with eagerness, and for a while he and Martine make various toasts and clink glasses together. In the meantime I am chatting with other people in the group, and they all want to drink with me to my Nidan.

At some point I realize that Martine has abandoned her Brazilian conquest and is now standing very close to me, pressing her hip against mine.

"Hey, who was that man you were talking to before, by the water fountain?" she asks while refilling my glass.

"No one," I reply quickly. "My uncle," I add after a short pause. I can't quite explain why, but I have decided to go along with Sergey's cover of being my uncle.

"Well, did you see how he looked at me? Do you think he liked me or something? He might be a bit too old for me, ha-ha."

"Don't be stupid, Martine. And stay away from that man. For your own good."

"Chill, girl, I was just kidding. You are so tense." She puts her hand on my back and starts massaging it. A little while later she pours more caipirinha for me and clinks her glass to mine.

As the caipirinhas take effect, the dark heaviness inside me gives way to a light pleasant sensation. I can have fun and be a part of this festive night just like everyone else. I can enjoy the laughter, the easy inconsequential conversations. Somebody asks me to dance and I readily accept and we go to the mat area where they have set up the sound system and a bunch of people are already dancing. I dance with one guy after the other giving in to the enjoyment of the music, the movements, the flirtation. Male hands are on my back, my hips, and my butt. I don't seem to mind, floating in some sort of a colorful fog. At one point I realize I am dancing with Martine, her strong arms leading me in the dance pressing my body against hers, and her mouth chewing on a strand of my hair near my ear. My chignon has by now collapsed, releasing my long, unwashed hair, but I couldn't care less at the moment.

*****

Someone puts another drink in my hand and I finish this one, too, as I walk around looking for something or someone. In a momentary flash of awareness I realize it is Liam I am trying to find. Yes, I've gotten off the improvised dance floor because suddenly I had a feeling his dark, severe eyes were following my every move. Now I need to find him and ask him something. What it is I want to ask I am not completely sure, I just know it's important I talk to him. I have no idea what time it is, but it must be really late as a number of visitors have started taking their leave.

Even though it is not as crowded as before, I still can't find Liam, and soon I give up and join a group of my friends, martial artists from the Dojo. They always stay until the very end of the party, or rather, their eventual departure in the early morning hours marks the end of the Winter Assembly festivity every year. I have another drink with them, not sure if it is still a caipirinha or something else, as I can't quite taste what I am drinking anymore.

At some point I hurry into the locker room to use the bathroom, suddenly feeling like my bladder is fuller than it has even been. I have trouble squatting unsteadily over the toilet. It takes some time and my quadriceps start cramping up. Later, standing at the sink, I stare for a long while in the mirror and do not know whom these dark unfocused eyes with their deep shadows and these salient cheekbones surrounded by long messy hair belong to. I am now feeling pretty dizzy and nauseous and splash some cold water onto my face, but it does not help much. I sit down on the floor in the locker room, my back against the bench, and close my eyes.

When I open them again, Liam is sitting on the floor next to me.

"What are you doing in the women's locker room?" I ask.

He does not answer and just looks at me. "You're drunk," he finally says.

"So? You're drunk too."

"Yep. Very."

We sit silently for a few minutes. I remember now what it was I so urgently wanted to talk to him about, but I can't bring myself to open my mouth and just say what's on my mind. My head feels so heavy. I really want to close my eyes again and go to sleep. Liam reaches over and touches my bare leg, moving his hand up from my knee to my thigh. He gets to the line of my dress, pauses for a moment, and keeps moving his fingers up along with the dress, exposing more and more of my skin. My reactions slowed down, at first I am just watching his hand. When it touches my panties I finally wake up and push his hand away forcefully. He turns toward me and tries to kiss me and I elbow him in the stomach. He does not try anything else and just sits motionless for a while.

"What the hell, Sasha?" he then says. "You dance with all these idiots, flirt with them all night. What about me?"

"What about you?"

"How am I supposed to feel?"

"What the fuck are you talking about?"

"What the fuck am I talking about?! I am talking about you and me. Or you just erased it all from your memory? How convenient!"

"It was one night last year. One night."

"Yeah, because you didn't want me anymore."

"Wrong. You know I wanted you. It wasn't the right time. It was not right. Both of us living here, training. It just wasn't right." How does he not understand this? It wasn't like those one-night-stands people have after meeting in a bar. Liam and I were close, and I had feelings for him, and that one night was amazing, but it couldn't continue. There are no express rules against a romantic relationship between the head uchi-deshi and a junior uchi-deshi—probably because there was no precedent for anything like that—but I was certain Sensei would not have allowed it anyway. I chose my training. I tried to explain this to Liam before—he never believed me.

"Bullshit! You simply didn't want to be with me. Why settle for one guy when you have so many admirers, so many guys to sleep with."

"Why are you insulting me? You know I don't sleep around. I do nothing but train."

I am feeling really dizzy and try to focus on one point on the wall to stop the room from going in circles. Liam wants me to look at him and takes my chin and makes me turn my head. He moves a strand of my hair away from my face and tucks it behind my ear, and then tries to kiss me again. I push him away and stubbornly remove that strand of hair from behind my ear.

"I know you are not sleeping around, but there *is* someone, isn't there? Someone you like?" he asks with pressing insistence.

"None of your business! What the fuck are you doing? One minute you sabotage my examination, the next you try to kiss me. That *tanto* switch was a fucking dangerous thing to do. Don't think I don't know it was you who did it. You are so fucked up, Liam."

So, there it is. I've said out loud to him what I wanted to say all evening. But it seems he has not heard a word.

"There *is* someone else then?" he asks, focused entirely on one thing. "I knew it. Who is he?"

"Oh, go to hell."

"Fuck this shit." He gets up and storms out of the changing room, hitting the doorframe with his shoulder.

*****

Coming out of the changing room on my unsteady legs I discover the reception area empty. I go toward the stairs and stand at the landing for a few minutes deliberating whether to go up and lie down in my room or go downstairs and hang out for a bit with the remaining people who must have stepped outside for a smoke or fresh air and whose voices and laughter I can hear. I choose to go downstairs as I don't feel like being by myself right now, alone with my thoughts and the spinning walls.

I am just about to make the first step down the stairs, when someone's hands push me hard in the back and I go rolling down the whole length of the steep stairway, hit my head on I don't know what, and black out.

When I come to, my first instinct is to get up as fast as I can. I have no idea for how long I've been out. Maybe I am still in danger and need to put up a fight against the invisible opponent. Trying to stand up, however, I see moving spots before my eyes and feel extremely nauseous and throw up. I then realize that there are people around me, multiple friendly arms trying to sit me back down, concerned kind voices, and the words *concussion* and *ER* pronounced several times. I think at that moment I start laughing. That laughter must sound very odd and rather scary to everyone. I suppose they believe I am in shock. I probably am. A heavy pain is driving through my head, shredding my rational thinking process into tiny fragments. Out of that painful chaos one thought emerges and sticks, and for some reason I find it funny—looks like I am going to the hospital after all. If the *tanto* did not quite manage to do it, then the push down the stairs did.

CHAPTER 8

On December 31st the last class of the year starts at eleven thirty at night. It is an old tradition at the dojo to meet the New Year on the mat training. No visitors are allowed in this unique class. Only some twenty or thirty of the most dedicated regular dojo students and us, the three uchi-deshi, are here.

Sensei is in a very good mood, smiling and telling jokes, and the overall ambience on the mat is intimate, light, and festive. We are practicing a standing *ude-garami*—a top shoulder lock—also called a figure-four lock. I like joint manipulation techniques a lot and *ude-garami* is one of my favorites, but I also know that Sensei tends to do them in conjunction with a throw, and so I'm a bit nervous about what's coming. These days, hard throws are not exactly within my comfortable range.

Yep, I was right. Soon Sensei calls a combination of *ude-garami* and a throw. It is a pretty brutal technique and I can feel every muscle in my body tense up. Out of the corner of my eye I see Sensei look at me. I think he half expects me to ask permission to sit this technique out. But I don't want to do that. I will keep on training.

I am partnered with Hiroji and he performs all the motions including the cranking of my shoulder and elbow very hard, but at the very last moment, right before the actual throw, he lets up and puts me on the ground very smoothly. I breathe out with relief and move my lips in a silent thank you to Hiroji. He does not say anything but gives me a slight nod of the head.

After my fall down the stairs and the resulting concussion, Hiroji has proved a really good friend. I was back on the mat within a few days but haven't been able to take hard falls yet without feeling dizzy and getting a headache. Doctors said that the symptoms would soon go away, but for now my training has been somewhat limited, and Hiroji has been very protective, partnering with me often and making sure I am being thrown in a controlled manner. He also started teaching me how to take *ukemi*—all types of breakfalls—the Hiroji-style.

Practicing traditional Japanese martial arts, which originated in combating fully armored samurai on the battlefield and developed a system of the most effective techniques—joint locks, choke holds, pins, and, above all, throws—it is inevitable that you are going to be thrown down *hard* innumerable times. So it is crucial to acquire safe breakfall skills early on in order to minimize the risk of significant injury.

During training sometimes we do up to a hundred breakfalls in one class, and Hiroji has really perfected his way of taking ukemi, focusing on adjusting body positions in the air in such a way so as to land on the mat as safely as possible, even when being thrown extremely hard. What he is able to do with his body might sometimes even seem to be beyond human capability, but I know it is just many years of dedicated practice. Often at nighttime he goes onto the mat and works on his ukemi alone for hours on end.

In the past he has pointed out to me that my ukemi needs improvement. Sometimes when I am being thrown, my body angles are off, he says, which exposes me to potential injuries upon hitting the mat. That's why he was looking at me so critically that time on the mat when Liam was throwing me really hard in a shoulder throw. Hiroji did not think my ukemi was good enough. And after my fall down the staircase he even went so far as to tell me that if I had had better ukemi, I might have been able to roll down the stairs in a more controlled manner and possibly avoid the bad concussion. He says it's a matter of getting your body accustomed to taking perfect ukemi, no matter what the circumstances of the throw might be. So now he's taken to instructing me in his method of taking ukemi, and I am so very grateful to him for sharing his skills and secret knowledge, which he has worked years on acquiring and perfecting and is really not obligated to reveal to anyone.

A few minutes before midnight, the training pauses, we watch the Times Square Ball Drop on the big screen, drink a glass of symbolic non-alcoholic champagne, hug each other, and then get back on the mat for another hour of training. Afterward, everyone takes a shower and gathers in the reception area for real drinks and dinner. It is not a loud rambunctious party as the one during the Winter Assembly. This one is more intimate and quiet, though people will most likely stay up until morning, drinking and talking. The food is also better and more substantial than what was served to the hundreds of visitors. Sensei is treating and has ordered from a nearby restaurant, and there are delicious mini cheeseburgers, salads, roast beef with grilled vegetables and roasted potatoes, and cheesecake and two types of pie for dessert.

Throughout the dinner I try to call Danilo several times, but he does not pick up. When he finally answers the phone, I abandon my food and hurry up to my room to have a quiet conversation with my brother. After a few minutes I grab my coat and come out onto the roof, because it is nearing two o'clock and I want to be able to see the street down below. It is freezing up here and I am wearing a dress, the same short off-white dress as on the previous occasion, since it's pretty much the only dress I have—all my other clothing being gis, sweats, hoodies, sweaters, and jeans. I would have been more comfortable in jeans and a sweater of course, but I had my reasons for putting on the dress tonight. Now, standing on the roof I am very cold and I wrap my coat tight around me and pull the hood low over my face. I can still feel the frozen wind, especially on my legs, but don't want to go inside.

Danilo is at some party and I can hear music and loud voices, but his own voice doesn't sound happy or festive at all. I ask him what's the matter, but he doesn't want to say.

"Danny, tell me, are you physically OK?"

He mutters something unintelligible.

"Can you please step outside or something? I can't hear what you are saying."

There is a very long pause, then finally the music and noises get quieter.

"Can you hear me now?"

"Yes. I was asking if you were physically feeling OK."

"Yeah." He sighs.

"Then what's wrong?"

"Nothing. Why do you think anything is wrong?"

"Oh, please, I know you too well. What's going on?"

Another sigh. "I have to go now, Sash. I'll talk to you later. Happy New Year." And he hangs up.

I dial his number several more times, and again he doesn't pick up. I am about to dial again, when I see a car pull up to the curb on the opposite side of the street. I go inside, and in the living room there is Liam sitting on his red couch with a plate of food. We haven't really talked since the Winter Assembly and I have tried to avoid him as much as possible. It's not easy of course, living in the same space, but I know his daily routine by heart and have adjusted mine so that we are rarely in the living room or kitchen at the same time. On the mat, I also train far away from him. I think Sensei might have started suspecting something strange going on as I notice him give Liam and me curious looks, but he hasn't said anything.

I wish it didn't have to be this way, but I really do not want to interact with a person who sabotages my test in a very dangerous way and then throws me down the stairs. Just as I suspected, the investigation about the real tanto did not lead anywhere. But I have no doubt it was Liam who removed it from Sensei's office and then put it back. He would have had access and opportunity. I don't have any proof, either, that it was Liam who pushed me down the stairs, but in my mind I'm sure it was him. He seemed so jealous and angry—no, beyond angry—storming out of the women's locker room that night. He was enraged and heavily drunk and in a sort of a frenzy. It couldn't have been anyone but him.

I cross the living room going toward the stairs, pretending not to notice him at all.

"Where are you going wearing a coat?" he demands to know.

"To get some snacks. There is plenty of alcohol, but no snacks for later when everyone gets hungry again." I hasten my step so as not to give him an opportunity to say anything else and prohibit me from going out.

*****

Stepping out the front door of the dojo I don't cross the street to go to the car. What if Liam has come out to the roof to spy on me? I walk, staying on my side of the street, and I can hear the car follow me and then see it pass me and turn the corner of Sixth Avenue.

This is the first time I am out of the dojo in a while and the avenue seems so busy and lively. There are people, cars, and the regular noises and movements of the ever-revolving Manhattan life. Being shut in for weeks on end makes you see all of this with new eyes each time. Our dojo is like a small island, where time and traditions run their own course, but all while tucked in the midst of a bustling modern city. And right now, going to Drago, for a split second I have a strange sensation of doing something I am not supposed to be doing, as if I were distancing myself from the dojo and all it means to me. This dark ominous feeling comes over me but is gone within a brief moment. The exhilaration at seeing Drago pushes all other thoughts aside.

"Are we playing spies?" Drago asks when I get into the car. "You are beautiful and dangerous, uchi-deshi girl." He smiles. I have already noticed before that he has several very different types of smiles, but this one now is absolutely wonderful—genuine. It crinkles up the corners of his eyes and lights up his whole face.

Before settling down on the seat, I make sure to take off my coat so that he can fully appreciate the dress. I can see that he does, his gaze moving from my naked shoulders, down my body, and to my equally naked legs, though he is trying to be somewhat discreet about it and pretends to look only at my face when I catch his eye.

I hardly recognize myself when I am around this man. I don't really like it when men stare at me and much less when they want to touch me. Ever since boys first started paying attention to me, I have elbowed a great number of them in the stomach or in the ribs when they tried something. But with Drago, I am fully aware of wanting his eyes on my body, his hands on my body, his body on my body.

I touch his cheekbones, his jaw, and the side of his neck. He places his hand behind my head and kisses me and I know that this kiss is what I have been dreaming of since the last time I saw him. No one had ever kissed me like this before, or perhaps I had never felt this way when other men kissed me. I had no idea that a simple kiss can at the same time be so overwhelmingly satisfying and yet leave you hungry for more. When our mouths separate and his hands move away from my body, I have an almost painful sensation of craving his touch again.

"How did you manage to sneak out of the dojo?" he asks. He is breathing heavy, and his voice sounds very deep and somewhat hoarse.

"Told them I was going to the corner store for some provisions."

"Hmm, that does not give us much time. Should we go into a bar and have a quick drink?"

"Everywhere is going to be really crowded. Let's just drive around for a bit."

"Whatever your ladyship desires."

We drive slowly through the streets and then get onto the Henry Hudson Parkway and the car picks up speed. I lean back looking not at the road but at Drago's profile. He knows I am looking at him and smiles. I can see the smile in the corner of his mouth. I feel I am caught in a strange moment where time stands still, where the world outside is of no importance, and this little space inside the car is all that really exists in the whole universe. I am also intensely conscious of feeling happy. I guess I never really knew before what this word meant, but now I know. I am happy right now, in this very moment. Happy just sitting in the car next to him. When I say it like that it sounds so simple, but if you really think about it, it is quite overwhelming. Being happy just because another human, a specific human being, is next to you. Out of a multitude of people, suddenly there emerges one person, who has this effect on you. Hmm, not so simple after all.

*****

On 125th street in Harlem we stop across the road from a low, windowless building with a sign that says, "Cotton Club."

"I need a cigarette," Drago says, gets out, sits down on the curb next to the car and lights up.

I open the door, and we sit like this for a bit, me inside the car, he just outside, smoking and looking at me, and trying to blow the smoke sideways. I usually cannot stand cigarette smoke and its smell, but for some reason Drago's smoking does not bother me.

"This used to be a very famous nightclub during the Prohibition Era." He points across the street. "Tons of famous people came here to watch musical shows, party, and drink liquor. Been here in this same location since the twenties. I wanted to show it to you."

I nod and don't tell him that the original Cotton Club was not located here at all but first on 142nd Street and then somewhere in the Theater District. That this here is nothing but a modern reincarnation opened sometime in the seventies. I am not sure why I don't tell him. I guess because he looks so proud of having shown this "historical" building to me, and I don't want to ruin it for him.

Suddenly two figures appear just a few steps behind Drago. I don't know where they've come from. I did not see them approach. I want to warn Drago, but he must have heard their steps already—he gets up quickly and turns toward them while simultaneously shutting my door. One of the figures pulls out a gun and very discreetly presses it against Drago's side. I don't know what they want from him. His wallet? But nobody carries much cash on them these days. There is also a chance they would like to escort him to the nearest ATM and have him take out money. Drago does not wait to find out their intentions. He grabs the wrist with the gun, locks it out, twists it in one brusque motion, the gun falling right out of it, and throws the man on the ground, while tossing the gun aside. I can see that the man's head hits on the concrete pretty hard. I suppose he never learned how to take ukemi safely.

The second individual might be a boxer. He assumes a boxing stance and starts throwing punches. Drago hits him right on the jaw and then throws him down as well. At that moment a car drives up, brakes with a jarring noise, and hits the bumper of our car. Three men jump out and pounce on Drago. While he is fighting the newcomers, the original men manage to scramble to their feet and rejoin the bout.

So now it's five against one, and I decide I should help Drago instead of just sitting in the car and waiting to see how the situation plays out. I open the door, but Drago yells "stay the fuck in" and slams the door shut once more.

As I watch him battle his opponents, I realize he does not need my help at all. I have never seen such mastery of technique, precision, and speed, such explosive power. He seems to be facing all five of them at the same time, never giving his back. All of his moves are perfectly timed and controlled. He is not wasting any of his energy on unnecessary motions. Each strike connects with a vital point. Every lock produces a dislocated or a broken joint. And when he moves in for a throw, his target ends up on the ground within a split second.

At one point, the first attacker manages to locate his gun. Before he can pick it up, though, Drago deals him such a blow on the temple that he simply slumps to the ground on top of his gun and does not get up again. Without their guns, these guys never stood a chance against a fighter like Drago. His level of fighting is many degrees above anything I have ever witnessed, inside the dojo or out.

After only a few minutes, all of the attackers are plastered on the ground, limp and semiconscious. For the briefest moment Drago stands above them surveying his work, then he gets in the car and we drive off. I want to say something, to comment on what I've just seen, but I cannot seem to find adequate words to express my admiration of his skill, and so I keep quiet.

He stops the car after a while to wipe the blood from his mouth and examine his teeth in the mirror.

"That boxer asshole landed me a pretty hard one. Didn't even notice in the moment."

"Did he knock out a tooth or something?" I ask.

"Nah, my teeth are stronger than his knuckles. I bet he broke his hand, the idiot."

"What did they want?"

"They were tourists, asking how to get to the Statue of Liberty and got impatient because I did not know the way."

I laugh and want to kiss him.

"Ah, careful now." He touches his lower lip, which has already started to puff up.

I kiss him on the neck and inhale deeply his scent. It is a mix of Dior's Sauvage cologne and cigarette smoke, and to me it seems the most intoxicating and arousing smell in the world.

"I need another cigarette," he says and lights up, but throws it out the window after only a few drags. He then leans in and starts kissing me with that characteristic strength and decisiveness of his that have such a thrilling effect on me. His mouth has a bitter cigarette taste, but that does not turn me off at all.

"Can you drive to your place now?" I whisper into his ear.

"Yes." He gives a quick and firm reply. "No," he says after a pause. "No, I must drive you back to the dojo." And he takes my hand and kisses it.

He gets out of the car one more time, goes into a twenty-four-hour corner store, and comes back with a bag filled with potato chips, salted almonds, and a few other items. "Your alibi," he says giving me the bag.

*****

Back at the dojo, Liam meets me at the main-floor entrance. How did he know I was returning right at that moment? Did he hear me coming up the stairs? Or did he maybe stay up on the roof, leaning over the parapet the whole time, observing the street down below? Hmm. In any case he pretends that it is an accident, us running into each other like this, does not say anything, and moves aside, letting me pass through the doorway. Our bodies within a few inches of each other, I notice him sniffing at my hair and making a face. Liam is very sensitive to smells and can't stand cigarette smoke and must have sensed it on me. I am not about to give any explanations, but I am sure he has drawn some conclusions of his own. He glares at me from under his knit eyebrows and his furious dark eyes say plenty. Silently, I hand him the bag with the snacks and go in.

People are still up, sitting down at the mat area, their backs propped against the wall, watching a samurai movie on the big screen. They welcome with great enthusiasm the arrival of the snacks. I sit down next to Martine and watch the movie for a while. At some point I probably close my eyes and take a short nap. When I wake up, the samurai movie is still playing, but Martine is gone. She returns a few minutes later saying that there is somebody who wants to see me downstairs. In my confused half-awake state I imagine it might be Drago who's come back for me. I do not think anything else and do not ask Martine what she was doing downstairs in the first place. I suddenly feel so very happy and can't stop smiling. This momentary exhilaration dies down and gives way to gloom as soon as Martine tells me that it is "that man from before, your uncle."

"An uncle?" Liam asks. Sitting nearby he must have overheard the conversation. "An uncle?" he repeats with great suspicion. "Didn't know you had an uncle. Well, tell him to come up. I want to meet your relative, if that's what he is."

"He doesn't have time to come up," I say.

"Do tell him to come up," Liam repeats in a harsh slow manner placing emphasis on each word.

So, I go downstairs and stop halfway down the staircase, observing Sergey's silhouette in the tiny and poorly lit foyer. It is strange seeing him stand like this, leaning against the wall in a sort of a patient and weary pose. Somehow it does not go with his usual self-assured pompous image. I rather thought he would be waiting outside, seated comfortably in his car. I also wonder who has unlocked the front door for him and let him in. Must have been Martine.

Without even greeting him I beckon to Sergey to come up. He hesitates a moment, and then follows me up. He is wearing a tuxedo and looks very tired, his face pale, almost ashen.

"So, you are Sasha's uncle," Liam asks once Sergey steps inside. He also offers him a bottle of beer.

"Pleased to meet you," Sergey replies and makes a brief motion with his hand rejecting the beer.

The two men shake hands, after which Liam visibly loses interest in my "uncle" and walks away. Ha! I know why he was being so suspicious. I bet he thought Sergey was my secret man, the one he'd been so jealous of this whole time. Now he must have realized it's not him. Perhaps upon taking a close look he saw that Sergey is in his late fifties. Or maybe it was the fact that he did not smell like cigarettes. I did notice how Liam sniffed at him while they were shaking hands. In any case, Liam gets back to watching the samurai movie with the others, and Sergey and I sit on a bench in a quiet corner, right by the Christmas tree.

"I've had a very long night, Sasha," Sergey says in an unusually subdued tone. He rests his elbow on his knee and props his chin in the palm of his hand as if his head weighed a ton. I think he is overplaying it. Somehow this weary and quiet demeanor of his does not strike me as entirely genuine. An image of a big wild cat setting up for an attack pops up in my head. All the time I can sense his heavy gaze on me. Am I imagining it? I cast a quick glance at his face, partially hidden in his hand, and meet an alert and intense eye staring right at me.

"Are you having a good New Year's?" he asks.

I don't reply. I am waiting for him to state why he is here. I have the dark heavy feeling inside me again and I've already sort of made my peace with the fact that something very unpleasant is going to be unleashed on me now. I certainly don't want to hear it, yet at the same time would rather it be out in the open as soon as possible, so I can deal with it.

"Talked to your brother recently?"

"Why?"

"Well, you must already know then that he ran up a new debt."

"What? How much?"

"So, you don't know, hmm. Twenty-five thousand."

"That can't be! How is it possible?"

"He spent a few full nights playing poker, and he obviously thought his poker skills were better than they really are."

I remember Danilo's voice on the phone. He sounded so dejected and could not bring himself to tell me the reason.

"He gambled in one of *your* establishments again?"

Sergey scoffs. I realize it was an unnecessary question. Of course my brother went back to 2 Gild Street, where Sergey owns half a building and runs his shady businesses.

"Listen, Sasha. I am dead tired, and you don't look like you are very happy to see me. So, let's try and not drag out this conversation, all right? Here is my offer. You do one Dark Fight for me, just one fight, and your brother's whole debt is paid off. The entire debt. He will not owe me a dime."

"No," I reply right away. "I will not do the Dark Fights."

"No? Ok. Well, then I guess our sweet Danilo will have to get into the cage again. There is a Dark Fights night coming up."

The image of my brother in the ER appears before my eyes. I recall so vividly him sitting there with his broken ribs, dislocated shoulder, his bruises and cuts.

"Let's just hope our dear Danilo does not end up like that unfortunate boy. You know the one I mean? They call him Dav. He had his spine broken and will never walk again." Sergey looks me in the eyes and holds my gaze for a few intense seconds. "You know what I am talking about, don't you?"

Well, now I know. Dav. The fourth uchi-deshi. Now I know what really happened to him. I try to breathe in and out deeply to keep myself in check, turn away from Sergey, and fix my gaze at one of the silvery bright spots on the Christmas tree.

"Yes," Sergey pronounces with significance, "yes, that boy had talent, but he was not a true fighter. It just was not in his blood. You should have seen what he looked like when they carried him out of the cage that night. You don't want the same fate for your brother, now, do you?" He waits for me to say something, to ask questions, but I keep quiet. So he continues, "Yet, I wonder how our sweet Danilo will fare if he gets into the cage again. When was the last time he even trained? Hmm, I guess he's just too busy partying and drinking. Here, take a look." And he shows me a few pictures of my brother slumped on a couch next to a couple of girls in party dresses, a drink in his hand and that stupid drunken smile on his face. "Do you think he is in a fight-ready shape? Yet fight he will, for the debt must be paid off."

Damn it. How I wish I could by some miracle have that money in my hands right now so that I could throw it in this bastard's face. Twenty-five grand. All I have left in my savings is a couple thousand.

"What if I lose the fight?" I ask after a rather long pause.

"No matter. You get the money, win or lose. I am being very generous with this offer, beauty. And I always keep my word. So, what do you say? Do we have a deal?"

I nod without looking at him.

"I will need you to actually say it out loud."

"Fine. We have a deal. I will do one fight."

"Good. We will not have anything in writing of course, but historically verbal agreements are binding in New York, and you may rest assured, I am an honest businessman." He offers me his hand.

A "businessman" he calls himself. A fucking "honest businessman." I believe he is a mobster. Perhaps that word is not even used these days anymore. They all call themselves "businessmen" now. Well, they were mobsters, all right, in the nineties and in the years before. From the few words Grandpa mentioned here and there, I put the picture together more or less. The Russian Mafia was huge in NYC back then. And now? Well, maybe just the terminology's changed.

"I will never shake your hand, Sergey."

CHAPTER 9

"The car is waiting on the corner of 7th and 16th. Hurry up."

This comes late in the evening, two weeks after my last conversation with Sergey. He told me to be prepared to receive the "invitation" at any moment within the next month, as the exact date and place of the Dark Fights are never fixed in advance and might be arranged at the very last minute.

I am rather glad that the waiting is over. It hasn't been easy. The last few days have been especially nerve-racking, the tension building up and not letting go of me. I tried to make myself not think about what was coming, to focus instead on my everyday activities, but the pressure was building within me all the time, and I couldn't relax for a moment. Exhausted after hours of training, I would then lie in my bed unable to fall asleep, or I would fall asleep for a few minutes and then wake with a start. I even had half a mind to ask Martine to bring me some pot, but decided against it.

Now I feel a strange sort of relief to find out that within a few hours it will all be over. I have no idea how the night will end for me, but just knowing that it *will* end makes me feel better.

I put on a pair of *vale tudo* shorts, made of nylon and spandex with grip lining on the leg openings to prevent them from riding up, and a sports bra. While getting dressed I notice that my armpits have a tiny bit of a stubble and I pause for a moment unsure whether I should shave them or not, but then decide that I really could not care less if my armpits do not look quite perfect tonight—it's not like I'm going on a date.

I have already planned and tested a sneaking-out strategy that does not involve going through the living room where Liam is firmly installed on his red couch. I zip up my warm hooded coat, open wide the window in my room, and hook the fire escape ladder that I bought on Amazon to the window lip. True to the online description, the ladder has a tangle-free design, anti-slip rungs and, nylon strap rails and it's fast and easy to deploy. And what's most important, it does seem pretty sturdy. It's supposed to be able to hold the weight of up to one thousand pounds, so I should be all right. It would have been easier and more secure of course if there were a real, permanent fire escape outside my window, but historically buildings in NYC that had fewer than five stories did not have fire escapes installed. I never quite understood that—in case of a fire you are not expected to jump down from a fifth floor, but from a fourth or third you'll be just fine?

I climb down my makeshift fire escape ladder and land in the backyard of the parking garage that rents the first floor of the dojo building. I go in through the garage's back entrance and out the front, waiving on my way to the friendly nighttime attendant. Turning the corner of 7th Avenue, I don't immediately know which car is the one waiting for me. The driver of a metallic gray BMW sedan gets my attention by blinking his headlights, and so I approach the car and get in.

The period of inactivity during the ride is difficult to bear. I feel the tension starting to build up inside me again. My lips are dry and peeling. With my teeth I catch a bit of the dry skin and rip it off leaving behind a small patch of raw flesh. Damn, I wish the car would just get to wherever it is going already. This ride seems interminable, even though I know it hasn't really been more than ten minutes or so. I try to calm myself down by doing some breathing exercises. I also crack my knuckles and stretch my neck muscles.

The chauffer lets me out at Wolf Flannigan's pub on Molten Lane in lower Manhattan. "Just go in. You are expected," is all he says. I walk into the pub and immediately, from a table near the entrance, a brawny bald-headed man in a dark suit and white shirt gets up and gestures for me to follow him. As we walk past the counter the bartender looks at me and I can see that he recognizes me. I nod to him and he smiles and is about to nod back but then he glances at my companion and the expression on his face changes right away. He lowers his eyes, pretending not to know me.

We go into the back room, then down a staircase to the basement, where we walk for quite a while along a narrow cement-floored hallway. We are both wearing rubber-soled footwear that doesn't make a sound. The only words the bald-headed man says are "the party girl number two has arrived," and he speaks them into his lapel mic. We reach a metal door, which opens into a wider hallway. I think we have crossed into a different building and wonder if perhaps we might be under 2 Gild Street now.

After walking for some time in the wide hallway we stop in front of another metal door and my taciturn companion says something very brief into his mic again. The door opens and he hands me over to a second man in a dark suit and white shirt. They are both of pretty much the same height and shoulder span, the only difference being the second one is not bald but has a military-style buzzed haircut. The door closes behind me and the second white-shirted man gestures for me to stay put for a moment and speaks into his mic.

A third man, strikingly similar to the first two, a tattoo on the nape of his neck, stretching up over the back of his head, setting him somewhat apart, arrives and leads me through a smallish chamber that connects to a much bigger one, at the other end of which I can discern an entrance to yet another. The ambience and the decor is absolutely not what I expected to see in an underground fights locale. I think, in my mind I pictured some sort of a bare space with nothing but a fighting cage and maybe some naked light bulbs for illumination. Around me I see comfortable elegant sofas and armchairs, low coffee tables, bar counters, waiters with bowties. A large number of men in dinner jackets and women in evening dresses and high heels walk around and sit in elegant chairs, drinking, eating, conversing, and clinking glasses. Some are dancing. The music is loud but not as deafening as in a regular nightclub.

In the middle of the second chamber there is indeed a fighting cage, its platform elevated a few feet above the floor level. It's empty now and I can see very visible blood stains on the light canvas.

*****

I am led to a round booth where Sergey sits in the company of several men and two very pretty blond women in sparkly dresses, their lips painted bright red. Sergey invites me to take a seat on the couch next to him and everyone stares at me with great curiosity.

"Would you like something to drink?" he asks.

I shake my head.

"Here is some water." He pushes a glass toward me, but I ignore it.

"Nervous?"

I do not answer. Sergey smirks and looks away and does not pay attention to me for a few minutes, talking to the two blondes.

"Take a good look around," he then whispers into my ear. "See how many fine people have come to see you fight. I have high expectations of you. You won't disappoint me tonight, now will you?"

"I need to use the bathroom," I say and get up.

Sergey beckons the guy with the tattooed head, who is standing nearby and tells him to accompany me. He leads me to a small bathroom near the backdoor that we originally came through.

When I am washing my hands, a guy in very tight pants and with an elaborate hairstyle comes in and stares at me, his eyes squinted and his head inclined sideways.

"The boss sent me," he declares.

"Who are you?"

"I am Ricardo the Stylist."

He sits me down on a bench.

"We'll start with makeup," he says. "Not too much. The boss wants you to look fresh and bright. We'll just accentuate these gorgeous eyes of yours."

Finished with the makeup, he lifts up a few strands of my hair, a pensive expression on his face.

"I was going to put it up in a tight topknot," I say.

"N-no, I don't think so. That won't hold. We need to braid it first."

He separates my hair into several parts, braids it rather tightly—at one point I even have to ask him to stop pulling so hard—and then gathers the braids up, using only soft elastics without any metal parts.

"Ok, good. That should be it. Oh, wait," he exclaims and all of a sudden reaches in and feels my breasts.

"What the hell?" I protest and hit his wrist with the blade of my hand.

"Ouch! That really hurts!" He makes a grimace and is shaking his hand.

I am sure he is exaggerating the pain level, since I didn't hit him hard at all.

"You are so jumpy! What are you hitting me for? I am not interested in your lady parts. I was just checking if you had the boob guards in. And you don't, ha!" He pouts and looks away blowing on his wrist. "How are you gonna go into the cage without the boob plates?"

Damn, he is right. I haven't thought of that. I did bring my mouth guard, but the breast protector completely slipped my mind.

"Ricardo, can you help me out, please?"

"Ha, first you beat me up, and now you ask for my help."

"Nobody beat you up."

He is still pouting.

"Look. I'm sorry."

Immediately he cheers up.

"Don't move. Wait here." And he rushes out of the bathroom.

Through the open door I catch the announcer's words, "Ladies and gentlemen, the second fight of the night will begin shortly."

Ricardo the Stylist brings me a sports bra with the breast guards inserted securely into the cups. I take my bra off and put the new one on. It feels uncomfortable with my breasts squished in, but I know that during the fight I might be quite grateful to have this protection.

"I do hope you won't get too badly damaged tonight," Ricardo the Stylist says and starts sniffling. Is he about to cry? I wonder what he might have seen go down in that fighting cage that makes him feel so sorry for me now. Well, I guess I can imagine.

Still sniffling, he gives me a hug and a kiss on a cheek and takes his leave.

*****

The door opens again, and a man in a black shirt and black pants comes in and introduces himself as the referee.

"It's your first time, right? Ok, listen up. Here it goes." The words come out very fast. "There are no rules except for no eye gauging, biting, or groin strikes. There are no rounds, no time limit, no weight category, no gloves, no cutman to treat wounds during the fight, and there are no judges. Bout will only come to an end by either a knockout or submission. In case of a submission you can tap out—if you are still able to move your hand, that is—or you can yell 'tap out.' Questions?"

I shake my head.

After the referee leaves, the door opens once more and this time the big tattooed guy steps in. He frowns, scratches his chin, and generally looks uncomfortable.

"Eh, the boss wants to know if you need anything," he says.

Despite his large muscular stature and overall tough appearance, something tells me this guy is not unfriendly. Right now I could use some help, even if it comes from one of Sergey's men.

"What's my fight strategy?" I ask.

"What? I am not your fight coach."

"Ok, but maybe you got some tips?"

"Your strategy is to stay alive and to try not to get too badly damaged yourself—and to inflict bad injuries on your opponent."

"Oh, ok, thanks. Very helpful."

"I'll give you one tip." He takes my hand and makes a fist with it and hits it against his jaw. "In a no-gloves bout, bone against bone will break your hand before causing your opponent any serious damage. So you better go bone against soft." He touches my fist to his solar plexus. "Go palm-heel under the nose and such. And don't forget to use elbows and knees and—" But before he has a chance to finish his words, the bathroom door opens yet again, and in comes Sergey himself.

He tells the tattooed guy to go and wait outside and looks at me for a few moments, no doubt appraising the stylist's work. I believe he is satisfied with what he sees.

"So, listen, beauty," he then says. "It is almost time now. The fight is about to start. Here's the final instruction for you. People out there did not pay a lot of money to watch a boring monotonous exchange of punches. They want to see something spectacular. So do those wild takedowns, joint breaks, choke holds that you are so good at. All those impressive techniques. Yes? That's what the audience wants to see."

I look him in the eye but do not say anything.

"I hope we understand each other. And one more thing. You do get paid win or lose, but if by any chance you are planning to tap out too quickly to end the fight, just know that that's not going to work. In such case, the referee has been instructed to have the fight go on. Got it?"

"Got it."

"Let's go then."

*****

The announcer's voice comes on. "Ladies and gentlemen, for the second fight of the night, welcome the Formidable Frightening Freya."

While being patted down hurriedly, and with obvious lack of attention, for foreign objects, greasy substances, long nails, open wounds, and such, I steal a glance at my opponent who is already inside the cage. Formidable Freya is only a bit taller than me and probably stands at five feet eight inches, but is much bigger-boned, and I'd say is around a hundred and forty pounds against my current weight of one hundred and eight.

"And presenting the newcomer," the announcer continues, "the Little Samurai Princess!"

"What?" I turn to my tattooed friend, who has escorted me to the cage and is now holding my coat.

"What? That's you."

"Little Samurai Princess—that doesn't make any sense."

"Got a good ring to it." And he nods with what seems like genuine encouragement. Then he tells me to stay still for a moment while he is putting petroleum jelly on my face, to prevent punches from splitting the skin. Before a sanctioned bout an official cutman would usually perform this service. But this is a Dark Fight—no rules, no rounds, no time limit, no weight category, no gloves, no cutman. Most likely nobody here gives a damn if I get cuts on my face. The audience probably would even prefer to see more blood. I realize that, given the circumstances, I am lucky to at least have some assistance.

Stepping into the cage, I have a strange feeling as if time has altered its pace and I am caught inside one second that stretches like some sticky, viscous substance. I look at the crowd, which has gotten quite dense as most people have left their couches and armchairs and gathered around to watch the upcoming spectacle. They are all craving some good entertainment and it is not particularly pretty to think that the other fighter and I will soon be beating each other up and inflicting pain solely for the thrill and viewing pleasure of the elegantly dressed, bloodthirsty audience. I try to empty my mind of all such thoughts. They are useless and distracting.

I am inside the cage now and, when the door closes behind me, time resumes its usual speed.

"Fighter, ready?" The referee looks at the Formidable Frightening Freya.

"Fighter, ready?" The referee turns to me.

"Fight!"

For the first ten to fifteen seconds we are just walking in circles, trying to measure each other up and guess at our opponent's martial arts style. From the Formidable Freya's stance I can deduce that she's had judo training, so she must be good at throws and takedowns. No doubt she has a full arsenal of other skills as well.

After we exchange a few tentative punches, I shoot in for a *kata guruma*, the fireman's throw. I get under her, wrapping my arm around her thigh, a move that is illegal in many sanctioned fights. I load her on my shoulders and drop her forward onto the canvas, rolling on top of her.

Kata guruma is really a visually stunning technique, and right away the audience erupts in applause and cheering. But this seemingly brilliant move doesn't give me much advantage, because now we are both on the floor, and Formidable Freya demonstrates amazing groundwork skills. We attempt a series of arm bars and leg locks and I can barely escape from her *juji gatame*—a perpendicular arm bar executed in a supine position.

Back on our feet, Formidable Freya's fist connects heavily with my jaw.

It rattles me quite a bit, but I'm pretty sure that with the punch she's done damage to her hand, maybe even broken a bone. Still, she manages to deal me a couple of hard ones, right on the breasts, though I myself have completely refrained from hitting her in that specific area.

As she attempts a kick to my ribs, I catch her leg, move in, throw her down, step over her leg, and get her in a knee bar. I know she must be in a lot of pain, and I think she might tap out now. That doesn't happen. Formidable Freya is tough and skilled and is able to get out of the leg lock.

Immediately we scramble back up, I shoot in for an *uchi mata*—an inner thigh throw. My *uchi mata* fails, and we move into a clinch, where her looping hook connects with my kidneys. She manages to repeat this sharp stabbing motion several times, and the stinging pain nearly brings me to my knees. She then does a beautiful *sacrifice throw*, grabbing me and falling backward on the ground, rolling back, and hurling me over her. The motion propels me forward and down hard. Luckily Hiroji's instruction has improved my ukemi tenfold and I manage to adjust my body angles and fall down safely.

She almost tags my head with a knee. A knee to the head of a downed opponent would be illegal in an authorized fight. At the very last split second I am able to move my head and avoid a potential knockout.

My strongest weapon in this bout are throws that are performed while simultaneously applying joint manipulation. They are prohibited in many competitions. Now, the audience goes wild when I execute them. At one point I have my opponent's elbow so dangerously locked out that, if I finish the throw, the elbow will just break. This realization flashes across my mind and in a split second I make the decision. Something in me simply refuses to proceed with a technique that will definitely cause her a grievous injury.

I release the control of my opponent's arm allowing her to escape.

The next instant, *pow*! I catch a devastating blow from her knee to my stomach.

The brutal knee strike leaves me reeling, and she grabs me and throws me against the fence, where she continues kicking and striking me and then gets me into a guillotine choke, pushing against the fence to make the choke stronger. I am determined to fight it off, tightening my neck muscles, trying to yank her hand off my neck or at least get a bit of the pressure off. None of it works and the choke gets tighter.

I remember what Sergey said about tapping out too soon. So, for a few more seconds I still do all I can to get out of the choke, but it is of no use. Everything starts to darken before my eyes. During training I have been put to sleep on several occasions with this choke. It comes on so suddenly you don't even have time to realize it. One moment you are still conscious, the next you are waking up from being out and not knowing how much time has lapsed. I don't want this to happened now and so I tap out. I hope I actually tap out and not just hallucinate doing it. At the very last second before I feel I am going to pass out, the referee pulls my opponent off of me.

*****

The referee announces that the Formidable Freya has won the fight. I get out of the cage and the tattooed guy leads me back into that small bathroom, which I guess has been designated my locker room for the night. There I sit on the bench for a few minutes alone. With the adrenaline still pumping, the exhaustion and the pain have not quite set in yet. My mind is racing. I want to make my thoughts stop but cannot get them under control. I catch myself going over the bout again and again, reliving the most dangerous moments of it. Damn, I don't think my body had ever performed at such level before tonight, giving everything it had, working at the height of its capabilities. But then again, never before had I participated in a fight like this, where every wrong move or a split-second-delayed reaction might and probably would cause you a serious injury.

My thoughts are interrupted when a physician comes in. He examines me and to my great relief states that I have not been badly injured. He works on my nose, which is bleeding but is not broken, puts my knuckles in ice and applies ointment to cuts. He also tells me to hold ice to my jaw and head where the opponent's strikes connected. My head is ringing, but the doctor says I don't have a concussion. He is a rather worried about the repeated strikes to my kidneys. They are very sensitive to the touch now and he says I might be passing blood in my urine for a few days.

I realize that my left elbow hurts like hell. The doctor examines it and says a ligament or tendon might be damaged and that he can put a sling to immobilize my elbow and let it heal. I thank him but refuse the sling.

After the physician leaves, Sergey comes in.

"It was a good fight. Exactly what the audience wanted," he says. "They loved you. You executed some very spectacular and dangerous techniques. It was great entertainment."

"Ok."

"That was a very stupid thing you did though, taking pity on her and not finishing that throw."

"It would have broken her arm."

"That should not have been a deterrent. You see, your momentary weakness cost you the win. Your opponent's injuries, however grievous, should not worry you in the least."

"Sergey"—I look him full in the eye—"what happens to the fighters who do get badly injured? Do they just get patched up in a bathroom and are then dumped somewhere?"

"That's right, ha-ha-ha, my men just point them in the direction of the nearest ER and instruct them to say they got beaten up in a rough neighborhood, or better yet to keep their mouths shut altogether, ha-ha-ha."

He laughs, yet I cannot figure out if he is joking or not.

"You see me in such dark colors." He puts on a fake horrified expression. "What am I, a monster? No, no. I certainly am not. In really dangerous cases—but I am not talking about a broken arm or rib or such—they do get taken to a hospital and I take care of all the expenses. I pay a lot of money to some really good doctors who provide excellent services and don't ask questions."

Yeah. I bet he has a whole network of underworld doctors who "do not ask questions." Damn it, how far does his empire stretch? Where else does he have people who "do not ask questions?" Police, for sure.

"I look after my fighters," he declares in a suddenly serious tone of voice, "especially the ones who show great potential. As I want a long-lasting and successful collaboration, I am very generous with them. You will see."

What? What the hell is he talking about now?

"No!" I say with as much firmness as I can muster. "My fight is done. My brother's debt is erased. Right?"

"Well, yes. As per our agreement."

"Good. Then I want to get out of here."

"Why rush out? Wouldn't you rather have a few drinks, maybe a late dinner with us?"

"No. I want to go back to the dojo."

"All right. The car will take you. See you, beauty."

"No. You will not. It's all finished." And I really do believe that accruing this huge debt has served as a sort of shock-therapy for my brother, that he has come to his senses, and that he will have no more dealings with Sergey, ever. And neither will I.

"If you say so."

I am escorted out, and then in the company of the first of the white-shirted men retrace my steps along the underground corridors and up the stairs that lead to the back room of Wolf Flannigan's. The car is waiting for me outside the pub and it takes me back to the corner of 7th Avenue and 16th Street. I walk toward the dojo, but then change my mind. I suddenly feel such a yearning to see the man in the fisherman's sweater, to be near him, to touch his skin and smell its sense, that even though it is around two o'clock and I know I'll wake him up, I call and ask if I can come over.

"Yes, of course," he says, his voice very sleepy. "Should I come pick you up?"

"No, I'll take a cab. Just tell me the address."

CHAPTER 10

The cab turns the corner of 2nd Avenue and 103rd Street, and I see Drago outside walking a huge Rottweiler. He comes up to the driver's window and pays for my ride. As I get out, I pull the hood of my coat low over my face hoping Drago would not notice, at least not right away, that it is swollen and uneven. In the building entrance the light is pretty bright, but he is not looking at me, busy with picking up his dog and then carrying it all the way up to the third floor.

"She's old and very sick," he explains as I follow the pair up the stairs.

Inside the apartment, I immediately ask him to dim the lights. He does not question my request nor makes any comments, and yet somehow I get the feeling that he has already observed the poor condition of my face and is purposefully choosing not to say anything about it.

"You okay?" is all he asks coming up to me and offering to take my coat.

"Yep. Had an overly-intense training today, that's all," I say and keep my coat on. Don't want him to see the attire I have underneath. "I am very cold though. Can I take a hot shower?"

He points toward the bathroom.

"Can I have something to wear? Sweats and a T-shirt or something."

His eyes are fixed on my face for a moment, taking in, I am sure, every detail. He does not ask anything else though. He goes into the bedroom and brings me clothes, a towel, and a pair of white hotel slippers still in their original packaging.

In the bathroom I peel off with relief the *vale tudo* shorts and the sports bra, and then stand under the shower for a rather long time, washing my hair and letting the warmth penetrate and revive my stiff beaten-up body.

As I come out, Drago hands me a sweatshirt. "Put this on too. It is cold in the apartment. Are you hungry?"

My first reaction is to say no, but I realize that I am actually starving.

"Here, come, take a look." He guides me to the fridge. "There are bread and cold cuts. I can make a salad or cook some pasta or eggs."

"Can I have an egg-and-cheese sandwich and some hot tea?"

"Go sit over there." He points toward the couch.

I settle down arranging several pillows under my back and my head. The Rottweiler comes over on her unsteady legs and lies down against my feet. I stroke her head and she looks at me out of her kind and sad eyes. A cat jumps down from a shelf and starts walking back and forth across my lap and then finds a spot it likes the best, on a pillow next to my thigh, and lies down. One of the cat's eyes is hollow. I am not too much of a pet person, but I immediately like the Rottweiler and the one-eyed cat. Sitting on the couch in their company I feel so very cozy. In fact, everything in this apartment, its whole atmosphere have this calming, comforting effect on me, as if I had known this place for a long time and belonged here.

Drago brings me a plate with the egg-and-cheese sandwich and a salad and a large mug of steaming hot tea. Without saying a word he also hands me two ibuprofen and goes back into the kitchen and stands there smoking near an open window. The food he's made for me is delicious, and I would be enjoying it more if my jaw did not hurt so much with every bite that I take.

Drago joins me on the couch and winces as he tries to find a comfortable position.

"What's wrong?" I ask.

"Have a herniated disk from an old judo injury. Must have aggravated it when lifting the dog."

"Do you have any good ointment to reduce inflammation?" I ask after I finish eating.

He finds some ointment and I sit behind him, help him take off his sweatshirt, and start massaging his back. I discover the spot where a nerve is pinched, and I can tell that he is in substantial pain because of it. My own body is sore all over and my left elbow hurts like hell, but I really want to help Drago and so I keep massaging his back for a while. Having to use a lot of strength because his muscles are as hard as stone, and only being able to work with my right arm, I finally get exhausted and have to stop.

Still sitting on my knees behind him I lean on him and put my head on his back. I stay like that for a while and then start moving my lips against the nape of his neck and breathe in, deeply inhaling the scent of his skin, that mix of Sauvage Dior and cigarette smoke. I kiss the side of his neck and he turns his head and then our mouths are kissing. He gets up and picks me up in his arms.

"Your back!"

"It's already messed up," he replies and carries me into the bedroom.

He puts me on the bed, and I pull him down onto me, and it feels amazing to have the full weight of his body on top of me.

I want him to turn the lights out, but he refuses.

"I want to see you," he says and takes all my clothes off.

We kiss so hard that it's possible we're hurting each other, and yet it doesn't feel like enough and I want him to kiss me harder still. His hands are on my breasts, my stomach, my hips, my thighs, pressing hard into me, and yet not as hard as I am craving. Nothing feels like it's enough or ever will be. I want more of him. All of him. I have never wanted anybody like this, nor have I ever known it is possible to want somebody like this, to have such an urgency for somebody's body.

His finger is inside me, and then it's not his *finger* anymore. I push him away and move my hips from under him.

"A condom?"

"Don't have one," he mutters, holds me firmly against him, and is immediately inside me again. I push him away once more, and he grabs my arms and holds them with one hand above my head, and with his other hand guides himself into me, and this time I don't resist at all. "Just don't come inside," I murmur as I raise my hips and wrap my legs tight around him.

*****

On my way back from the bathroom I make a detour to the kitchen, find a yogurt and some dark chocolate and bring them to the bedroom, and sit on the bed naked, eating. I try to keep my hair over my face, especially the right side of it.

"I want to smoke," Drago says.

"Well smoke then."

"What am I, a barbarian to smoke in bed?" He gets up and leaves the room but comes back only a minute later with a pack of cigarettes and an ashtray, and some more chocolate for me. He lies down and smokes and I keep sitting across the bed from him, eating, and we just look at each other and don't speak.

"When did you start smoking?" I ask after a while.

"A few years ago."

"A judo master who smokes."

"Doesn't matter. I don't compete anymore. Did my final competition three years ago."

"Were the competitions very important to you?"

"Of course. How else does a man know that he is the best?"

I lie down next to him, put my head on his chest, and run my fingers over his ribs, his stomach, his hips, and back to his ribs. His body is beautifully proportioned and is in an amazing shape, lean and muscular. Two of his ribs are strangely salient, ruining somewhat the flawlessness of his figure.

"Broken," he says.

"Only these ribs?"

"Nah, have more than twenty broken bones."

"All from judo?"

"Nah."

I pick up his hand and examine it. His index and middle fingers are somewhat misshapen. Breaks that did not heal properly. I touch his arm. His muscles feel perfectly hard even when he is not flexing. Above the elbow the skin is of a different color and pattern. I look at the other arm, and it's the same thing here.

"What are these marks?"

"Nothing."

"Why can't you tell me?"

"Ok. I was burned. Also on my face and my feet. Doctors had to peel the skin from my upper legs and do the skin transplant. And I got to watch them do it."

"What?"

"Yup. I am resistant to pain medication and anesthesia. They could not put me to sleep and I had to be awake and conscious. Hey, that's not the worst thing I had to deal with."

I ponder his words for a while. "How did you get burned?" I then ask. "Were you in some sort of a horrible accident?"

"Wasn't an accident."

"Somebody did that to you on purpose?"

"Doesn't matter."

"Tell me."

"I don't remember. It was in another life and should stay there."

"Wish you could tell me. I want to know about you."

"Why?"

Because I think I love you. I have never fallen this hard for anybody before. I don't know when or how this happened, but I love you now. I don't say this out loud, but I'm not sure what's stopping me. It's not the fact that he would not say it back to me. I don't care about that. I am filled to the brim with feelings that I had no idea existed in real life. It cannot be anything other than that thing that books and movies talk about and call "love," and it's rising up inside me, about to spill over, and I could say it a hundred times to him, shout it out, but instead I remain quiet and just hold him tight.

"And besides," he says, "there is nothing to know about me. I am just another asshole on this overpopulated shithole called Earth."

"Ha, perhaps you are right. I mean I wouldn't argue with the self-evaluation of such a wise man as you."

"*Such a wise man?* Nah, girl, I am not wise at all, but I'll take the unde-served compliment."

With my hands propped on his chest I lift myself up a bit and look into his eyes for a few moments.

"I can't figure out if you are totally good or totally bad, Drago."

"Well, I'm not completely rotten."

*****

Loud thudding noises emanate from right above us.

"Ah, the hookers are home," Drago says. "A car usually brings them back at this hour, and they walk around in high heels for a while."

"You have interesting neighbors."

"Yup, this is an exciting neighborhood and a lively building. They'll quiet down in a bit."

He shuts off the bedside lamp.

"Let's go to sleep, girl. Try to fall asleep before I do."

"Why?"

"I snore like crazy. Nose broken several times."

Lying on my back I reach for his hand. He picks up my hand, kisses it, places it back under the covers, and keeps holding it. Within a few minutes his breathing changes, and then, first in a sort of a hesitant tentative way and after that louder and with more assuredness, he starts snoring. Well, he was not kidding about that. I am pretty sure the neighbors on both sides, and above and below, can hear him. Thinking that I probably will not be able to fall asleep to such loud snoring, I decide that I will just lie here for a bit and then go back to the dojo. But minutes and minutes pass and I can't seem to be able to bring myself to get up. Lying next to him feels so incredibly good. Everything in me just wants to be as near to him as possible. I turn on my left side, put my leg on top of his and my arm around him. Being in this position hurts my injured elbow, but I don't care. I close my eyes and stay like this, my thoughts flowing softer and softer and finally disappearing altogether.

When I wake up, it is almost seven and I immediately think that I've overslept and am in big trouble now. Then I remember it's Sunday and classes do not start till nine. Sunday. If I go back to sleep now, Drago and

I can wake up together hours later and then stay in bed. He is lying on his side, breathing softly, not snoring anymore. For a moment I am very much tempted to curl up next to him and close my eyes again. But no, I can't do that. I must get up now and return to the dojo.

I get out of the bed as quietly as I can and get dressed in the living room. The one-eyed cat is nowhere to be seen, but the dog comes up to the door to see me off. I've asked Drago the names of his pets, and he said their official names are Uchimata and Morote Seoi Nage, after his favorite judo throws, but he mostly just calls them Cat and Dog. It is difficult for the dog to be standing up, so while I am putting on my boots, she lies down. I squat down beside her and she puts her head on my knees and I pat her on the head for a while, and then all of a sudden, I just start crying. It is the strangest thing, but I believe I am happy and am crying from happiness.

Outside it is so cold that when I inhale the frosty air the snot freezes inside my nose. I think about getting a cab but prefer to walk a few blocks to the 96th Street station, where I can catch the Q train. I walk very fast, that feeling of happiness I had earlier still within me and growing with each step I take. I become more and more acutely aware of being the most alive I have even been, my whole body filled to the brim with effervescent joy.

*****

It is not easy to climb a hanging ladder up to the third floor when a sharp pain shoots through your whole arm if you as much as try to move the elbow. Damn, I realize that my right knee is fucked up too and putting a lot of weight on it is not very feasible right now. What should have taken me only three to four minutes becomes a slow and laborious ascent and I wonder what the neighbors across the courtyard might think, and do, if they happen to observe me. What if they assume I am a robber and call the police? Nah, that probably won't happen. This is New York City, a place where people believe deeply in the live-and-let-live adage and do not interfere in others' affairs. Besides, seeing a woman climb a ladder hanging off a window on a Sunday morning is not nearly enough to surprise the hardy residents of this town. They'll just think I am doing some sort of a sports activity.

Back in my room, I pull the ladder in and store it under the bed. I consider whether to lie down for a bit, but, despite having slept for only a few hours at Drago's, I feel wide awake, and so I decide to go downstairs instead and wash my hair, which smells like cigarette smoke.

After the shower I stand in the middle of the locker room examining my naked body in the mirror. By now the bruises have gained a very definite bright-blue coloration. There is an especially huge one on my shin. I touch it and it's very swollen and painful. This hematoma might not dissolve on its own, and I should probably get some treatment for it.

Straightening up, I suddenly see the reflection of Liam's figure standing a few feet behind me.

"What the hell are you doing here?" I pick up the towel from the bench and wrap it around me.

"Inspecting the locker rooms, which is my job, you know."

"Get out."

"What are *you* doing down here so early?" he asks and does not move from his spot. "That is some nasty bruise." He points at my leg. "And what the hell happened to your face?"

"I fell while taking a shower."

"Repeatedly?" His reply to my blatant lie can be nothing but sarcastic of course.

"Liam, get out!"

For a few more seconds he stands perfectly still, looking at me with great suspicion and clearly wanting to ask more questions. Then he turns around and walks away. Lifting the curtain that separates the locker room from the hallway he pauses and says, "Listen, are you okay?" Strange as it is, but it seems to me there is real concern in his voice.

"What the fuck do you care?" I reply instead of just keeping quiet.

He walks out without saying anything else.

*****

Throughout the day I manage to take it easy. In the first class I partner up with Martine. I give her the same legend about slipping and falling badly in the shower. I am not sure she buys it, but she doesn't question me further. Even though she usually prefers to train very hard, she now goes softly and slowly, and I am very grateful to her for that. In the following classes I work with beginners at the back of the mat showing them the basic footwork, and so am able to let my sore body rest a bit.

Before the last class of the day, which is taught by Sensei, my luck changes. I notice Sensei glance at me, his forehead furrowed and the corners of his mouth drawn down. He doesn't ask me anything directly but inquires through the head uchi-deshi if I am all right. I bid Liam to let Sensei know that I am absolutely fine, and that these are just a couple scratches that won't hinder my training in any way.

At the beginning of the class, Liam bows to me, which means he extends an offer of training together. It is against the dojo etiquette to refuse to partner with a person who has bowed to you, especially if the invitation comes from a higher ranked martial artist. Usually lower-ranked persons are to seek out and bow to higher-ranked ones, and it now strikes me as very strange that Liam should be inviting me to train.

"Sensei told me to do it," he pronounces curtly as we start working on the first technique.

Liam and I have not trained together in quite a long time, definitely not since the eventful Winter Assembly. I have tried to avoid him on the mat, never bowing to him at the beginning of classes and, if a certain technique is practiced in groups, waiting to see which group Liam chooses and then going to a different one. I must admit that I am . . . well, not exactly scared of him, but definitely wary.

I have a piece of blue tape on my left sleeve to indicate that my elbow is injured. Usually people are respectful of the blue tape and when training with an injured person make an effort to be careful. A thought crosses my mind that Liam might pretend that he has not noticed the blue tape. That would be very much like him. I have half a mind to tell him, but something in me does not allow me to say out loud that my elbow hurts and to ask Liam to take it easy on me. I don't know why I can't just say it. I guess I don't want to sound like I am complaining or asking for special treatment.

To my surprise Liam acknowledges my injury and, when executing techniques that might put pressure on my left arm, he lets up and proceeds with care. In general, he seems to be going at a slower pace than usual and does not display any of his habitual enthusiasm and passion for training. Even his smirk is gone. He does not look directly at me either. Unless he is in a very bad mood, he always looks his training partner right in the eyes, especially when attacking. Now it's as if he does not even see me, gazing at the wall behind me or down at the mat.

During the whole class Sensei remains nearby and keeps a watchful eye on me and Liam. He never once says anything to us, but by his serious and almost severe expression I can tell that he is not happy.

"It sucks training with you," Liam whispers when doing a pin, which immobilizes me on the ground. "Why do you think Sensei partnered us up? He wanted to see some good training out of you. And instead he sees this. You think this is a Nidan-worthy training?"

Lying flat on my stomach, with my head turned in the other direction, I can't see Liam's face, but I can imagine what it looks like at this precise moment, those very dark eyes of his blazing with suppressed fury. I tap out and he releases the pin. Up on our feet, we do not immediately resume training, but stand very close for a few moments, just staring into each other's eyes. Then Liam's gaze shifts downward at my elbow with the blue tape and I realize that I am holding and slightly massaging it. Ah damn, it probably looks as if I were trying to draw his attention to my injury and thus make an excuse for my subpar training.

"If you can't train, you shouldn't be on the mat," he says. "Or maybe you shouldn't even be at the dojo at all."

*****

Toward the end of the class we are practicing a two-hand shoulder throw. Our pace has slowed down even more, Liam going through the motions in an exaggeratedly uninterested and aloof way, as if to show that he would rather be doing anything else or training with anybody else but me. Several times he mutters under his breath something about me being worthless on the mat and again suggesting I should leave the dojo. I feel more and more annoyed and frustrated. I do my best to ignore Liam's games and focus on the technique, using the slow pace to work on my angles.

When it's my turn to throw, I grip Liam's sleeve and lapel, unbalance him, and shoot in, going lower than his belt. But something is off and I can't seem to fully engage my messed-up elbow. I am taking too much time, trying to adjust my position.

"The fuck are you doing? You don't even know how to throw?" Liam says.

He is clearly trying to provoke me. I do not reply anything, take a deep breath to keep the irritation under control, and am about to finish the throw by extending my legs, bending forward, and turning.

Suddenly my right knee buckles under me. I fall down, losing all control of the technique and sending Liam into a haphazard free fall.

For a split second it seems he would land right on top of my knee and break it, but he makes an almost impossible adjustment in the air and misses me by an inch and falls down at the most dangerous angle, his neck going straight into the mat.

Everything just stops.

There are no sounds, no visuals, no movements—nothing exists for me at this moment, only Liam lying on the floor, seemingly unconscious.

I am on my knees beside him, feeling scared, so very scared. I want to check his pulse, but instead just touch my fingers gently to his skin and withdraw my hand. I am so scared. What if he's already dead? This thought invades my head, and my whole body goes numb with a sudden and unbearable pain. In an instant, all his terrible behavior toward me is of no importance—all I remember right now is that this is Liam, with whom I had such close, complicated, but almost intimate friendship in the past, and then that one that night turned into passion. And maybe it was more than just passion. There was tenderness and . . . and I don't know what else. Liam. Please, just be alive.

I am not aware at all of how much time passes. Probably no more than a few seconds, but these seconds are interminable. Then Liam stirs, sits up, and moves his neck back and forth and sideways, making sure it's not injured.

"Liam." I pronounce his name several times. He does not look at me.

People have gathered around and I can hear someone's voice ask quietly, "What the hell was that? Did she throw him like that on purpose?"

"Liam . . ." I move in close to him. "It was an accident." For fuck's sake, he must know that it was not revenge on my part, that I would not deliberately throw him in such a dangerous way. He must believe me.

He doesn't reply and gets up without once looking at me.

*****

After the class ends and we bow out, Sensei does not immediately step off the mat as he usually does, but remains standing in the middle. We keep sitting in *seiza*, waiting for what he will do next.

"True martial art is about the precision and perfection of the technique and the self-control of the martial artist," Sensei says.

We all listen with the greatest attention and deference—it is not often, if ever, that Sensei gives a speech.

"Control your opponent through being in control of your own body, your emotions, and your force. True martial art is not about inflicting injury on your opponent through loss of self-control. Anger, frustration, resentment have no place on the mat."

We bow to Sensei again, and after he leaves, we bow to our training partners.

"Liam, it was an accident," I repeat.

Yet once more he turns away from me.

I don't get this man. I simply don't get him. He hates me and probably thinks I hate him too—he deliberately tried to harm me during the Winter Assembly, he often lashes out at me, he makes my life at the dojo very hard, and yet just now when, because of my failed technique, he would have fallen on my leg and broken it, I saw him make an almost superhuman effort to land away from me, risking a severe injury to himself.

CHAPTER 11

A week later, my face has sufficiently healed, and looking in the mirror I examine it with attention, trying to finally figure out what it looks like. Oval shaped with a regular nose, a small mouth, big brown eyes, and high cheek bones, framed by light brown hair. Strange, I can study for a long time every separate feature, and yet the whole picture still evades me. I wonder if it's only me, or if others also have problems knowing their own faces.

I have not used makeup in all my time living at the dojo, well, except when Ricardo the Stylist put some on me before the Dark Fight. I remember that he said it was a good idea to accentuate my eyes, so I do the same now using eyeliner, eyeshadow, and mascara. I also comb my freshly washed hair with special care. Sweating for hours on the mat every day, putting it up in a tight topknot, and not paying much attention to it for a long time—all that has quite damaged my hair. So earlier today I put tons of coconut oil in and left it for a while before washing it out, and now the result is pretty great. For once, my hair is soft and shiny. All in all, I am happy with my reflection in the mirror, except perhaps the cheeks being too thin—but at least they do not look as hollow, and the cheekbones are not as salient as on some other days when I train intensely on not enough sleep and food. Last night I had a good night's sleep and made sure to eat well throughout the day today. I had a large bowl of oatmeal with raisins and walnuts for breakfast, a tuna sandwich for lunch, and then ate some sushi which Hiroji shared with me after the last class of the day.

Thinking about food makes me hungry again, and I wonder if I should eat something quickly, but realize it is five to eleven and Drago must already be waiting for me. I climb down the ladder outside my window, walk through the garage, and find him chatting with the garage attendant. I told Drago about my slipping-out strategy and he thought it would be a good idea to give a little something to the friendly man, who leaves the garage's back door open for me. So today he brought him a bottle of good whiskey and some cash.

"That's how things work in the Balkans," he says when we get into the car.

"But this is not the Balkans."

"I am pretty sure this is how things work everywhere. You are too young to know that. You'll learn. The importance of money especially. You hungry?"

I tell him that I am a bit hungry and we drive a few blocks to Le Midi, a French restaurant on 13th Street where they play old French and American movies on a big screen. We sit at a small table in the bar area and I have a glass of Sauternes and Drago drinks cider. We want to order something to eat and they say the kitchen has already closed but they can still make us the Le Midi salad. The salad is delicious, especially the poached pears, candied walnuts, and Roquefort, but that's not enough food, and so the waiter also brings us bread, pâté, an assortment of cheeses and some fresh fruit.

Tonight they are showing *The Charade* with Cary Grant and Audrey Hepburn. Drago and I both like old movies and *The Charade* is a really good one and we watch it in silence for a while. When a highly stylized and rather fake-looking fight scene between Cary Grant and one of the gangsters comes on, we look at each other and smile.

"You any good in a fight, uchi-deshi girl?" Drago asks, wrinkling the corners of his eyes. "If we were to venture into a bad neighborhood, would I be safe by your side?"

"Nah, I suggest you learn some martial arts yourself. Oh, wait, I forgot, aren't you supposed to be a fifth dan in judo?"

"Who, me? Nah. Fights scare me. What if I get a bruise?"

Then his face grows serious. "How old were you when you started training?"

"Nine."

"Why did you start?"

Usually when people ask me about what got me into martial arts, I shrug my shoulders and tell them I don't really know or don't remember. But I don't want to lie to Drago. I keep silent for a while taking slow sips from my glass.

"My parents died some time before that," I say after a rather long pause. "I was scared. All the time I just felt scared. My grandfather thought doing judo might help. He was right."

I worry that Drago might want to know how my parents died. If I say, "they were killed by shots from a passing car," that will just provoke more questions. Grandpa never explained much, even though I got a feeling he knew the whole backstory. From his brief unwilling explanations I gathered that in the '80s, when he and my parents came to this country, there were great turf wars between two powerful Russian Mafia gangs in NYC. Racket and extorsion were ubiquitous. It was practically impossible for a recent Russian immigrant to work and prosper in this town without choosing a side and having the protection of one of the Mafia bosses. My father tried to stay neutral for as long as possible, but in the end was forced to seek an "association" with a person of influence. He trusted that person and even invited him to family events. I think it was in the retinue of that person that I saw the then young Sergey for the first time. Some years later there seemed to arise a disagreement with the trusted person of influence. As a result, my parents were mowed down by the gunshots. When I think of that, a spasm starts somewhere in the depth of my stomach and goes up and my throat tightens and closes up.

I am really not prepared to talk about my parents, not even with Drago. Good thing he leaves the matter alone.

"Where did you do judo?" he asks instead.

"My Grandpa had been a judo master and then a coach in the USSR and he ran a very small dojo here as well, just for neighbors and friends."

I gather my thoughts before going on.

"Stepping into that small dojo and seeing people throw each other had a strange effect on me. Instead of making me more scared it made me feel calm and as if shielded. My brother was already training there." I look at Drago, and he nods with encouragement.

"I remember the first day I put on the gi. They didn't have the right size for me and the sleeves were much too long, but the rules don't allow you to roll the sleeves . . . I looked pretty funny in that huge gi, but I liked the feel of its heavy cotton against my skin. At the end of the class I learned to do the basic *o goshi* throw. It felt good. I enjoyed it."

"What happened with that place?"

"My grandpa got too old to teach, and the little dojo closed, but I kept training at various locations in the city. I did judo for quite a while. Then my brother started sambo with some Russians and hand-to-hand-fighting, and I got into that too. Judo and those other martial arts were very good, but they are relatively new, and I dreamed about switching to a really traditional Japanese martial art, so came to Sensei's Dojo, first as a regular student, then as an uchi-deshi."

"And how long are you planning on being an uchi-deshi?"

"As long as I can. As long as Sensei allows. Dojo is my home now and being Sensei's uchi-deshi is who and what I am."

"That's not a very normal life you are leading, you know."

"Someone once told me not to use the word 'normal.' It's devoid of meaning."

"True." He nods his head. "But hey, listen, being shut inside the dojo for so long, with all the rules, the intense training, the hard work—don't you feel you are missing out on . . ."

"What?"

"Hmm, life."

I don't say anything to that.

"You sure you are not just holding onto a sort of a sanctuary, a safe harbor you found to avoid dealing with the messiness of the real world?"

Still, I remain silent.

"They say she is tough. I think she is pretty fragile," Drago mutters under his breath and takes a long drink of his cider.

"Are you talking about me?"

"Nah." He stares into his almost-empty glass. "And why such fascination with *traditional Japanese* martial arts anyway?" he suddenly asks.

"Well, I think, when I was little." I pause and smile, "I really liked the samurai. Hey, I still do. I think they were awesome with their strict moral code, rules, loyalty, and honor."

"Ha, girl, you've seen too many samurai movies. Sorry to burst your bubble but what those movies show is just a romanticized fairy tale."

I take a sip from my glass and raise my eyes to glance at him.

"Yup, all these beautiful words—strict code of honor, moral principles, noble actions—had no meaning or presence in the samurai world," he pronounces with conviction. "It's a myth. The real samurai sold their martial arts skills to the highest bidder. Their loyalty was to the money only. They were paid killers who in the time of peace bragged about how great and honorable they were, and in a battle used any means necessary, however ignoble and treacherous, to kill their opponents."

I look at him in silence for a while.

"Well, don't get all upset." He signals to the waiter to bring me another glass of Sauternes. "To give them some credit, they *were* exceptionally skilled and highly dangerous fighters, these samurai of yours. We do owe a lot to them. Japanese jujitsu, daitō-ryū, aikido, judo—all have roots in the samurai fighting style," he explains, and I listen with great attention. "The techniques are deadly and are meant for a quick and efficient kill. Of course, in modern martial arts rules were introduced in order to make them more like sports and reduce, as much as possible, the occurrence of injuries in competitions, but the basics are all the same."

"Are we trained to be killers then!" I ask after finishing the strong wine in one gulp.

"See, that's the thing." Drago leans forward and looks at me with intensity. "True martial arts teach you these deadly techniques while at the same time teaching you to be strong in body and mind, disciplined, in control. How you apply these skills is ultimately your choice. You understand? For example, a situation where you must defend your life or the life of your dear ones is very different from instances of unrestrained aggression and violence for money."

"Have you ever been paid to kill?"

"I was paid to do my job, which at times might have resulted in somebody getting killed, but only if circumstances left no other option."

"And you could not refuse the money?"

He gives me a long look and does not reply. He drinks his beer and I can tell he's now done with the topic and probably regrets having said too much.

The conversation has touched something very deep in me, something really important and meaningful. I want it to continue in the same serious vein, but I sense Drago would rather switch to something lighter now. He sits back, his face relaxing, wrinkles on his forehead smoothing out, and a half smile hovering on his lips.

"Do you want another glass of Sauternes?" he asks.

*****

The restaurant was still pretty full when we arrived, but by now has become almost empty and the man who stood behind the bar counter comes over and introduces himself as the owner and asks if we want anything else. Drago invites him to join us and he sits down for a bit at our table and has a glass of wine with us. After he goes back behind the counter, I want to ask Drago more about his life and work in Europe, but all he does is smile and reply that he doesn't remember.

"At least tell me how you got into judo. Or is that also a restricted topic?" I ask.

"*That* I can tell you. I was six years old and the only things for boys in my little town were judo and soccer. I went for judo. I knew nothing about it, of course, but it sounded cooler than soccer. When I just started, there were about twenty boys in the group. By the time I was sixteen, it was only me and my best friend. Soon he gave up too. The training was just too intense."

"But you stuck with it?"

"Yup. I was a wild kid, always a troublemaker. Judo kept me in check. And I always enjoyed the competitions." He looks pensive for a moment and then starts laughing. "In the little spare time I had, I took ballroom dancing, believe it or not."

"What? A judoka taking dancing classes?"

"Yup. Salsa, tango, all that."

I look at him in disbelief.

"It was to pick up girls, ha-ha-ha. That was the only reason. Wasn't a single girl doing judo in my small town. So, I had to be inventive."

I smile picturing this tall, muscular man, who walks with a sort of a sailor's gait, doing salsa moves.

We are both having a very good time, sitting in the empty restaurant and talking, and if it were up to us we could spent another hour or two here, but we can tell that the owner wants to close for the night, and so Drago pays the bill and we get up to leave.

"Should we go find another place to have one more drink?" he asks. "Or what do you want to do?"

"Well, I'd like to go dance some salsa with you."

"What? No! And how do you even know how to dance salsa?"

"Ha! I've lived in NYC my whole life. Of course I can dance salsa. Come on, let's go, yes?"

"I don't know, girl. I am too old for that."

"Too old! What are you, thirty-five? Thirty-six?"

"Something like that. And my back hurts too."

"Oh."

I place my hand on his lower back and starts massaging it. He looks me full in the eyes and smiles, and I wish he would put his arm around me or touch my thigh or just kiss me or something. Why is he keeping his distance? I am craving his touch and I am sure the same thoughts are going through his head. I can feel such a strong sexual pull between us. Is he resisting it on purpose?

"Well, all right," he says, "let's go dance some salsa. Is there a place nearby?"

"But what about your back?"

"You'll have to massage it for real later."

*****

El Hogar y la Leña is only a couple blocks over on Broadway, and from a while back I remember that late at night on the weekends the floor above the restaurant turns into sort of a salsa dancing club. It's not really much of a club, the space is small and there is no live band, but it's the nearest locale I can think of. We leave the car, so as not to lose the good parking spot, and walk to Broadway and East 12th and go through the restaurant and up the stairs in the back.

Upstairs they charge a cover and want to see our IDs, which I don't remember from before. We also have to check our coats. It is pretty hot and I wonder if I should also check my sweater. I probably won't be comfortable dancing in it. Underneath I am wearing a silk-and-lace camisole over my bra. I decide that in the semidarkness the camisole can pass off as a top, and so take the sweater off.

Inside it is packed. There is a bar counter, a few tables—all occupied—and in every square foot of available space there are people dancing or just standing around and watching. We stay near the entrance for a bit and take in the crowded, loud, hectic, and sweaty ambience.

"Well, this is my idea of hell," Drago shouts to me over the music.

"Do you want to leave?"

"They are not even playing salsa."

He is right. Merengue and bachata music have been on this whole time. I motion to him that we can leave, but at that moment the merengue song ends and people stop dancing and hurry toward the bar, leaving the floor pretty empty. Then introductory notes of a salsa song come on.

"Well, since we are already here," Drago extends his arm, "Would your ladyship like to dance?"

He leads me to the center of the room and puts his right hand on my back, I put my left hand on his shoulder, and for a few moments we stand still. I look up at him and he seems to be very focused on listening to the music. By the way he is holding me I can sense he is somewhat tense. Is it possible that the man in the fisherman's sweater is nervous? Ha, I believe he is. When he is around people, he almost always has this expression on his face—a tiny smirk, a certain look in his eyes—which reads as if he knew something that others don't. Well, now this expression is gone.

He makes the first few steps, checks if I follow his lead well, if my body responds to his moves, realizes that I am perfectly pliable in his arms and react to his slightest motion exactly the way he wants me to, and immediately regains his usual self-assuredness.

I've guessed from the start what sort of a dancing partner he will be. His lead is strong and protective at the same time. As the music continues, the floor becomes packed again, but Drago makes sure that nobody ever bumps into us. He does not do any overly complicated combinations or wild turns that some dancers do just to show off and that could be dangerous in this crowded room, and I feel comfortable and secure in his arms.

Salsa songs come in a sequence of three of four and for the duration of this sequence, which is maybe some twenty-five minutes or so, I am completely surrendered to Drago's control, and it feels intoxicatingly good. My body is fully attuned to his and he guides with confidence and precision my every turn, every step. At one point I even close my eyes for a while and feel with each particle of my being this perfect combination of music, movement, and voluntary surrender.

"That was quite something," he says when the music stops. "The things you make me do, girl."

He won't admit it, but I can tell he's actually enjoyed dancing with me very much.

He asks if I want something to drink and gets a bottle of water for me and a beer for himself. We stand in the corner by the bar counter for a while and watch people dance merengue and wait for another salsa sequence to come on. When Drago goes to the bathroom, some guys who are sitting at a nearby table and have already consumed a heavy amount of alcohol, start asking me to join them. I do not reply, and one of them gets up and comes up to me and, standing on rather unsteady legs and struggling with words, tells me that they are celebrating his friend's birthday and would very much like for me to have a drink with them. I decline the drink. He then asks me to dance and tries to grab my arm. I get him in a wristlock and apply a bit of pressure, not aiming to injure him, just to make him understand that his advances are not welcome. Despite being pretty far gone on cheap booze, he gets the hint and retreats, staring at me as if I were an alien or something.

Another guy from their company wants to try his luck too and approaches, shouting to the bartender that my drinks are on him and explaining to me that I will definitely be dancing "the next one" with him. He starts executing some dancing moves right in front of me. I am not sure what to make of the situation and so just back away from him until I am all the way in the corner and he is dancing barely a few inches away from me. I am very tempted to punch him in his red, perspiring face, but don't want to make a scene. Drago appears behind him, towering a full head above the guy. He puts him in a light rear naked choke and, in a careful and friendly way guides him back to his chair and drops him onto it.

"Can't leave you alone for a minute, can I?" He wrinkles the corners of his eyes at me. We look at each other for a few seconds and then his expression grows serious and he focuses his gaze on my mouth and I feel the excitement build up inside me because I know what he is thinking and I am absolutely certain we are thinking the exact same thing at this moment.

From the table yet a third guy gets up and, speaking in a cautious and respectful manner, tells Drago that there has been some misunderstanding and that he apologizes for his friends who did not realize that the lady was accompanied, and that it is his birthday that they are celebrating and offers Drago a beer. Drago accepts the beer, clinks bottles with the birthday guy, but does not drink from it and leaves it on the counter.

Standing at the bar, he puts his arm round my waist and presses his fingers into my hipbone and my thigh, then touches his chin to my naked shoulder and kisses it.

"I am all sweaty and salty," I say.

"Yes, you are. What should we do now? Dance some more or go to my place?" he asks.

A new group has just come in. They are maybe eight or ten people, and Martine is one of them.

"Definitely go to your place. Let's leave right now," I say and, as we walk toward the exit, I try to hide behind Drago and stay out of Martine's line of sight.

*****

In Drago's apartment I take a shower and he comes into the bathroom and asks if he can get into the shower with me. I tell him no, because I absolutely do not see a point of two people taking a shower together, and that he will have to wait for his turn. He chuckles, closes the toilet lid, sits down, and watches me shower through the transparent curtain. When I step out, he hands me a towel and says I should stay and entertain him with stories while he is taking a bath. I do not believe that he will actually take a bath, but he does indeed fill the tub with water, adds some salts and such, and gets in.

"My back is really out. This helps," he says.

"Ok, enjoy your bath. I'm going to bed."

"Nope, I wasn't kidding. Stay and talk to me."

So, now it is my turn to sit on the toilet lid. I tell him stories about the dojo and he especially likes the one about a rat jumping out of the toilet early one morning and trying to bite Hiroji and then the guys attacking the rat with the swords.

When he is done with his bath, we go to the bedroom, and I tell him to lie down on the bed, face down, so that I can massage his back. I take my towel off, sit on top of him and rub the ointment into the sore spot on his lower back and massage it in. After a few minutes of lying still, he starts touching my legs, tentatively at first, and then with more insistence. I bend down and push my breasts to his skin, and then lie fully on top of him. He turns over brusquely, trapping me under him, and then is inside me and moving strong and hard.

"Ah, damn it," he exclaims after one particularly strong motion and stays still.

"What's wrong?" I ask.

"My back. Did something to it just now."

I help him roll over and lie next to him.

"Is it really that bad?"

"Nah, I am faking. Just wanted to take a little break."

He tries to reach over to get a bottle of water from the nightstand and winces in pain. I hand him the bottle and he can barely sit up to drink, and then he lies back down and closes his eyes.

"Drago, I'm sorry I made you go dancing. I didn't know your back was really hurting."

"It's all right. I'll go see my doc tomorrow. He'll give me a shot or something."

Lying side by side, we are breathing deeply, wanting each other really badly. He is still very hard, and I reach with my hand and start touching him. He tries to pull me on top of him, and I get on top, but do not let him inside me yet. I lean in and kiss him hard on the mouth and bite his upper lip. He grabs the back of my head and kisses me for a long time. I pull away and look at him and then touch his shoulders, his chest, his stomach. I never knew it was possible to derive so much pleasure from just touching someone's skin, inhaling its scent, kissing it. Every touch seems to reverberate inside me. Why this man? What is it about him that makes me feel as if a small fire, pleasurable and agonizing at the same time, started burning in me every time there is contact between us? It is as if I had taken some sort of a drug that makes all my sensors work at their highest mode when I am with him.

I take him in my mouth.

"If you keep doing this, I will come," he says after a short while.

I show him a thumbs up.

"No," he gently pushes my head away.

"Why?"

"Because I want this," he says and sits me on top of him.

After some time he suddenly grabs me and lifts my hips off of him, so as not to come inside.

*****

Afterward we are both terribly hungry. I suggest I can bring stuff from the kitchen, but he says we'll both go and eat at the table like civilized people. It takes him several minutes to swing his legs off the bed and pull on his jeans. He can't stand up very straight and his gait is slow and uneven.

"Yup, look what you did," he says and tries to smile.

"And taking painkillers won't help at all? You have ibuprofen, don't you?"

"Helps with inflammation. Does not do anything for pain, not for me. Told you, I am resistant to pain medication."

As we turn the light on in the kitchen, a number of roaches run in different directions from the sink.

"Yeah," Drago says. "They don't like it when someone turns the light on unexpectedly in the middle of the night. Disrupts their pastime."

"Yeah, I noticed the first time I was here. Thought it a very picturesque feature of the apartment."

Drago rummages in the fridge and takes out bread, Brie cheese, radishes, blueberries, strawberries, and a mango. He also finds some dark chocolate. We put everything on the table and sit down—me in one of his Henley shirts, which is pretty big and hangs off one shoulder, he in his jeans—and eat. After a while he gets up because it hurts his back more when he is sitting down and continues to eat while standing up and leaning against the counter. I put my naked legs up on the empty chair and he stares at them. I study the tattoo on his arm, but I'm more interested in the discolored patches of skin and the story behind those. I try to ask again.

"When you were burned, was it in an explosion?"

"Nope."

"What then?"

He shakes his finger at me. "Give it up."

"Tell me."

"All right. It was napalm mixed with gasoline, in a fire extinguisher. It shoots fifteen feet. Napalm burns through the flesh. Nothing can extinguish it."

I put down a piece of mango I am eating at the moment. "Why did they do that to you?"

"Well, I guess they must have been angry with me."

"Why?"

"Probably because I tried to arrest them, and they had different plans for their immediate future."

"So basically, it was your fault?"

"Exactly. I brought it on myself," he laughs.

"Did it happen in your country?"

"Nope."

"Where?"

"In Austria."

"What were you doing trying to arrest people in Austria?"

"Don't remember."

"Were you working for Europol or Interpol or something?"

"Ha! You know many interesting words, girl. Are you done eating?" He asks staring at my legs again.

"Why?" I get up and come up to him looking him in the eyes. He puts his arms around me, pulls me in close, and moves his hands down my back, my ass, my thighs, and then under the Henley shirt.

"Thought it wasn't good for your back?"

"It's not. Tomorrow, I won't be able to move at all," he says and then turns me around and leans me against the counter.

CHAPTER 12

I wake up and look at Drago. He is lying on his back, breathing heavily and breaking into short and torturous bursts of snore every few seconds. Before we fell asleep, he said that it was not cool how I had just left "in the middle of the night" the last time, and that I should definitely wake him up this time and, if his back was not too bad, he'd give a ride to the dojo. But we went to sleep so late, not before four in the morning, and he still turned around in bed for quite a while before he could find a more or less comfortable position for his back. And now, two hours later, I just can't seem to bring myself to wake him up. No, I won't do that. Let him sleep. Maybe his back will feel better after he's gotten some rest.

The Rottweiler walks me to the door again, her kind and sad eyes watching me with great attention while I put on my coat and boots. The one-eyed cat makes an appearance as well, first sitting at a bit of a distance and then coming up and rubbing against my feet. They both look awfully drowsy, and I kind of envy them, knowing that as soon as I leave they will go back to sleep.

After I close the door behind me I stand in the hallway for a few moments, picturing the apartment I have just left. Drago in the bedroom. The dog and the cat in the living room. Roaches in the sink in the kitchen. Damn it, I miss it all already, and I haven't even gone five feet away.

Once again I take the Q train, but this time I get off after only one stop, at the 86th Street Station. I walk to 82nd and 1st to check up on

Danilo. The last few days he hasn't been answering my phone calls. I know there is very little chance he will be at the apartment now. He's most likely spending the night anywhere else rather than at home. Still, I decide to take a look. If he is in and sleeping, I won't wake him up, and will just leave quietly.

I go up to the fifth floor and open the door with my key.

Walking into the bedroom, I sort of gasp and stand still for a few moments, leaning against the wall.

Danilo is lying in bed, on top of the covers, awake. His neck is in a brace, right arm in a cast, he has an eye patch over one eye and nose inserts sticking out of his nostrils, his lower lip is cut badly and swollen to triple its normal size, and when he opens his mouth I can see two teeth are missing.

"Hello, Sash," he pronounces with great difficulty. "My face is ruined."

"Oh, Danny, what happened?" I sit at the side of the bed and blink rapidly so as not to start crying.

He does not answer and just looks at me with his one good eye, and his gaze is sadder than the Rottweiler's.

"You did another Dark Fight?"

"Yeah."

"Oh no! Why? Never mind. Just tell me, how bad is the neck injury?"

A cervical fracture is something all fighters probably fear the most. Danilo being in his bed and not at the hospital means he does not have a severe break, and I guess I should not be this scared. But seeing him like this, with the cervical collar on, I cannot help but feel terrified. Even a minor fracture would have my brother bedridden for weeks and might have serious complications and require a surgery later on.

"There is no fracture," he pronounces slowly, some of the sounds coming out messed up or disappearing altogether.

I realize I have been holding my breath, and now breathe out with relief.

"Are you sure?"

"Yeah."

"And the eye?"

"Something called a hyphema."

Oh, he must have been punched or elbowed really hard right on the eye.

"Can you see at all with that eye?"

"Not too well."

"Will you need a surgery?"

"They said probably not."

"Ok, well, then things are not so bad." I try to smile to reassure him, but I don't think my smile comes out very bright and cheerful at all. I sit silent for a while, looking at my brother and biting the inside of my mouth.

"My face is ruined," he repeats. "Nose broken again . . . and these." He points at his missing teeth.

"The nose will heal again, and we'll get you to a good prosthodontist for the teeth."

"Sergey says he'll pay for the dental work and stuff," Danilo sighs deeply several times.

I don't reply anything out loud, but in my head I deliver a few choice words about Sergey.

"I found one of the teeth," Danny then says, struggling to pronounce the words clearly and pausing to swallow the saliva. "I tried to put it back into the socket. You know if you put it back in within an hour, it will reattach itself."

"It might." I nod.

"But it fell right out again and I swallowed it."

I can see a tear appearing in his good eye and hanging on his long lashes.

"It's all right, Danny. It's all right," I say and stroke the arm that's not in the cast. "We'll get your face fixed. Don't worry."

We are silent for some time. I want to ask him so many questions, but somehow they just don't seem important at the moment. What matters most is that none of my brother's injuries are life-threatening. The mere notion that I might lose my brother gives me the same deep spasm in my stomach and the tightening and closing of the throat that I feel when I think about how our parents were taken from us.

"Danny, why did you fight?" I finally ask.

"Owed him money again," he says and closes his good eye.

Ahhhhh! I feel so frustrated I just want to scream. I was so sure that my doing that one Dark Fight and paying off my brother's full debt would be the end of it, that he would come to his senses and stop his gambling and would stay away from the 2 Gild Street lifestyle for good. Damn it. I was so stupid, naive and stupid, and too ready to believe what I wanted to believe.

I feel the anger boiling inside me, but it's not directed at my brother. I know how it is. It is that bastard Sergey that would not let him out of his clutches. That fucking "honest businessman." If he were in the room right now, I don't think I would have been able to contain myself, and he would have been in acute danger of serious physical damage. With no outlet for my anger and frustration, I breathe in and out deeply until I feel a bit calmer.

"I am kind of hungry," Danilo says. "There is stuff in the kitchen. I had it delivered from the store."

I go to the kitchen and find several large jars of apple sauce and cartons of mango juice. I feed Danilo the apple sauce from the spoon. He can probably manage the spoon with his left hand, but it makes me feel better to be able to do something for him now. I then give him some juice to drink from a straw.

There is an almost full bottle of oxycodone on the nightstand. "Do you want your pain medicine now?" I ask. I wish he didn't have to take that highly addictive stuff at all, but I don't want him to just suffer through the awful amount of pain he must be in.

He hesitates.

"Nah," he mutters then, and a grimace runs across his already distorted features. "That shit started giving me terrible itches all over my body. Pour some white rum in my juice instead."

I bring a bottle and add a small splash of rum into the glass.

"A bit more, please. Come on, pour a good amount in."

"Danny," I say after he finishes his drink. "Listen to me. Focus, please. You must promise me that you will not do any more Dark Fights ever again. Not ever again. Do you hear me? And that you will stop the gambling. Once and for all. Promise me that. And this time you must really mean it."

He is silent.

"Danny?"

"Ok, Sash, I promise."

*****

Having climbed up the hanging ladder, I am back in my room just in time to get changed and start on my morning chores before we open the dojo. Passing hurriedly through the living room on the way to the stairs I almost bump into Liam. I mutter an automatic "morning" and want to get around him, but he catches me by the elbow and starts sniffing at me.

"You smell like a man's cologne and cigarette smoke again," he declares and looks at me out of his sleepy eyes that gradually gain a stern, angry expression.

I shouldn't respond. I should just walk away quietly, but because I am in such a bad mood, such an *agitated* mood, I cannot contain myself.

"Yeah? So what? You gonna throw me down the stairs again?"

A momentary shudder runs across Liam's face. He releases my arm, steps back, and lets me pass, just watching me, his mouth tightened into a narrow line, his eyebrows furrowed.

This time he does not know for sure I spent the night outside the dojo. He is full of suspicions but has no definite proof and won't find any. Unless . . . hmm. What if Martine did see me last night? Would she snitch? If she does, I'm screwed. Ah, damn it, right now I really can't focus on any of that. All of my thoughts are about Danilo.

Intense training helps me relieve some of the turmoil I feel inside after having seen my brother in his horrible condition. I have my anger somewhat under control now and no longer feel the urgent need to choke Sergey to death. Still, I don't feel quite like myself and, immersed in my gloomy thoughts, I don't want to talk to anyone. After the class, I am sitting on the bench in the empty locker room, staring at nothing in particular, folding and unfolding my black belt. What worries me the most is whether Danilo can keep his word. Damn it, I really hope this time he can.

Martine comes in and sits by me.

"What are you so gloomy about?" she asks.

"I'm not. I'm OK."

"Come on. I can see something is wrong. Was it your boyfriend that upset you?"

"My boyfriend?"

"The man I saw you with last night at El Hogar."

Damn. So she did see me. I look her in the eyes for a moment and then turn away.

"Don't worry, I won't tell anyone you sneaked out of the dojo. I understand how it is," she says and pats me on the knee.

It is strange hearing her refer to Drago as my boyfriend. *Is* he my boyfriend? I never really thought about that. I do not particularly like the term "boyfriend," either. People say it left and right and it's become such an overused word that I am not sure I know what it means exactly.

"Don't be sad." Martine puts her arm around me and kisses me on a cheek. "Oh, I know how to cheer you up. Wait here! Don't move," she exclaims and runs out.

She returns some ten minutes later. I am still sitting down on the bench in the exact same position as before and playing with my black belt. She takes the belt from me and places a warm ham-and-cheese croissant in my hands.

"Your favorite thing for breakfast, right? I got it at the coffee shop across the street, not at the food cart. And the coffee, too, just as you like it, with almond milk, no sugar."

"Oh, thank you, Martine," I say and almost start crying.

Such acts of kindness from people who do not want anything in return have always had a rather powerful effect on me, but not to the point of tears. Now my friend bringing me a croissant and a coffee makes me choke up. I wonder what is going on with me. Have I gotten so used to being the strong one and feeling responsible for and trying to take care of and protect my brother, that *receiving* feels utterly unexpected and throws me off? Could be that, or maybe it's just my hormones acting up. I've read somewhere that if a woman abstains from sex for a while and then suddenly starts having sex, her hormonal balance gets completely messed up.

"I hope Liam did not see me running out on the street in my gi." Martine laughs.

Wearing gi outside the dojo is against martial arts etiquette.

"Thank you, Martine," I say again.

"Listen. Don't worry about your boyfriend. Whatever he did is not worth your being so upset. Maybe you should not even be with him anyway. He is too old for you."

"Huh?"

"Well, how old is he?"

"I don't know. Midthirties."

"Hmm. I doubt that. He looks older."

Well, his body certainly does not. I do not say this out loud. "I'm not upset because of him, Martine."

She looks at me waiting to hear more, but I do not elaborate further on the topic.

"Hey, remember how we used to go dancing together before you became an uchi-deshi? I miss that," she says. "I'm a bit jealous you go now with that guy and not with me. It used to be our thing. Maybe one of these days you can sneak out and we can go to El Hogar together." She puts her arm around me again and kisses me on the side of my head and then on my neck.

*****

Sometime after the noon class a basket with food items arrives. It has a French baguette, foie gras, camembert cheese, and a number of other delicacies, including a small tin of caviar. The card says, "to my niece." My first reaction is to throw everything in the garbage, but on second thought I go outside, cross the street, hand the basket to Amadeus the Homeless Guy, who is sitting there under the scaffolding, and quickly come back to the dojo.

A little while later, while I am on duty at the reception desk Sergey calls on the dojo phone.

"Can you talk?" he asks.

I look around. There is nobody on the main floor. Hiroji and Liam must be resting upstairs.

"What do you want to talk about? About my brother maybe? You fucking nearly got him killed."

"Did you like the food basket?

I look out the window.

"The homeless guy I gave it too seems to be enjoying it very much. The caviar especially."

"Ha-ha-ha. That's all right. I'll send you another one."

"How could you let my brother into the cage again?" I ask pronouncing the words slowly, trying to control the rage that is starting to boil inside me once more.

"Well, why not? The *pretty boy* is quite the darling of the audience. I give the people what they want. Interesting how they enjoy witnessing a beautiful face and body get destroyed."

"You fucking bastard."

"Easy, easy. Calm down now."

"What do you want from me?"

"I'd like to offer you a new deal."

"Damn it, why won't you just leave me alone?"

"Well, beauty, I cannot very well do that, now, can I? Let me be fully open with you. Even though you lost your first Dark Fight, the audience absolutely loved you. They were ecstatic. Such a combination of great martial arts skills and innocent beauty is not easy to come by, and I would very much like to hold on to you. So here is my offer. You come back into the Dark Fights, do a series of five fights and get paid ten grand for each win, and—this part you will like the most—I *never* have your brother enter the cage again. This is an incredible deal, don't you think?"

"Go to hell. I won't make any more deals with you," I say and hang up the phone.

As I turn around, I see Liam standing by the entrance to the men's changing room looking in my direction. Hmm, so he was not upstairs after all? I don't know how much if any of my phone conversation he was able to hear.

*****

Every year in February Sensei goes to Japan for the whole month and classes at the Dojo are taught by other senior-ranked instructors, and with each year Sensei assigns more and more classes to Liam. I must say Liam is a gifted teacher and his classes have excellent dynamics, and he has a natural talent for explaining in a clear and precise way even the most complicated of techniques. In the past, with great frequency he would call me to the center of the mat to demonstrate a new technique on me. He would also watch me closely throughout the class, correct my mistakes, and give me instructions, which always helped me execute techniques in the most effective manner. Now he completely ignores me, calls other people up for demonstrations, and never once approaches me to correct a mistake or offer advice.

Strangely enough, I feel somewhat disappointed that he's ignoring me in this way on the mat, but maybe it's for the best. Things have been quiet and I want them to stay that way. Martine has kept her word and didn't tell anyone she saw me outside the dojo that night, and Liam hasn't raised the topic again. My conflict with him will probably never ever be resolved, but at least for the time being his anger and resentment against me are burning somewhere under the surface, and I don't want them to flare up again. So, the less interaction I have with the man, on or off the mat, the less chance there is we might get into a bad altercation of some sort.

With Sensei away, attendance goes down, the classes are smaller than usual, and get smaller still when the flu hits the dojo. This year it hits us pretty hard around the second week of February with students falling ill one after the other. Liam, Hiroji, and I are taking tons of vitamin C, eating oranges and tangerines, but of course it is all pretty ineffective. Being in close contact every day with coughing, sneezing, sweaty people on the mat, it is inevitable that we get the bug too. It starts with feeling very tired all the time, exhausted, all your muscles sore, then your throat gets dry and scratchy, and then you wake up one morning completely sick.

I usually don't run fevers, even when I'm pretty sick, and on those rare occasions that I do, it affects me in a strange way. I guess my body feels it too acutely, and if my temperature goes up even a bit, I start feeling incredibly cold, like I'm freezing, and shaking, breathing real fast, and even hallucinating.

Lying in bed in my room I'm not sure who it is that brings me hot tea and pills, helps me sit up while I drink, walks me to the bathroom, and lays me back down and covers me with blankets. Somehow in my mind I picture that it's Drago's hands that hold the cup to my lips and gently push the hair away from my face. It seems to me that I am having a conversation with him, and he tells me jokes and I laugh.

In the moments when my temperature goes down and the fog clears, I see Liam's unshaved face by my side and his very dark eyes looking at me. Has it been him taking care of me this whole time? I am too exhausted to think this out, and then the fever starts in again and my thoughts get all muddled and the images confused.

At one point I open my eyes and lie very still, trying to leave behind my hallucinations and adjust my mind to the reality, and I become aware that it is indeed Liam sitting on the side of my bed. He looks very tired, exhausted. How long has he been sitting here?

"Sasha!" he exclaims. "You feeling better?"

"I think so."

In an unexpected gesture, he takes my hand and kisses it several times. He then notices me looking at him with dismay and drops my hand.

"You gave us quite a scare. The doctor said you'd be fine, but I was really worried."

"*You* were worried about *me*?" I ask unable to believe it is the same Liam who hates my guts talking to me this way now.

"Yes, me, worried," he mutters under his breath.

I look closer into his eyes and see tenderness and affection in them. Can it really be? Perhaps I am hallucinating again.

"You were delirious before. You were talking about some Drago. Who the hell is Drago?" he asks.

I don't answer and turn my head sideways so that I won't see his eyes that seem to be peering deep inside me. We are both silent for a while, and the next time I glance at Liam, the tenderness and affection in his gaze are gone, replaced by his usual stern look.

*****

Just when I begin to recover, Hiroji and Liam fall ill. It is now my turn to cook light nutritious foods for them, make them tea with honey and plenty of lemon, and give them pills that are supposed to help with the sore throat and body aches. I also try to convince Liam to move from the red couch to his real bed, where there are sheets and pillowcases, and where he would be much more comfortable, but the stubborn man refuses. At one time, when I am sitting by his side on the couch, he takes my hand and holds it in his and falls asleep, not letting go of my hand, holding it fast. I don't want to wake him up, so I lie down next to him and stay like this for a long while until he turns over and releases my hand.

It seems like an especially persistent strain of flu this year, because just when you think you are getting better, all of a sudden you are worse than before, and it goes on and on for days. And then a terribly annoying cough sets in. We are all walking around like ghosts, pale, with deep shadows under our eyes, and coughing all the time. It is only toward the end of the month when things are starting slowly to get back to normal.

One evening Hiroji and I are alone upstairs, Liam having gone to one of his bouncing gigs. I am in a bad mood, because I really wanted to see Drago tonight, but he is now sick with the flu too and told me not to come over. I thought about going anyway against his expressed wishes, but he must have guessed my thoughts and said he might not even open the door. I keep playing his words in my head again and again and only manage to upset myself more. I don't understand why he does not want to see me. I guess he is one of those people who prefer to be by themselves when they are not feeling well. But this conclusion does not cheer me up a whole lot.

Hiroji orders dinner from his favorite Japanese restaurant and invites me to eat with him. I know from before that this restaurant's food is delicious, but I don't have much appetite and only eat a few pieces of salmon and a seaweed salad and then go to my room and lie down. I am almost falling asleep when I hear the dojo phone ring in the living room. A minute later Hiroji knocks on the door and says my uncle is sick and a car is coming to take me to him. I ask who it was that telephoned and why that person did not want to talk to me.

"How should I know?" Hiroji shrugs his shoulders. "They seemed in a lot of hurry. 'Tell Sasha her uncle is sick and a car will take her to him,' was all they said and hung up right away. So, will you go?"

All this seems awfully suspicious to me. What the hell is Sergey up to this time? I deliberate for a few moments.

"I think I'll go, yes."

With Liam out, Hiroji is the one in charge and he gives me permission to go and says he will explain to Liam that it is a family emergency.

*****

I approach the metallic gray BMW and the driver steps out and greets me very courteously and opens the door for me. It is the same driver who took me to and from the Dark Fight, and, thinking that we are at least not total strangers, I ask him what is going on. He does not answer my question and tells me to please get in the car as there is little time and we must be on our way. After hesitating for a few moments I get in. However, I don't feel like just sitting here quietly not knowing where I am being taken. I question the driver again and again about our destination and the purpose of this ride. The only thing he says, again, very politely, is, "You will find out once we get there. It is not very far."

We cross to the east side and drive into Chinatown, and then turn into a maze of narrow streets, where we have to slow down significantly. The car pulls up to the curb, and the familiar bald-headed man appears on the sidewalk, opens the door for me, and asks me to follow him and to hurry up. He leads me into a side street and we enter what seems like the back door of a rather big and boring modern building, which sticks out discordantly from the row of old and disheveled neighboring dwellings. Baldy leads me along a corridor that must be going deep inside the building. We open a door to a large hall where there are at least a dozen Ping-Pong tables. At the end of the hall there is another door and it opens as we approach. Behind the door is the gentleman with the buzz cut. The whole set up in fact strikes me as familiar, with several changes, such as the different neighborhood and the absence of the underground tunnels.

Inside, the fight seems to be in full swing. The excited, loud, elegant, and sweaty crowd is packed tight around the cage. I cannot see the fighters, as they are probably engaged in the groundwork at the moment. Buzz Cut hands me over to the tattooed one, who nods at me with as a sort of a friendly recognition, but for some strange reason avoids looking me in the eyes. I think he will lead me to Sergey like he did the last time, but he does not. Instead, he opens the way through the crowd for me, and helps me get right up to the cage.

What I see next sends me into a momentary shock.

There is my brother trying to scramble to his feet, his legs giving out under him, blood streaming down from his forehead, his nose, his mouth. But can this really be happening! He hasn't even had enough time to fully recover after his last injuries to be in the cage again. This distorted nightmare can't be real. And yet it is. Danilo's opponent, twice his weight, actually helps him get up, and for a moment it seems that the two men are hugging each other, but then the big guy lifts my brother up and throws him down so hard, that my brother's head bounces off the canvas.

The referee does not stop the fight, and now the big guy is picking my brother up and is loading him up on his shoulders, setting up for a brutal *kata guruma*—a shoulder wheel throw—that will mostly likely kill Danilo right then.

At that, my mind just shuts off, letting my body take over the control, and the next moment I know I have somehow gotten into the cage and am now leaping toward my brother's opponent and thrusting a powerful kick into the side of his knee, which makes him go down, releasing his grip on Danilo. My semiconscious brother is sliding off of his opponent's shoulders awkwardly and is about to hit the floor hard, but I catch him and make sure he falls down smoothly. I then help him get up, wrap his arm around my neck, hold him around his waist, and walk him toward the cage door. Neither the big guy nor the referee interferes. The crowd however is going absolutely wild. Some are cheering, some are booing. Everybody, men and women, are shouting ecstatically at the top of their lungs.

"Wait, wait," Danilo pronounces with difficulty.

"What is it?" I can barely hear him through all the noise the mass of the excited people are making.

Danilo disengages his body from mine, kneels down with difficulty and picks something from the canvas. I do not understand what he is doing. I think maybe his mind is not working properly and he is hallucinating or something.

"Help me put this back in," he mumbles and shows me a tooth he is holding in his fingers and opens his mouth, the blood still dripping from it. He actually tries to place the dirty tooth back into the socket. I stop his hand and take the tooth from him and assure him a doctor will do it.

"Ok, but you must put it in milk for now. Not in water. You hear me, Sash, not in water!"

I walk my bleeding, disoriented, barely-able-to-stand brother out of the cage and toward the exit, with Head Tattoo making way for us. "In milk, not in water," Danilo mutters several times. He must have heard or read somewhere how to keep a knocked-out tooth alive, and now his concussed and muddled up brain is clinging on stubbornly to that idea.

Buzz Cut opens the door just as we reach it. Baldy is on the other side. No one tries to stop us. At that moment it occurs to me that Sergey has planned the whole thing. Yes, definitely. He wanted me to see, with my own eyes, Danilo inside a fighting cage.

Just before going through the exit, I look at Head Tattoo, who has always seemed the most human of all three of Sergey's men. He is, however, still avoiding my eyes.

"Tell your boss, I accept the new deal," I say while feeling my brother lean heavier against me and fearing he might pass out.

CHAPTER 13

Sensei is coming back from Japan in a couple days and Liam has us start on the preparations early and do an extra-thorough cleaning. Today he makes us lift all the mats and wash under them. Between Hiroji and me it would take us late into the night to finish this laborious task. Good thing that several of the dojo students, my friend Martine among them, stay after classes to help us. Afterward we order pizza and refreshments for everybody, and I think it is Hiroji who pays.

All day long Liam is following me around the dojo and giving me suspicious glances if I as much as disappear from his sight for a few minutes. When Martine and the others leave and I go downstairs to lock the door behind them and do not come back up right away, he comes down. I am reattaching the anti-slip cover on one of the steps and he watches me work, and even though it annoys me quite a bit, I do not say anything. I have no idea what has gotten into him, but I do not want any confrontation between us, especially today, and try my best not to set him off.

Later in the evening, while Liam, Hiroji, and I are eating and watching a movie in the uchi-deshi quarters, Liam's strange behavior continues. Every time I get up from the couch to bring something from the kitchen or to go to the bathroom he stares at me with suspicion and asks where I am going. I am starting to feel quite fed up with this and have half a mind to tell Liam in very unequivocal words what he can do with all his questions, but manage to contain myself.

Around eleven I say goodnight and go to my room. A little while later Liam knocks on the door. I am wearing my pajama shorts and a T-shirt. He looks me over with great attention.

"What's up, Liam?"

"Didn't you say you were going to bed?"

"Yeah, so?"

"I saw the light coming from under your door."

"So what? Do you want a full report on what I have been doing for the last fifteen minutes? Here." I lift up my foot. "See, I've been working on my calluses."

Taking care of the calluses is important for the uchi-deshi. When you just start out, training for many hours on the mat every day makes the skin on your feet crack and bleed. Nothing helps much—Band Aids and sports tape do not stay in place. We go as far as putting superglue into the cracks. With time the cracks heal and eventually calluses form, and you must take good care of them, applying special ointment, making sure they don't get overly dry. Calluses, such as the ones on the side of your big toes, help you get a good grip on the mat, and are a distinct feature of the uchi-deshi's feet. We are quite fond and a little bit proud of them.

Liam looks at my foot and nods. Then the suspicious expression returns to his face and his eyes scan the whole room, searching for I don't know what, and then zoom in on me again. I can tell he has further questions but doesn't know exactly what to ask. In the end he doesn't say anything else and walks out.

I lock the door and stand still for a few moments listening to his steps. I then turn the light out and get ready in the dark.

Before tonight's fight I do not feel as terribly anxious as I did before the first one. In fact, I am somewhat numb inside and have a strange sensation, as if the whole chain of preliminary activities—climbing down the ladder, getting into the car, driving through NYC's nighttime streets—were happening not to me but to another person, and I am just a neutral observer who does not care much about the upcoming event or its outcome.

*****

The car takes me to the entrance of a large hotel in midtown, where Baldy waits for me, and we walk through the lobby, take the elevator to the twentieth floor, and there switch to a different elevator. Baldy scans a card and the elevator starts moving, but instead of going up, as I thought it would, it goes down. As we get out I have no idea what floor we are on, as I cannot see any windows. It does not look like a hotel layout at all, either. Instead of hallways with doors on both sides, there is a space with a single door, behind which, according to the already established routine, I am received by Buzz Cut, who then hands me over to the tattooed one.

While Ricardo the Stylist braids my hair and makes my face look "fresh and bright," as per the boss's instructions, I sit on the bench slouching and picking at a hangnail on the index finger of my right hand, deliberating whether to tear it off or let it be. For some reason, I just cannot seem to focus my thoughts on the fact that within a few minutes I will be stepping into the fighting cage.

The announcer calls "Samurai Princess," and I don't even pay attention and Ricardo the Stylist has to nudge me on the shoulder several times to get me to wake up from my stupor-like state.

"Listen," Head Tattoo tells me as we make our way to the cage. "This girl you're gonna fight right now, she trained in *bajiquan* and *xing yi*. Her punches are fucking tricky. Might not seem like much, but will rupture your internal organs. Your best bet is to get her onto the ground."

"Where is Sergey?" I ask.

"Are you fucking listening to me? Pay attention. I don't want to have to carry you out of here choking on your own blood."

"No worries, just leave me choking on my own blood right there on the canvas. Surely all these fine people will enjoy such a show very much. Is your boss not here?"

"Oh, he is watching all right."

After the announcer's "Fight!" the *xing yi* girl attacks right away. I am protecting my central line and vital organs from her strikes while attempting to get in a position for a takedown. At one point I grab her wrist and do a powerful supinating wristlock throw, but the girl just jumps in the air and flips over her own arm, lands on her feet safely, and then strikes me in the ribs with incredible force. This attack is meant to rupture my spleen and end the fight right away, but at the very last moment I manage to change my body angle just enough for the strike to lose some of its penetrating force. I think it's at this point that I finally come to my senses and start caring about what's happening—and realize that I am not just an observer, but an actual participant in this damn fight, and if I do not fully apply myself, I will indeed be carried out of the cage very badly damaged or dead.

I block the next incoming strike, and she grabs my wrist and does the exact same throw on me that I did on her a mere minute ago. I too flip over my own arm, thus not allowing her to break it. The audience takes great delight in these visually spectacular maneuvers and erupts in loud cheering.

After some time, the girl's potentially deadly punches start to really worry me. I've already caught one or two and expect the next one might connect with a vital point and finish me off. I remember my tattooed friend's advice and so, at the first opportunity I drop down to the floor in a *tomoe nage*, a sacrifice throw, my foot catching her in the stomach, and hurl her backward over me, hard, and then roll on top of her. She does not seem to be very skilled in groundwork, and after a short while I am able to get her in a good position for a choke hold.

Right then my eyes start burning.

In an automatic motion I rub my face against my arm trying to relieve the scorching sensation, and at this she escapes from the choke hold, attains a dominant position, and strikes me in the head.

My eyes are filled with the stinging pain and I cannot see much, and I realize that this sneaky girl must have hidden a blob of something like Bengay behind her ear or some other place where it was not detected during a very sloppy pat-down before the fight. She then somehow got hold of it and smeared it onto my eyes during the full body-on-body groundwork. Damn it. A no-rules fight is one thing, but this sinks even lower than the whole no-rules concept. Now, with my vision severely impaired, she can do what she wants with me. She'll fucking kill me. Fuck this.

"She put something in my eyes!" I call to the referee as loud as I can.

He pretends not to hear me.

"I. Can't. See." I shout again.

Still no reaction from the referee.

I tap out several times. The audience hates for the spectacle to end so quickly and starts booing.

"Fight goes on!" the referee announces, and the crowd applauds. He then bends down near my ear and repeats just for me, "Fight goes on."

My eyes are burning like hell, and everything is a blur. Damn it, if I let this girl get back on her feet, I'm done for. I make a desperate attempt at tying her legs up, not just grappling with my arms, but utilizing my legs for control and, as we are locked in the same position on the ground for a long time without any visible progress on either side, the audience gets impatient and starts booing again.

Now the referee interferes and orders us to get up and again announces "Fight goes on!" to the great delight of the paying customers.

I know I only have a split second to act now. All I can see out of my damaged eyes is a vague figure before me and I charge right at that target, catching a punch or two as I do and moving through the explosive pain they cause. I then practically attach my body to the girl's, holding her as tight as I can, not allowing her sweaty, slippery flesh to get away. As I unbalance her, I throw her over my shoulder, and she falls down hard, her head going into the floor first.

I am aware that I am expected to finish her off with heavy strikes to the head, and the crowd is cheering me on to do so. Yet despite the trick with the Bengay, there is no rage against her inside me. As far as I am concerned, the fight is over. After the throw, she stays down and does not get up for a while. When she does, she is very unstable on her feet and looks disoriented. She can only make a few steps and then sinks down again. I am sure she has a bad concussion, and maybe a neck injury, and needs to be taken to an ER straightway. The crowd sees my inaction and starts booing once more. To hell with them. Hitting the girl on the head now can kill her, and I simply cannot bring myself to act so brutally.

*****

As I get in the car, sit back, and close my eyes, the door suddenly opens and Sergey gets in on the seat beside me.

"How are your eyes?"

I shrug. I washed them with copious amount of water right after I got out of the cage, and then the physician rinsed them out with eye solution and put cold compress on them, but the burning is not completely gone and things still look somewhat blurred.

"If you need, I'll arrange for you to see an ophthalmologist," Sergey says. "Listen, beauty," he goes on after a pause. "We need to have a serious conversation about certain aspects of your in-cage presentation."

"If it's my hairstyle or makeup that worry you so, talk to Ricardo the Stylist."

"Good one." He laughs with apparent gaiety. "I am glad that the long and difficult bout has not affected your sense of humor. Unfortunately, there is something more important than your braids and eyelashes that we need to address," he pronounces in a quiet voice that suddenly has very distinctive cold and hard notes. "I will let it slide this time that you tried to give up and tap out too soon. I must warn you, however, that such behavior might nullify our deal. You'll know better than to do that in the future. Also, I would very much like to remind you that the persons you are fighting in the cage are not your training partners, but your opponents, your enemies. They will do anything it takes to defeat you. You understand? You must treat them the same way. You cannot show mercy. You cannot walk away from a half-defeated enemy. You must continue until the end. Nothing less than that will do. Is that clear?"

I don't say anything.

"Is that clear?" he raises his voice.

"Yep. Can I go back to the dojo?"

"Certainly. I will leave you now. Have a good night, beauty."

*****

I turn the corner and approach the dojo walking slowly, my head bent down, lost in thoughts. Suddenly I hear a voice and realize it is my friend

Amadeus the Homeless Guy calling to me from across the street. He gets out of his sleeping bag and comes over.

"Look, look!" He points to the windows on the third floor of the dojo. Those are the windows of Sensei's room and they are now brightly lit.

"Oh." I stop in my tracks.

"Your chief is back."

What! Sensei has returned from Japan already. We weren't expecting him back until the day after tomorrow. So strange. As a head uchi-deshi Liam would certainly have been informed of any changes to Sensei's itinerary.

For a few minutes Amadeus and I stand together on the street looking up at Sensei's windows and not saying anything.

"Do you think your cover is blown?" he asks then.

"I don't know," I say trying to convince myself that everything is all right but cannot quite dissolve the dark premonition that quickly sets in. "Ah, almost forgot!" I give him his favorite tuna sandwich that I just got for him at the twenty-four-hour deli around the corner. As I hand over the paper bag, my eyes are still locked on the brightly lit windows and my thoughts are getting gloomier and more despondent by the second.

"Much appreciated." He takes the wrapper off and bites into the sandwich. "Well, if they throw you out, you are welcome to use my sleeping bag, and if it gets too cold I know where we can get shelter for a night or two. I don't forget my friends."

"Thank you, I think I'll go in now and see what's going on."

"Good luck."

I walk through the garage and come out into the backyard all the while telling myself that maybe all is not lost. Perhaps my absence has not been detected and I can still get to my room, and in the morning my life at the dojo will continue, and I will take Sensei's class and then do my chores as usual, and then more classes, and . . .

I get to the spot where the ladder must be hanging, and all shreds of hope disappear.

The ladder is not here.

Ah, damn it. So that's it then.

The light is on in my room, and I remember perfectly well having shut it off. I stand for a few long minutes huddled against the wall, trying to get my thoughts together and not knowing what my next move should be. Hiroji's head leans out of the window.

"Hey, are you down there?" he calls, and then tells me to go in through the front door and straight up to Sensei's office.

*****

The last time I was in Sensei's office was when right after my examinations he invited me in to congratulate me on my second-degree black belt. At that occasion the room was filled with high-ranking guests who were eating and drinking, and the ambience was fun and festive. Now Sensei is sitting behind his huge desk looking stern and sad at the same time, the corners of his mouth drawn down. The last time I had a cut on my side that bled a lot but was not too painful and I could stand up straight. Now, besides being bruised all over, I have two broken ribs and have to stand bending forward and a bit sideways taking shallow breaths. I would very much like to sit down or at least lean on the table, but of course out of respect for Sensei I do not do that.

"Those events you participate in, those Dark Fights, they go against the spirit and values of true martial arts." Sensei says passing his fingers through his thick white hair. "Martial arts teach you discipline, of body and mind. Responsibility. Self-control. Restraint. Honor. Respect for your fighting opponent. In that cage fighters get maimed and killed for no other reason than money and spectacle. That is not martial arts. The unrestrained, unchecked violence will corrupt your body and soul and will make you lose yourself. You must stop now, while it is not too late."

When Sensei talks to you, you are supposed to bow and reply "Yes, Sensei." Now, I do bow, but I cannot say, "Yes, Sensei." I cannot lie to him pretending that I am finished with the Dark Fights. I still have four fights to do.

"Promise me you will never step into that cage again."

"I am sorry, Sensei."

He waits for a few long moments looking at me with a mix of severity and deep sadness.

"You are not an uchi-deshi anymore," he says. "You must leave the dojo."

"Yes, Sensei," I say and bow, everything inside me filled to the brim with such utter misery that, if Sensei says just one more word, I might not be able to contain myself and simply break down. But no more words are said.

I go to my room and lie down on the bed and want to fall asleep and wake up in the morning and for this night never to have happened. Being an uchi-deshi has meant so much to me. It has been my life, my true existence, my real path. The dojo has been my home. If I am not an uchi-deshi, then what am I? Nothing at all. A homeless, purposeless woman, whose vision of the future does not extend beyond the four fights she must do to fully extricate her brother from Sergey's clutches.

*****

Hiroji knocks on the door and I tell him to come in. He leans on the windowsill and looks at me silent for a while. I don't say anything either. What is there to say? Everything is pretty damn clear. Oh, actually, there is one thing that is not quite clear.

"Hiroji, how did Sensei find out?"

He shrugs his shoulders.

"Was it Liam who told him?"

"I don't know. Listen." He comes over and sits on the bed. "Maybe you don't realize how fucking dangerous that shit is. Liam and I should have warned you, we should have told you about what happened to Dav, our fourth uchi-deshi, but we didn't want you to know that shit even existed." Hiroji's face is quite composed, but his hand is tightening into a fist, his knuckles becoming almost white, and I can tell how perturbed and upset he is. "We knew the underground fights were out there At one point we were approached by some people. We didn't want to have anything to do with that shit, though, and we didn't know any of the particulars nor who was really behind it—we sort of just closed our eyes to it. We acted stupid, I guess, like those birds, ostriches, sticking their heads in the sand. I don't know, I guess we thought you were safe from all of it here, inside the dojo. Somehow, those bastards got to you. Liam seems to think it was through your brother."

At this, my thoughts immediately go back to that phone conversation that Liam might have overheard.

"Look, let me tell you now about Dav," Hiroji says.

"I already know."

"And that didn't stop you?"

I do not reply.

"All right, look. I guess being crippled or killed does not scare you. But have you considered the other thing that might happen in that cage?"

"What other thing?"

"That you might actually cripple or kill your opponent. Do you have any idea what's it like to kill a person?"

"Do *you*?"

"Yes," Hiroji says in a low voice that has a ring of frightening certainty to it. His eyes gain that hard, cold shine that I have on several occasions observed in them before and that I have found quite unsettling. "Back in Japan I killed. And I am telling you, once you realize what you've done, you want to jump out of your own skin and not be you anymore." The scary light in his eyes fades, and he sinks his head onto his chest and sits motionless. Then he gets up and walks to the door. "I wanted you to know. I hope you do not repeat my mistakes. They are hard to rectify, very hard, Sasha."

*****

I keep lying down trying to gather enough energy to get up and start packing my stuff. My beaten-up body refuses to cooperate and prefers to stay in the horizontal position. I get frustrated with having to take careful shallow breaths, but every time I try to breathe in deeply, a sharp pain shoots through my ribcage as if I were being cut in half.

After a while there is another knock on the door and this time it is Liam who comes in. He remains standing by the door, completely immobile, looking at me and frowning. I wonder if he is going to say anything or will just stand there indefinitely, keeping silent and observing me. Finally, he unglues himself from the spot by the door, walks into the room, and . . . all of a sudden he kneels by the bed.

He is looking right at me, and his dark eyes are filled with the same tenderness and affection I saw in them when I was sick with the flu. But I don't trust him. He is not going to be able to trick me now. I am more than sure it was he who snitched on me to Sensei, so that I would get kicked out of the dojo.

"What do you want?" I ask adding as much coldness to my voice as I can muster.

"What do I want?" he mutters sounding a bit lost. He then gets up from the floor, takes a turn around the room, and tells me that he brings a message from Sensei. I don't have to leave right this minute. I can stay in my room for a few days, until I feel better and find new accommodations.

"Sasha . . ." I can see that he has something on his mind that he really wants to tell me but doesn't know how to put it into words. He comes up closer to the bed again. He touches my hair in a very tender but hesitant gesture. I move my head slightly and he withdraws his hand.

"Do you have a place to stay?" he asks, and by the tone of his voice I can tell that that was not what he wanted to tell or ask me.

"Yes, I do."

At this he simply flips out. "Where? With that smoker you've been seeing?" He cries out not even trying to conceal his sudden and seemingly uncontrollable fury. All the tenderness and affection go out of his eyes, instantaneously replaced by anger, jealousy, and irritation.

"That's none of your business. You must be so happy I've been thrown out of the dojo. You've wanted me out of here for a long time. Thanks for snitching on me. Now you got what you wanted."

"Sasha, you've brought this onto yourself. You've made some very bad choices."

"You don't know anything about my life." I raise my voice and try to sit up, but the pain blasts through me, and I lie back down and close my eyes. When I open them again, Liam isn't in the room anymore.

CHAPTER 14

"So where should I take you?" Drago asks after putting my suitcase on the back seat and getting into the car.

"I guess to 82nd Street?"

"Wouldn't you rather go to my place tonight?"

"Yes," I reply and cheer up a bit.

Packing up my *gi* and my black belt, going down the narrow staircase one last time, opening and closing the door behind me, all the while feeling like an outcast banished from the place that has been my home—more than my home, a place where I truly belonged—well, that hasn't been easy. Good thing I'll be with Drago tonight. Sitting next to him in the car already makes me feel better. I look out the window at the three-story brick building. Right now Sensei is teaching the evening class and they are all on the mat training. I suppress a sigh and turn away. From across the street Amadeus waves goodbye. I resist the urge to steal another glance at the dojo. The car turns the corner and I leave all that, my whole life behind.

Drago drives north on Park Avenue, but instead of continuing uptown, turns East on 57th and then gets onto Queensboro Bridge.

"Are you lost?"

"Nope. I moved."

"You don't live on 103rd Street anymore?"

"Nope. That place was a dump. Too small and filled with roaches."

"I can't believe you are not living in East Harlem anymore. That's so unlike you."

"I know. And just when I got to know every single rat and roach by name."

"I liked your old apartment."

"You'll like this one better."

We cross the East River into Queens and drive North on Vernon Boulevard, turn left, and get onto the Roosevelt Island Bridge and cross the East River again in the opposite direction.

"There is no direct bridge from Manhattan to Roosevelt Island," Drago says. "That's the only inconvenient thing about living here. Otherwise it's pretty amazing. It's considered a part of Manhattan, but it's like a different world here."

He parks the car in a garage and takes my suitcase out of the back seat.

"Why are you bringing it?" I ask

"Won't you need stuff from it?"

"Yeah, I guess."

His new apartment is in a large multilevel building on Main Street, whose architectural style is a mix of residential and industrial. We take the elevator to the tenth floor. He opens the apartment door and inside there is a staircase leading down into a huge living room.

"Cool, huh?" Drago glances at me to see if I share his enthusiasm.

The place is indeed pretty cool. The windows in the living room are floor to ceiling. The kitchen is modern and spacious. The bedroom alone is almost the size of the entire apartment on 82nd Street. And there is a huge walk-in closet. He got all new furniture too. A big sectional black-leather couch in the living room, large coffee table, bar stools, a huge TV. How could he afford this place?

"Did you win a lottery or something?"

He smiles but does not answer my question directly. "It's good to have some money," he says instead. "Money can be damned useful, girl. Useful and pleasurable. Who wants to spend their entire life with roaches, rats, and hookers for neighbors in an old dirty walkup?"

At first I think that I don't like the new place very much but when I see stuff from the old apartment—the same books in French, Russian, and German on the bookshelves, the same black-and-white photographs on the walls, his collection of old cameras—it starts to feel more like Drago's former apartment, where I felt so comfortable and secure.

There is an enormous wood-and-metal telephone, from the end of nineteenth century, standing in the corner.

"Yup, this is my phone. The one I use daily," he smiles.

This artifact somehow fits very nicely into the whole setup of the place.

The one-eyed cat jumps down from a shelf onto the couch and makes itself comfortable by my thigh. Yep, now it absolutely does seem like Drago's apartment. I find the whole ambience of the place so very soothing and calming. It envelops me and makes me feel the same way I did at his place on 103rd Street—I belong here all right.

"Where is the dog?" I ask.

"She had to be put to sleep."

"Oh. I am sorry."

I look him in the eyes and there is a momentary expression of deep sadness in them and he seems lost. I can tell he loved that dog very much. Within a second however he smiles. "Well, it's just you, me, and the cat now," he says. "Are you hungry? I'm starving."

This man does not show emotion very easy, does he? Is he always this tough? How deep does the toughness go? If you dig through layers and layers of this toughness, will there be anything under it?

He cooks dinner—tilapia with grilled vegetables. I come into the kitchen and want to help, but he jokes that he'd prefer if I didn't burn down the apartment on the very first night and tells me to go back to the couch and choose a movie for us to watch.

We both like Andy Lau, so I find *Firestorm*, and we start watching it in the living room with dinner. When we are done eating I put a pillow on Drago's lap and lie down with my head on it. He places his hand on my hip.

"Come on," he says after a while. "We can watch the movie in the bedroom."

Lying down in the bed, my raised knee blocks his view of the screen. He pushes my knee down with his leg. I raise it up again. He pushes it down one more time and leaves his leg on top of mine. I want him very much, the weight of his leg is so pleasurable it is almost burning through my skin. He places his hand on my stomach, then moves it down and his finger is now inside me. But it is not what I want. I push his hand away. I want to feel the weight of his whole body on top of me and him inside me. And it has to be right now. Nothing else will do. He puts his hand on my neck and kisses me hard on the mouth and lowers his body onto mine and guides himself into me. After a while he puts my legs on his shoulders.

In the morning his alarm goes off, and I don't want him to get up. I press my body into his and soon he is inside me again.

"Damn," he says afterward. "I have to go to work. You stay here and go back to sleep."

When I wake up again, it is almost noon. On the nightstand there is a set of keys and Drago's passport opened to the page with his birth date. He is forty-four, quite a bit older than I thought he was, but it makes no difference to me.

I spend the day in the apartment, reading on the big couch in the living room most of the time. I go out once, walk the short distance to the river and look across at the Upper East neighborhood of Manhattan, and then go back to the apartment and fall asleep reading, the one-eyed cat by my side.

Drago comes back in the evening and asks why I have not unpacked my suitcase.

"There's plenty of shelves and hangers in the closet for your stuff," he says.

"Do you want me to unpack my suitcase here?"

"Yup. I think it would be best."

*****

Living with Drago, the first few days are filled with him and being with him and thinking only about him when he is not around. My mind just blocks out thoughts of anything and anyone else. Then waking up late one morning I have a strange feeling that I am late, that I missed the first class of the day and have not even started on my chores. Liam will be furious with me. It takes me a few seconds to realize I am not at the dojo anymore. After that, the thoughts of the dojo do not leave me. I push them to the very back of my mind and try not to dwell on them, but I cannot help but miss my life as an uchi-deshi. Sure it was a tough life, filled with intense training, hard work, injuries, strict rules, the constant feeling of tiredness, but yeah, I do miss it now. I miss Sensei, my friends, and especially the structured training, the instruction from Sensei and other higher ranked martial artists.

I need to continue my training, and Sergey puts at my disposal a private gym he has at 2 Gild Street. I am not surprised he owns a gym. I have heard from my brother that half of the building there belongs to him. I am only allowed in the gym at certain hours, however, in the morning and in the evening. I guess Sergey does not want me to bump into other fighters who might be training there.

For my first training session I go around eight in the evening. I hop on the subway and head downtown to the Financial District and get off at Fulton Street. From there it is a couple-minute walk. I pass Wolf Flannigan's Pub on Molten Lane, glancing in the window and seeing the familiar bartender behind the counter, turn the corner, and continue under the archway on what seems like the narrowest sidewalk in Manhattan. Then the space opens up and 2 Gild Street appears in all its enormity.

It is a huge residential building and people are coming in and out of it in a continuous two-way stream. Delivery guys, partygoers, girls in high heels, dog owners in pajama pants—a lively ambience here. Inside, there are at least four or five doormen. I tell one of them my name and where I am going. Sergey said I would have to do this only once. From now on the doormen will always let me in without stopping me.

The gym is on the sixth floor and it is a full-size gym with a complete set of exercise machines, a boxing ring, a cage, and a tatami mat area. Everything is modern, brand new, and sparkling clean. At my allocated time I am alone here. I change in the beautiful and spacious locker room and come out and sit on the mat feeling sad and gloomy, missing the dojo very much.

A few minutes later the door opens and Head Tattoo walks in. I am suddenly so glad to see him I almost feel like I want to hug him and kiss him on a cheek, but I contain myself and we greet each other with a more appropriate fist bump.

"The boss sent me. I am to be your sparring partner," he grumbles under his breath. He seems rather uncomfortable and is standing a bit hunched over and shifting his weight awkwardly from one foot to another. As we start training he relaxes and proves a very good sparring partner. Despite his huge body size he is very agile and fast on his feet, and I can learn a lot from his footwork. His strikes are precise and powerful, and he teaches me a few good tricks for attack and defense. He also makes me work on strengthening my knuckles, so that I can hit hard surfaces like my opponents' jaws without damaging my hands. Together we do pushups on bare knuckles, which is his favorite exercise. Unfortunately, his throwing and ground-work skills are somewhat lacking—still, I enjoy training with him quite a lot and after a while don't feel so lonely and gloomy anymore. I go to the gym at 2 Gild Street every day, and later Sergey sends me other people to spar with—experts in BJJ groundwork as well as exceptional strikers—but I always prefer Head Tattoo.

This new type of training takes some getting used to. Exiled from the dojo, I am no longer part of a real community. There is no sense of belonging to something big and meaningful, steeped in traditions, values, and rules of conduct passed down many generations. Now I am training just for myself, for the sake of improving my fighting skills for the Dark Fights—nothing else. I realize there is no sense in comparing. What I am doing now is purely utilitarian—I must do it in order to survive in the cage.

*****

On the day of my next Dark Fight, the metallic gray sedan comes to pick me up earlier than usual. Drago is not home yet, which is good, since I can just leave and don't have to lie about where I am going. I get into the car and there is a garment bag and a box with shoes on the seat. A cocktail dress and high-heeled shoes.

"The boss wants you to wear this," the driver says.

"In the cage?"

"There is a small event before the fight."

I start taking off my sports clothes and see the driver's eyes in the mirror. He averts his gaze, but I am sure he will look again within a second. I put on the simple sleeveless black dress and am glad it is modeled in such a way that does not require a bra or panties, since I am not wearing either.

We drive to a building on West 16th street, close to the river, and I feel weird being only a few blocks away from the dojo. The building is filled with small and large art galleries and Baldy takes me up to the eighth floor, where Buzz Cut receives me at the door and indicates for me to go right in. I find myself in a modern art exhibit, with people walking around drinking champagne and having hors d'oeuvres. I sit on the windowsill and look at these people, their smiling and chewing mouths. Sergey comes over and takes me to see a big painting on the opposite wall.

"What do you think?" he asks.

"Nothing."

"You are not very fond of modern art."

"No."

"Well, I just bought this painting for one hundred and thirty thousand dollars. To tell you the truth, I don't care for modern art either, but it's a good investment. I invest wisely. I strategize. I seek out pieces that will bring me good return on my money."

"Pieces?"

"Oh, yes. Fine Art. Martial arts. Martial artists." He looks me straight in the eyes and his lips are curved in a half smile. "Martial artists can be a very good investment." He takes a meaningful pause as if he wants his words to really sink in. "I really do not like to be disappointed, though." The half smile disappears, and his eyes gain a hard, steely expression.

*****

The space behind the art gallery is where the Dark Fight takes place tonight. After midnight all the guests abandon the modern artwork exhibit and start migrating toward the cage. Plenty of drinks are still being served here. This is just the continuation of the party for them.

Going into this fight I feel confident, having put in many hours sparring with Head Tattoo and other partners that Sergey provided for me. My fight plan is to take my opponent down with a *kata guruma* or a *te guruma* within the first minutes.

I am waiting for the right moment to move in, when all of a sudden, *bam*! She shoots in for a *te guruma*.

In this throw, you grab your opponent with one arm around their thigh and your second arm a bit higher than their waist, you lift them up, twist them in the air and throw them on their back. It is spectacular, highly efficient, and dangerous. In most sanctioned competitions it was banned several years ago. In many martial arts schools this technique is not even taught anymore. Grandpa showed it to me a long time ago, it was one of his favorite throws along with *kata guruma*, and I have practiced it ever since.

I am quite shocked now that my opponent preempts my move with her own *te guruma*. But I instantaneously detect mistakes in her execution of the technique and make use of them. She is bending her back instead of bending her knees, and her right arm is too high, which gives me an opportunity to get it into a *kimura* lock.

If played in slow motion, this will present a bizarre and horrifying sequence—

She is lifting me up and turning me upside down in the air, all the while I am locking her arm in the *kimura*.

She then finishes the throw, but instead of landing me on my back, she executes a piledriver, which means she is spiking me on the canvas on my head. And no amount of ukemi training from Hiroji could help me here.

I crash onto the mat with my neck taking the brunt of the impact in a horrifying fashion.

Did the *piledriver* happen because I was holding her arm in the *kimura* trying for a submission, didn't disengage, and thus couldn't maneuver my own body to break the fall? Was she in a lot of pain and so angered by my lock that she decided to slam me onto my head? Or was it her intention from the very start—instead of landing me on my back to smash me on my head? It could be either or all, in any case, the result is that the *piledriver*, illegal in most sanctioned matches, does happen now, and the audience goes wild, erupting in applause for my opponent.

Then, all is quiet. Has the room gotten silent, or the silence is in my head? Is my neck fractured? Damn, this is the injury many fighters are most scared of. Am I crippled for life now?

I stay motionless on the canvas for a few moments, then move my neck, slowly, very slowly at first, then I sit up and try for a wider range of motion with my head. It is OK. A small miracle. Well, not so small for me.

*****

The fight is not stopped. In a sanctioned match, I would be attended by a doctor on the spot and he'd be putting a neck brace on me right away. But no such "luxury" in a Dark Fight. The bout goes on.

I am quite rattled after the *piledriver*, and my opponent uses it to her advantage, attacking all the time, a number of her strikes connecting heavily with different parts of my body. I do my best to reciprocate, and after a while both our noses are bleeding. I don't think mine is broken, but I cannot be sure, of course. Blood is coming out of our mouths too. There is blood on our bodies, our clothes, blood mixed with sweat in our hair. There is so much blood on the canvas, it starts feeling slippery.

At one point she has me pinned down with her knee on my head, the weight of her whole body driving into my skull. I feel like it's going to crush my skull. Later on, she is in a dominant position again, and she pins and twists my leg in such a brutal way that something seems to tear inside my knee. Still, I somehow manage to scramble back up on my feet, and the fight goes on.

And then there comes a devastating kick to the head that fells me.

It is strange but I do not pass out right away. For a split second I am still aware of myself and of my surroundings—I see and hear in almost exaggerated and overly bright picture the audience shouting, applauding, their arms up in the air. I know that it was a KO and I've lost the fight and feel myself falling backward and cannot stop the motion. I know now I am going to hit the floor, but do not feel the contact. I probably pass out before my head touches the canvas. When I come to, all the sounds are muffled, as if I have cotton wool stuffed in my ears.

The physician who examines me in the backroom after the fight says I might have a fractured shinbone, a dislocated shoulder, a torn meniscus, and worst of all, a possible neck injury and a severe concussion. With the adrenaline still pumping I don't yet feel so bad, but I throw up a couple times and know that it cannot be a good sign. I hear the physician trying to convince Sergey that I should be taken to the ER for a CT scan or an MRI right away to rule out cervical fracture and intracranial hemorrhaging. Sergey first objects and tells the physician to try and fix me up the best he can right here, but then makes a call and says that it's all settled. I'll be taken to a hospital where a doctor on duty will not be asking questions.

As I am being led out of the backroom, I start feeling pretty sick and my thoughts get rather confused. I struggle to stay conscious and I think Head Tattoo asks me questions and I try to answer but am not sure if the words come out right. His voice reaches me as if from the far end of a long tunnel and then fades out altogether. Instead, as if out of nowhere, Sergey's prefight remark "martial artists can be a very good investment" pops up in my concussed brain. I catch on to that phrase and play it in my head again and again. Oh, I get it—he agrees to send me to a hospital only because he wants to protect his "investment." The bastard. Didn't he once tell me that badly injured fighters who no longer serve him a purpose are just dumped somewhere to fend for themselves the best they can? I suppose I should feel lucky to receive preferential treatment. Yeah, "lucky." Damn it.

I pass out in the car on the way to the hospital and then come to and throw up again. My stomach is empty and only bitter liquid comes out. During the MRI, I fall asleep inside the narrow tube despite the horribly loud noise. Later on they give me some meds and I am sleepy and groggy the whole time I am in the hospital.

After the night in the ER and a bunch of tests and examinations that rule out cervical fracture and intracranial bleeding, they release me and the driver wants to take me to Roosevelt Island, but I tell him to drive to

82nd Street instead. I don't want Drago to see me in my present condition. Head Tattoo rides with me and then practically carries me up to the fifth floor and helps me inside. Danilo is not in. Head Tattoo tells me something, but I cannot understand what he is saying and cannot focus my thoughts on anything at all. I lie down on the bed, close my eyes, and immediately fall into a strange sleep which borders on unconsciousness.

When I wake up, Danilo is sitting by my side. I have a terrible headache, a bitter taste in my mouth, and I feel awfully nauseous. When I try to move, a big iron ball starts rolling around inside my head. The doctor did mention something about it being a very bad concussion. Well, I guess he knew what he was talking about. My neck is stiff and sore, but they said it was not fractured and that I should thank my luck for that.

Danilo is holding a drink in his hand and the sight of alcohol intensifies my nausea and I throw up. Danilo cleans up the mess, gives me some lemon-ginger tea to drink, and sits on the bed again. He strokes my arm with his knuckles in his very own gesture of affection

"Sash," he pronounces in a very feeble, plaintive voice. "You can't go on like this. Please."

"I must finish the five fights," I say, every word ringing hard and loud somewhere in the depth of my brain.

"Let's chuck everything and move to Amsterdam together."

"Again with your Amsterdam."

"You can't continue fighting."

"I only have three fights left."

"They'll kill you."

"No. I just need to prepare better. I know what kind of training I need."

After a short while I fall asleep again. I don't know how long I sleep for, but when I wake up, Drago is in the room. He and Danilo are talking.

"You told him?" I ask my brother.

"Yeah, he knows."

I ask Danilo to leave us alone for a bit. He says he'll go make himself another drink.

Drago sits on the side of the bed. He frowns and shakes his head.

"Listen, girl," he says, "you gotta stop doing that. You'll get killed."

"No. I won't get killed. Not if you train me."

He looks at me and doesn't say anything.

"Drago," I say. "You won't tell me what kind of work you did back in Europe or what type of training you had apart from judo. But I know you know how to fight. To fight for real. Train me."

CHAPTER 15

I wake up with a start and don't immediately know where I am. It takes me a few moments to figure out that I am in bed with Drago in the apartment on Roosevelt Island. I've been back here from 82nd Street for over two weeks now. Drago is lying on his back and breathing with difficulty. It is a bad position for him, and I gently roll him over on his side and he breathes easier. My T-shirt is damp. I must have been sweating in my sleep. Did I have a nightmare? I think I did but can't remember what it was. I've been having nightmares almost every night since the last Dark Fight. Sergey's doctor says it is most likely an aftereffect of the concussion.

Drago cries out something and turns over brusquely almost hitting me with his arm. I block it just before it strikes me in the face. Drago does not wake up and rolls on his other side again. He does this a lot, the shouting out, the moving in his sleep. He usually quiets down in the first hours of the morning.

I get up and put on a fresh T-shirt and walk to the kitchen for some water. I am still limping because of the injury to my knee. I was really lucky the meniscus was not torn. If it had been, I would have needed a surgery and the rehabilitation time would have been several months, at least. I go to physical therapy three times a week and it's helping with the pain somewhat, but I will pretty much have to live with it and ignore it for a while.

I walk up and down the hallway and around the kitchen trying to step normally, bending and straightening both knees in the same way, without coddling the injured one.

It feels very hot in the kitchen and in the living room, so I open a window and then sit down on the couch in the dark. I almost jump up when the couch starts moving.

"Damn it, Danny. You scared me."

He has been doing this often now, coming over and spending the night on the couch in the living room. Drago gave him a spare key so that he wouldn't be waking us up at odd hours. On the good days he arrives just in time for dinner and we three have a nice meal all together. Drago and I have to hide all the liquor bottles, however. We normally have some wine or brandy standing around, but when my brother is here, we gather all the bottles and lock them up in a cabinet. Sometimes Danny comes in late at night, already drunk and brings a bottle with him and continues drinking while we are sleeping. Now I see there is a glass and a bottle standing right on the coffee table, and from what I can discern in the dark, the bottle is half empty. I reach over to pick it up and take it away, but Danilo holds my arm.

"Come on, Sash. I feel like shit. I need a drink."

"It's the middle of the night. And you've already had enough. Go to sleep."

"I haven't had enough. I am telling you I feel like shit. Worse than that. What is worse than feeling like shit? I'll tell you. It's when a guy knows that his sister is risking her life in a fucking cage for him, and there is nothing he can do about it."

"It'll be all right, Danny. Don't worry about it. I'll train better and I'll be fine. The fights will be over soon. We'll be OK."

"Yep. Most definitely. But let me have another drink now."

I know I must not let him, but I don't know how to go about it. It's awful having to fight with him every single time. He pours himself half a glassful and starts drinking and I take the glass from his hand. We struggle for a while.

"Shh, be quiet, Sash," he tells me. "We don't want to wake the Grumpy up."

Initially Danilo just took my relationship with Drago as a matter of fact, but then I think he rather warmed up to him. I think he is a bit fascinated by him and even looks up to him in a way. They do argue a lot, though, always about Danny's drinking.

He now picks up the brandy bottle quickly and drinks right from it. Then he rummages among the plates and such on the coffee table and finds a piece of pizza and offers it to me. I refuse, and he bites into the pizza and takes another drink from the bottle.

Drago comes into the living room, turning the light on, his face sleepy and angry.

"Oh, good. See what you did. Now he's up," Danilo mutters under his breath and tries to hide the bottle behind his back. Drago snatches the bottle from him and starts yelling at him. Danilo yells back. For a few minutes the room is filled with yelling and cursing. The one-eyed cat jumps up onto a high shelf and watches from over there.

In the end, Drago out-yells and out-curses Danilo. It has happened a number of times before and always ends in the same way. My brother promises he will not touch alcohol again.

"Why the fuck is it so hot in here?" Drago wipes the perspiration off his forehead and then looks in the direction of the kitchen. "Wait a minute . . ." he walks toward the stove. I get up and follow him. I have already guessed what happened.

"Ah, dammit," Drago exclaims and shuts off the oven. "Your drunkard brother was heating up the frozen pizza and forgot to turn off the oven again. One day he's gonna burn down the house." He turns to go back to the living room, his face angry and determined. Danny moves to the far side of the couch and barricades himself behind some cushions. I grab Drago's hand, but he frees himself from my grip and walks quickly to the couch and stands towering over Danny for a few moments.

"Ah," Drago just waves his arm in the air and does not do anything else. "Come on, girl, let's go back to bed."

"You go. I'll sit with him for a bit."

Danilo lies down on the chaise section of the sofa and complains that he won't be able to fall asleep now. He moves around for a bit, arranging cushions this way and the other. Within a few minutes his breathing changes and I know he is sleeping. From the bedroom, Drago's loud snoring issues. The one-eyed cat jumps down from the shelf and makes itself comfortable next to my thigh. I sit for a long while and stare into the darkness of the room that merges with the darkness of the outside through the floor-to-ceiling windows.

*****

When I am sufficiently recovered from my injuries from the last Dark Fight, Drago and I go to the small gym on the ground floor of the building. We go late at night so that there are no people there. At this time we have the whole place to ourselves. Drago has ordered judo mats online and fixed it up with the super to store them in the gym. He now places them on the floor and we start our practice.

At the dojo I got too used to training in a traditional Japanese martial arts *gi* and to grabbing my opponent's *gi* sleeves and collar for throws and choke holds, which has been to my disadvantage during the Dark Fights where no *gis* are worn and all you can grab is sweaty slippery flesh. I must work on completely breaking my old habits. Now I only have tight shorts and a sports bra on, and Drago is dressed in sports pants and a T-shirt.

He has refused to wear any type of back support, and I am somewhat worried about how his lower back will hold up. It was badly injured in the past and every once in a while gives him trouble. It has been all right for some time now and he has been getting treatment for it, but I don't want one brusque motion to mess it up again. As we do some warm-up exercises I tell him to be careful, especially when we get to the throws. He smirks and asks who I take him for. He's dealt with much heavier stuff in his life than a bit of a "fucked up lower back" and trained and fought on tons of injuries.

"Enough talk—let's get down to business," he says then, his face acquiring a serious and focused expression and his words sounding very much like an order.

He demonstrates an exceptionally effective takedown. As soon as we are on the ground and his body is on top of mine, I breathe heavier, feeling that I want him. I know it's not right. At the moment he is my instructor, and these training sessions are crucial for me, and I should be fully focused on learning the technique, but I just can't help it. I want him.

We get back up on our feet and now it's my turn to try and throw him. Instead of grabbing his arm as he has just showed me, I move my hand slowly along it, feeling his muscles with my fingers. I then raise my eyes and look into his. He puts his hand under my chin, my neck between his index finger and his thumb. When he touches me like that I feel that I must have him right that moment or the whole world would just end. He kisses me hard. I sweep his leg and he falls backward onto the mat. I fall on top of him, a quick thought that this cannot be good for his back crossing my mind. I want to say something, but he closes my mouth with his and holds me tight with one hand while untying his pants with the other.

Afterward we are both pretty tired and decide to continue the training another day. We return to the apartment, take a shower, and go to sleep.

*****

Around two o'clock at night the phone rings.

"Sash, the fucking F train is not working. I can't get to the island." I can hear my brother is pretty drunk.

"Take a cab, Danny."

"Can't. Don't know where my wallet it. Only have my metro card. But the fucking F train has signal problems and is not working."

"What's going on?" Drago asks.

"Danny lost his wallet."

"Tell him to take the damn cab and I'll meet him downstairs and pay," Drago grumbles, rolls over on the other side and I can hear him swearing.

"Danny, listen to me . . ." I start saying.

"Never mind," he interrupts me. "I'm taking the air tram. My metro card works for the air tram."

"Danny, take a cab."

"No! I want a ride in the air tram." And he hangs up.

I get out of bed and start dressing as quick as I can.

"Where are you going?" Drago asks.

"Go back to sleep. I'll be back in a few minutes."

I go outside and hurry toward the tramway's terminal which is about ten minutes of brisk walk along the Main Street. I get to the terminal just when the tram is arriving. Two police officers are escorting Danilo out. They say he's been making trouble during the ride, scaring other passengers. They tell me they'll let him go if I promise to take him straight home. I give the police officers my solemn word.

It takes us almost an hour to get back to the building, because every few feet Danilo wants to stop and look at the sky and try to find some constellation or another. We don't see any stars at all, and he gets frustrated. Finally at the building, he does not want to get inside and crosses to the other side of the street and sits down on the bench by the Church. I sit next to him. Nights are still pretty cold in April and after a while I start shivering. Danny takes a flat bottle of cognac out of his coat pocket and offers it to me. I refuse and he drinks alone.

Drago comes out of the building in a coat and pajama pants. He sees Danilo with a bottle, grabs it from him, and yet again they start yelling and swearing at each other.

The two police officers appear again.

"You promised you would take this one straight home," they say. "And now there's two of them making trouble."

"We live right here," I tell the officers. "We are going in right now."

"Oh, yes," Danilo puts in. "We are not making any trouble. We are just enjoying the quiet and lovely night. Won't you join us?" and he tries to offer the police officers a drink from his bottle.

"Just shut the fuck up." Drago locks Danilo's arm behind his back and makes him get up from the bench, and walks him in that position, the arm locked out behind his back, across the street and into the building. I say goodnight to the officers and follow Drago and my brother inside.

*****

Several days later a phone call from Danilo wakes us up again in the middle of the night. This time Drago picks up. When he hangs up, he starts getting dressed right away.

"He is in some bar in the Bronx. Drunk off his ass. I'll go get him."

"I'm coming with you," I say and put on the first things that I see lying around, jeans and one of Drago's Henley shirts.

We are out of the door in less than two minutes and once outside we walk fast to the garage. We don't talk at all, each immersed in our gloomy thoughts. The weather has been shifting. It is very humid and muggy out. An occasional strong gust of wind flings my long messy hair into my face. Before we get to the garage, we hear a loud thunder and see several flashes of lightning.

"What a fucking lovely night to be outside," Drago mutters.

It starts pouring while we are driving. When we get to the bar from where Danilo called earlier, Drago tells me to stay in the car and he runs out and disappears through the bar door. I hate sitting in the car and just waiting and decide that if he is not back within five minutes I am going in too. He returns very quickly however, completely drenched, swearing. Danilo was not in the bar.

There are several other bars on the block and Drago checks them all, and Danilo is not there either. We drive slowly around the neighborhood. There is nobody out, no people, no cars, just our car creeping through the walls of rain. It is almost impossible to see anything, and I don't know what this driving around can accomplish and I start feeling pretty desperate. Drago does not give up and widens the search area, turning down each side street, one by one, his face tense and focused, his eyes narrowed. After a while it stops raining, and a few rolls of thunder and an occasional lightning appear again, but farther in the distance.

As we turn into yet another side street, I see a body lying on the sidewalk, huddled against the wall of a building, and three huge guys standing over the body and pissing on it. Drago accelerates, drives two wheels onto the sidewalk, hits the brakes, jumps out of the car, and within a split second is throwing down one of the guys and knocking out the second one with a strike to the jaw. The third one pulls out a gun, but Drago grabs the guy's wrist and locks it out. A shot issues, hitting the wall of the building. I think Drago breaks the guy's arm, because I hear a shrill cry of pain as he sinks down on his knees.

While two of the guys struggle to get up on their feet and their knocked-out companion is still lying down, Drago picks Danny up in his arms, throws him on the back seat of car, gets in, and we drive off. I think the whole incident on the sidewalk did not take more than two or three minutes.

I unfasten my seat belt and turn toward the back seat and try to check on Danny.

"Leave him alone," Drago says. "He's fine. Not injured or anything. Just passed out. Fucking drank himself into oblivion."

"What happened with the gun?" I ask.

"Nothing. Don't worry about it."

When we get back to Roosevelt Island and are about to go into our building, Drago suddenly pauses, leans Danilo's semiconscious body against me, runs across the street and disappears in the direction of the East River. He comes back in two minutes and we all go inside.

In the apartment he puts Danny in the shower to wash and revive him, then helps him out of the bathroom and lays him down on the couch in the living room. I put a pillow under his head, cover him with a blanket, and sit by his side for a long time. Drago puts a movie on and stares at the screen, but I know he is not really watching. He has this expression on his face that I know quite well by now and know that I should not even try to talk to him at the moment. After a while he shuts the movie off, throws the remote control on the table with a loud bang, and turns to me.

"Your brother is an alcoholic. We should check him into some sort of a program."

"He won't go."

"We won't ask him. I'll take him to a rehab in Nassau County on Long Island. They also offer treatments for gambling addictions. I'll drive him tomorrow morning."

"I'll come too."

"No, better that you don't."

"But Drago . . ."

"You are not coming with us." And by the tough and resolute tone of his voice, which I have already heard on numerous occasions, I know that it would be useless to argue with him.

CHAPTER 16

Like a guillotine over my head. This is what my life feels like now. Every day I dread being summoned to do my next Dark Fight. I am intensely aware that on any of these occasions I might get severely crippled or killed. This awareness makes my senses heightened, my nerves overstrung, and every moment of my existence overly bright and full. I wonder if it also has an effect on my feelings for Drago. With each day, with each night they intensify. I think about him constantly. Every time we have sex I give all of me, as if it were the last time, and in the morning I wake up filled with aching tenderness and desire to hold him in my arms and never let him go.

I do not think about the future though. My life after the Dark Fights just seems too remote, behind the line of the visible horizon. I guess I'm superstitious and don't want to tempt fate, so I chase away dreams of what it would be like to get out of the last Dark Fight alive and well. I live day by day, hour by hour, being with Drago, falling more and more in love with him, and training, training, training. All I know is that for me to have any shot at a possible future I must become a better—a much better fighter.

"Listen, girl, you are so fond of that historical, legendary martial arts stuff," Drago tells me one evening when we are sitting on the mat in the little gym in our building, taking a break from practicing a combination of a takedown followed by *juji-gatame*, a perpendicular arm bar. "Those beautiful fairytales of honor and valor. Listen, they did not originate from real battles. No, they were invented during peacetimes in Japan, when armed fights were outlawed and your beloved samurai had nothing to do but sit around, organize friendly matches from time to time, and invent stories of high standards and moral codes. This is all pretty and nice but does not work on the battlefield. You understand?"

"Are you saying a fighting cage is a battlefield?"

"Yes, once you step into it, the rules and values you learned at the Dojo do not exist. You understand?"

"How do you honestly feel about the Dark Fights?"

"It's a dirty, fucked-up business, and you should not be doing them. You'll do the three remaining fights, we'll get you so well-trained that you win them spectacularly and not get injured in the process, and then you are done with the whole thing and will not step in the cage again. You understand me?"

"Yes."

"Good. And since you love all that old Japanese martial arts stuff so much, here's one advice a legendary Japanese martial artist gave to his students after a long grueling day of practicing techniques. He said, 'When you are in a real fight—every technique your body executes must be reinforced with your mind's unwavering strength to inflict pain and damage.' Now, you see, *he* was a smart guy, and understood the reality of the world. All right, girl, get your butt up. Let's get back to training."

As soon as I am up on my feet Drago attacks me and throws me down and gets me in a choke hold so fast that I have absolutely no chance at resisting or countering. Hell, what am I saying, "resisting or countering!" He moved so fast, I couldn't even see his arms reaching for me, let alone even think how to resist or counter. If the words "faster than the speed of light" can be applied to the execution of a throw, then that's how fast he threw me.

I tap out and he lets go and gets up. I remain lying on the floor and probably have a rather astounded expression on my face. Drago smirks, gives me his hand, and pulls me up. "Don't worry," he says. "You'll get there."

After that first failed training session, when we ended up on the ground doing other sorts of 'techniques,' the following sessions have been going a lot more according to a plan. We both take this very seriously and do not let ourselves get distracted again. I am in absolute awe at Drago's teaching abilities and absorb his every word of instruction, every move he shows me.

He makes me work hard on breaking certain fighting habits that are not practical in the cage. Relearning can be very difficult and even frustrating at times, and it takes great patience and determination on both Drago's and my side. He starts by retraining me how to do a number of basic throws on an opponent who does not wear a gi. Without being able to grab gi sleeves and the collar, some of my throws in the cage will not work. Drago shows me how I can still use them effectively. For example, *ouchi-gari*—major inner reap—can be done very well in a standard clinch situation using underhook and overhook instead of grabbing the gi. One of the highest scoring techniques in judo, *seoi-nage*—shoulder throw—can also be executed with great force in the cage by grabbing the opponent's arm instead of the gi. It turns out that pretty much most of the throws with the exception of a few can be done without the gi, and once again I am amazed at Drago's great expertise in all matters concerning real fights, where no rules, uniforms, or score cards exist.

He identifies my weak and strong points and we work for hours and hours until the weak points become strong, and the strong ones turn into a formidable force able to end a fight. When we just start out, I feel frustrated because my favorite *juji-gatame*—perpendicular arm bar—seems to be ineffective on Drago, or rather I fail most of the times to overcome his defense and get his arm into the right position where his elbow would be vulnerable. As the training progresses, I am able get him into a successful *juji-gatame* with more and more frequency, and later on I hit an almost nine out of ten rate.

We practice various throws and take downs, *ne waza* (groundwork), and strikes to vital points such as the eyes, throat, back of the neck, and a number of highly effective choke holds and joint locks. We work on moves which are illegal in regulated fights, such as downward elbow strikes. Drago also teaches me some extreme techniques, for example the brutal grab with the fingers under the ribs reaching for internal organs, which are perfect for a no-rules bout. We work a lot on my defense, so that an opponent cannot execute a *te guruma* or the like on me, or kick me in the head, or put me to sleep with a choke hold.

"What about defense against sneak attacks, like the one with the Bengay?" I ask at one point.

Drago frowns and shakes his head. Even he, with his skeptical view of martial artists' code of honor and his very realistic ideas of what goes on in the fight cages . . . even he thinks that such tricks are a complete disgrace. "Fucking cheaters," he mutters under his breath and proceeds to train me how to take control of my body and mind, to continue fighting, and to not panic in extreme circumstances.

I have no doubt that Drago has a natural talent for teaching, and he seems to think I make a rather good student. We train at the little gym for several hours almost every day, and I also continue sparring with my tattooed friend and other partners at 2 Gild Street and practice on them the skills I learn from Drago. All in all, I get in as much, if not more, training as I used to when living at the dojo, only now the training is geared specifically to the no-rules Dark Fights. I try not to dwell on the past or the future at all. It is a strange life, existing intensely in the present moment only, and at times I feel there is something unnatural about it, but I try not to think about that either.

*****

Drago bought an espresso machine, and on the day of my next Dark Fight I make a mistake of drinking strong black coffee throughout the morning and afternoon thinking it would keep me alert in the evening and at night. It's almost midnight now and I am crashing. The driver turns toward me and says I look awful.

"Here, take this." He hands me a small plastic bag with two pills in it.

I deliberate for a moment, but then give it back. Instead, I find pressure points on the inside of my elbows and massage them as hard as I can. After a few minutes I feel somewhat more energized.

The car drives up to an impressive building on Fifth Avenue. Baldy meets me at the curb. Before we go in I pause for a moment. Wait a minute, I know this building. This is one of the oldest private clubs in NYC, The New Amsterdam Club. It's extremely exclusive, and you can only become a member if you are recommended by a member. Women were not allowed in until about twenty years ago. Membership costs some twenty grand a year and you have to spend another five grand a year in the club's restaurants and bars. They have amazing training facilities for various sports, an Olympic-size swimming pool, a decent-sized judo dojo, and besides that a formal dining room, a grill room, bars, lounges, a conference room, and a number of guest rooms for members and their guests.

I've been inside once, when years ago I was presented with a ticket to a judo tournament. And just like now, I had to go in through the side door. The club has a very strict dress code and only those in a formal wear may use the front entrance.

Baldy and I take the athletic elevator, the one for people not in formal attire, and go up to the ninth floor. Buzz Cut meets us in the elevator vestibule, and then hands me over to Head Tattoo, who leads me to the door of a locker room. Inside, Ricardo the Stylist is already waiting, absolutely excited about how big and beautiful the room is. It is indeed the most impressive locker room I have ever been in. A faint smell of raspberries hangs in the air. There are big soft armchairs, floor to ceiling mirrors, stacks of soft white towels, bottles of lotions, and numerous hair products on the sink counter.

Ricardo is ecstatic, "Oh, I wish all the Fights could be held at this location. It is so luxurious."

Sitting in a comfortable armchair while he is working on me, I almost fall asleep. Ricardo tells me he can go get something that will help me stay awake and be super alert and, in his words, "a few other things." I know now what he is referring to and say no again and massage the pressure points on the inside of my elbows once more.

Head Tattoo leads me to a large beautiful chamber with a direct view of Central Park. The setting could not be more glamorous, with what I guess is real antique furniture, marble sculptures, genuine paintings . . . all of that combined with the most stunning and authentic decoration of all—the park just outside. The crowd is more elegantly dressed than during the other Dark Fights events. All men are wearing dinner suits and bow ties, and the few women that are in attendance are dressed in elegant gowns and exquisite jewelry. The expressions on their faces are the same though. It is that mix of excitement, exhilaration, and almost hunger for the bloody spectacle to start.

I am the first one inside the cage this time. The announcer calls "Martial Marty" and the audience reacts rights away, a number of voices chanting, "M-M! M-M!" with great enthusiasm. Hmm, this mysterious MM must be quite a crowd pleaser. By now I am familiar with the tastes of these people and can't help but wonder what kind of brutal stunts MM has pulled in the cage in order to gain their approval.

When my opponent appears and takes off her hoodie, for a few moments I am not sure if my eyes are not deceiving me.

Could it be? Is it really? Yes, there is no doubt about it. The girl I am fighting tonight, this MM, is in fact Martine, my best friend from the dojo.

She has always been strong and very muscular, but now her muscles, especially her biceps and triceps, look almost abnormally huge. Besides working out like crazy, she must have been taking steroids. After stepping into the cage, she starts doing side jumps, not stopping for a second. She seems wired and hyper. I wonder if this might be the effect of those pills that the driver offered to me and that I refused. I bet Martine didn't refuse them.

For a moment, a deep sadness permeates my whole being. How is it that we have come to this, my friend and I? I must push this feeling away though and only focus on the bout ahead. I take several deep breaths in and out.

"Fighter, ready?" the referee asks me. I nod.

"Fighter, ready? He turns to Martial Marty.

"Ready!" she shouts.

"Fight!"

Martine keeps jumping around the cage in almost a frenzy. I watch her motions with attention. She attacks with a high kick going for a KO. No doubt she knows that was how I lost my previous fight and thinks that defense against high kicks is my weak point. Her kick does not connect, and for a moment she loses balance but then does a backward flip and lands on her feet. After an exchange of strikes we move into a clinch, both attempting a takedown.

"What are you doing here, Martine?" I ask while we are fighting in a tight embrace, our bodies wrapped around each other, every gap closed, our sweat mixing.

"Did you think you were the only one good enough to be invited into the Dark Fights?" she shouts into my ear.

It feels more than strange for me to be fighting Martine. I am so used to sparring with her at the dojo, to her being my training partner, not my opponent.

"This is weird," I say to her. "We're friends."

"Friends? How can you be so fucking stupid? We are not friends. I've always hated you." She spits out these words and I catch a glimpse of her contorted face, and immediately afterward our faces are pushed together by the force of the fight and our lips land on each other in the creepiest kiss ever possible.

"What?" I manage to pronounce when there is an inch of space between our mouths again.

"You came prancing into the dojo, all pretty and innocent, and Sensei loved you and chose you to be an uchi-deshi. You! That position should have been mine. You took it from me!" At this she sweeps my leg and throws me down on the canvas and goes for a *kimura* arm lock from side control, lying across me, her hips pressed against my chest. I do not allow her to get a full control of my arm and to crank my elbow, so she abandons the *kimura*, and tries to assume a position for a choke hold. At one point her eyes are only a few inches from me and they are full of such deep hatred. Suddenly it dawns on me.

"Was it you who threw me down the stairs?" I pronounce with difficulty, fighting off her attempts to get me in a choke.

"Who else?"

"And the tanto switch during my examination?"

"Yesss," she hisses into my ear. "I switched it. I also slipped you something in the water before your test. It slowed you down." I don't know why she is confessing this stuff now. I guess she's out of control, all fueled up on the natural adrenaline or the drugs.

"And you told Sensei about my Dark Fights!"

"Oh, yes. Sergey ordered me to. He wanted you to be kicked out of the dojo."

We get back on our feet and she continues her attempts at kicking me in the head, going for a KO. I know that, at all costs, I must avoid another terrible concussion. I remember Drago's words that the fighting cage is a battleground and the other person is not my training partner but my enemy. Martine is my enemy now.

A punch to her solar plexus. An elbow to her sternum, a strike to a pressure point on her neck, and a full-force strike to the eye. "Every technique your body executes must be reinforced with your mind's unwavering strength to inflict pain and damage."

She seems quite disoriented now, and I throw her down and go for the *juji-gatame* arm bar, her trapped elbow tight against my hips, extending her arm, arching my hips to overextend her elbow. She does not tap out. Does she not feel the pain? I know her elbow is being severely injured right now. It's possible that those pills, aside from giving her extra boost of energy, also numb the pain. Still, she must be aware that her elbow is about to break. I relax my grip a bit, and she tries to get out. We struggle, and she hisses, "I will kill you."

I regain my position and get her into the *juji-gatame* again and arch my hips once more overextending her elbow. You can visually see her arm bending backward. The audience is roaring with excitement at this point. Still she does not tap out, but a terrifying cry of pain and rage issues from her wide-open mouth. Then she taps out.

*****

After the fight I am sitting alone in the plush armchair in the locker room. The physician has just left after treating my cuts and bruises. I don't know where Martine is. The last glimpse I caught of her was when she was being loaded into a different elevator. I feel sad and gloomy. Ricardo the Stylist runs in all excited and I am glad of his company. He brings a garment bag with him and smiles and looks all mysterious.

"The boss sends this," he says. "I won't show you yet, but it is beautiful."

I reach over and want to unzip the bag. Ricardo slaps me on the hand.

"Get your dirty paws off this delicate beauty," he says. "Take a shower first. Are you familiar with the concept of taking a shower, you . . . you . . ." He pauses looking for a word. "You *fighter*."

After I come out of the shower, he covers the swelling and bruising with makeup and arranges my hair in long flowing waves. Finally, he opens the garment bag and takes out a dress that is indeed beautiful, elegant, and almost ethereal. It is made of some very thin fabric, light peach in color, with a very slight sheen. He holds it in his hands delicately and when he puts it on me it feels so light, as if I were not wearing anything. The dress is long, covering the heels of my shoes almost to the floor, but it has a high slit on one side and so does not restrict my steps.

When Head Tattoo sees me in it, he stares for a few moments, his head inclined sideways, his mouth opened slightly. And then he does something that quite impresses me. He offers me his arm. I smile and put my arm through his, and he guides me to the elevator, a very proud look on his face. This time we ride in the elevator for the formally dressed people. We get out on the second floor and go into the grill room.

The grill room is large and dark, its walls paneled with wood that looks very old. Sergey meets me at the bar.

"Oh, my beauty," he exclaims right away. "You look stunning. Please, sit, sit, have a drink with me. Oh, I am so pleased. It was an amazing fight, your best fight. Absolutely captivating."

"You call this an amazing fight? Her elbow is severely damaged now, practically destroyed," I say as I decline the drink and take a sip of ice water.

"Her elbow should be the last thing on your mind right now. Try to relax and have a good time. Hmm, still thinking about her?" He asks after observing me silently for a while. "That girl is a decent fighter, but she's started to give me trouble. She's too argumentative. Anyway, she's served her purpose. I have no further use for her. She needs to disappear."

"What?" I stare at him.

He laughs. "Nothing like that. You have a wild imagination. She needs to go away is all. A call to a friend at the USCIS has already been made. Martine has extended her legal stay in this country and will be sent back to France. Come on, beauty, cheer up, I will introduce you to some of my friends."

Sergey leads me to a large table around which about ten men are seated. As I approach they all rise and a waiter moves my chair for me. Sergey introduces his friends by their first names only. They are all about Sergey's age and are perfectly nice and polite, and their conversation is quite interesting. They do not make any reference to the Fights at all, and after a while I relax and, as I feel awfully hungry, order a crab cake appetizer, a filet mignon, and a mojito. With the food and the drink in me, I like the ambience of the place and the company more, and everything seems rather comforting and pleasant. Even Sergey's heavy Russian accent does not grate on my nerves as it usually does. He asks me if I want something else to eat, a dessert perhaps, another drink.

I don't know how much time passes, but at some point I get up to go to the bathroom. All the men at the table rise again. After I come back I do not go up to the table, but stand at a distance for a while observing the whole room. As I look around, it suddenly dawns on me that I do not belong here, I should not be here at all. Head Tattoo comes up to me.

"Get me out of here," I say to him.

He hesitates, looks at his boss, then nods, and walks me to the door.

*****

Back at home, I go into the bedroom. Drago isn't sleeping. He's watching a series on Netflix.

"Wow," he says when he sees me in my elegant outfit. "You look good, girl. Really good."

I take off my dress and walk around the room in only my high heeled shoes, feeling his eyes on me.

"Come to bed, girl."

I sit at the edge of the bed, my back to him, and he puts his arms around my breasts.

"How did the fight go?"

"Fine. I won. Only two more left to go. Turn the TV off, please."

"Why? Are you going to tell me about the fight?"

"No. That's not what I want to do right now."

I lie on top of him, prop my arms on his chest and look him in the eyes for a while. I kiss him on the side of his neck, inhaling deeply his scent of cigarette smoke and Sauvage Dior, and then I kiss him on the mouth as hard as I can. He rolls me over, traps me under him, and stays on top.

Afterward, lying next to him and holding his hand, I put my head on his chest. This is where I am supposed to be. This is home.

Later in the night I wake up and walk naked to the window and stand there looking at the dark river and the lights of Manhattan across it. Drago gets up and comes up to me and puts his arms around me. It feels wonderful, standing like this, in his arms, in the middle of the night, as if we had tricked time and carved out a unique slot just for us. I don't know how long we stand like this, but I guess at some point I get cold. A shiver runs across my body. He picks me up and carries me back to bed.

CHAPTER 17

On a very warm evening in late June, my brother and I are sitting on a bench on Roosevelt Island. It is one of those rare New York nights when the weather is hot but not humid, and we are enjoying the breeze from the river and don't feel like going inside. We are eating ice cream—Danilo chocolate, I green tea. I haven't had sweets in a long time, because they are bad for your muscles and make you sluggish, but now that the Dark Fights are done with, I can relax and eat as much ice cream as I want. I can only finish half of mine though, finding the taste too sweet, and I give the rest of it to Danny.

Danilo is back from the rehab on Long Island and is doing an outpatient program in Manhattan, and it seems to be going really well. He hasn't had a single drink in quite a while. We've just come from a modeling shoot in a studio in Hell's Kitchen, which he invited me to watch. He was worried about the look of his new teeth and his nose not being as perfect as before the two breaks, but it did not detract at all from his beauty and was barely if at all noticeable in the photographs. Sergey got him this modeling gig, but Danilo is quite optimistic he'll now be able to get more on his own.

"Isn't it great, Sash?" Danilo asks making a big gesture with his ice cream as if wanting to include the whole world in his definition of greatness.

"What is?"

"Well, everything! Things are starting to pick up for us, don't you think? You've finished all the Dark Fights and never have to step into the cage again!"

"Yep."

"Come on, show some more enthusiasm." He nudges me lightly with his elbow. "You must admit you are absolutely relieved and happy that the fights are over. I know I am."

"Well, yeah, sure, it's just that . . ."

"What?"

"I'll tell you, but you gotta promise you are not gonna tell Drago."

"Sure. I promise. I won't tell the Grumpy."

"Well, the thing is that the last fights went so well that I think I might have started to enjoy them."

"What! Are you crazy?!"

"Wait, let me explain."

"There is nothing to explain. It's just crazy."

"Look, I don't know how to put it exactly. It's this . . . the adrenaline rush, the excitement of the moment, the way your body and your mind function at the very height of their abilities. It is . . . I don't know what it is, Danny. It is fucking addictive, I gotta tell you."

"Really? And all the injuries, and the fear of not getting out of there alive, and the pain?"

"Drago trained me really well, you know. He taught me how to fight for real. Something changed. I don't feel like a passive scared creature in that cage anymore. I feel strong and ready to take on any opponent."

I'm not sure Danny is the right person to understand this. He's been in the cage but he never passed that point where the fear becomes one with the exhilaration and then dissolves in it, disappears altogether. When you conquer the fear and cross over that line, what a rush. The high you experience during the no-rules fight is so high, precisely because you've learned to transform your fear into something else and channel it into a driving force, and it drives you up and up, and when you come off of it, you feel sort of lost for a bit and don't know what to do with yourself and you crave more of that high.

"Well, I don't want to hear any more," Danilo says and even bangs his fist on the bench to really get my attention. "You've done the five fights. It's over now, OK? No matter how good of a fighter you think you are, every time you step into that damn cage you risk not getting out of there alive. You are done with all that, all right, Sash?"

"Yeah, OK. Chill. It's over."

"Just look at your face," he says and shakes his head. "Your lip is still swollen from the last fight. "Be grateful you didn't get a few teeth knocked out as well."

I touch my swollen lower lip with the tip of my tongue and smile. This is not from the last Dark Fight, it is from Drago. In the past he had always refrained from biting me, but after last night I have his teeth marks on my back, my butt, and yeah, he also bit my lip pretty hard. It was quite a night we had. We wanted each other again and again, until at one point we were both exhausted, and had to stop, him still inside me, still very hard. We took a break and ate some bitter dark chocolate and drank water, and then he wanted to be inside me again and I wanted him to fuck me for as long as there was an ounce of energy left in him. Every time I would come, it would turn him on even more, and he wanted to keep going. And those were not the superficial brief clitoral orgasms that I don't like at all. They were the deep, slow-building, and long-lasting internal ones, the real ones that are felt deep within and shut out the whole world and leave me shaking and then absolutely limp. He would wait until I recovered a bit, opened my eyes, and became responsive again, and would then keep going. I did not want him to stop either, I wanted him to empty himself completely into me. I wanted all of him. I don't know what came over us last night, and now I am pretty sore inside and my mouth hurts, and yet I cannot stop smiling. If it's even possible, now I feel more in love with that man than ever before.

"What are you smiling about?" Danny asks.

"Nothing. Are you finished with the ice cream? Want to go inside now?"

"Yeah, let's go. We don't want the Grumpy to get angry that we're late for dinner."

*****

Drago is not home. The one-eyed cat jumps down from the shelf and rubs against my feet, first meowing softly, then with more insistence, demanding food. A usual can of some nutritious seafood-y substance takes care of the cat's hunger. My brother, however, is not so easy to please. He has been looking forward to the rib eye steak dinner that Drago has promised us, and now doesn't want to settle for anything else. I offer to make him a sandwich or some pasta, or order Japanese, but he just says no to everything. He opens the freezer and his eyes sparkle as he spots a pizza. He then remembers what happened the last time he heated up a pizza in the oven, changes his mind, and shuts the freezer with a loud bang.

He walks around the kitchen humming a tune by You Bred Raptors?, a local band that we heard perform earlier today in a subway station. The melody has a strange combination of lively energy and deep suspense that kind of creeps under your skin. I really liked the song, but for some reason Danilo's humming it now bothers me. In his interpretation it just sounds too gloomy, almost chilling and ominous, and makes me shiver. I ask him to stop. He breaks off for a minute, but then continues, probably without even realizing.

He walks back and forth restlessly, looking at the old photographs on the walls, then starts going through the stack of mail on the counter. I tell him not to touch Drago's stuff. He picks up one envelope, and abruptly his humming stops.

"What the fuck!" Danilo exclaims staring at the envelope, a startled expression on his face.

"What is it?"

"The company that sent this to your boyfriend. I know the name. I got checks from them in the past for some of my modeling gigs."

"What are you talking about? Drago doesn't do modeling."

"No shit. Use your brain, Sash! Don't you understand? This company is a front for Sergey's businesses." With this Danilo rips open the envelope.

"Hey!" I protest but shut my mouth as soon as I see what's inside. It is a check for seventy-five thousand dollars. Danilo and I stare at it for a few long moments.

"Sash," he pronounces gently.

"No!" I interrupt him. "Don't say it. It can't be true. It just can't. There must be some other explanation."

"I don't think so." He shakes his head. "Your boyfriend works for Sergey."

*****

In the absolute silence I hear the front door open and close and steps come down the stairs that lead into the living room. Drago approaches, greeting us cheerfully and places a bag with what I guess are three rib eye steaks onto the counter. He smiles while announcing that the master chef will now demonstrate his excellent cooking skills and a superb dinner will be ready in no time. He wants to say something else but cuts himself short, taking a closer look at our faces and then at the check in Danilo's hand.

Drago's smile vanishes right away and his eyes narrow. He makes one quick motion going for Danilo's wrist. I strike with the blade of my hand deflecting his move. In less than a split second he counters my strike, reaches Danilo with his other hand, and holds him in a tight grip. Danilo's fingers release the check, letting it fall to the ground.

Attracted by the disturbance, the one-eyed cat comes up, and for a while the four of us just stand there, our gazes fixed on the rectangular piece of paper on the floor. I am not sure how much time passes. We all seem to be hypnotized, unable to move or avert our eyes.

In an involuntary gesture I crack the knuckles on my fingers, and the harsh grating sound startles everyone, the one-eyed cat jumping away and settling in the corner.

"Drago and I need to talk," I say to my brother. My own voice sounds strangely hollow and almost lifeless to me.

Danilo refuses to leave at first, but I give him *the look*, which he understands. I don't want him in the apartment now, and after some deliberation he heads out.

Drago pours himself a glass of water, drinks it in long gulps, and then sits on the windowsill in the kitchen, facing me.

"Just tell me everything," I say nodding at the check, which still remains in the same spot on the floor.

"Sit down." He points to one of the chairs and lights up a cigarette.

I remain standing up. "Tell me."

He shrugs his shoulders. "What do you want to hear?"

The truth of course. I want to know the truth. But do I really? Doesn't some part of me want him to make up a lie, a nice smooth lie that would miraculously erase this sinking feeling that I have inside me now and would patch over the rift that is already starting to form between Drago and me?

"All right, well, yes, the Russian paid me to train you."

I remember when I was a little girl and would play on a swing on a playground and would swing myself so high that I would get a chilling hollow sensation in my stomach. I get that same sensation right now.

So, there it is. The truth is out. There will be no merciful lie. The rift between us is growing bigger by the second, threatening to turn into an abyss.

"You knew all along I was in the Dark Fights?"

"Yes."

"And you didn't give a fuck."

He puts out his cigarette but then immediately lights up a new one. "Listen, girl, it's complicated."

I don't want to cry. I'm doing my best to suppress the tears. On the inside I'm screaming with pain, and, when a tiny moan issues from my mouth, I immediately shut my lips as tight as I can. I try to breathe deeply in and out through my nose to stabilize myself. I need to know more. I now doubt everything, our whole history together. "Was it a plan all along?" I ask in as even a tone of voice as I can muster. "Was I targeted from the beginning? You actually did track me, didn't you?"

Drago exhales loudly, as if exasperated by all this questioning. "You want me to say that our meetings were not a coincidence. OK, they were not. The Russian had this whole master plan for you, he wanted you caught in a 'spider web like a little moth'—his exact fucking words, not mine. But I'll tell you one thing, girl—I did *not* want you doing the Fights. I argued with the Russian for a long time. I found him other fighters. There was no use. He wanted *you*. He saw you were something very special and decided to invest in you. After that there was no changing his mind."

"So you gave in. Why? The money?"

"Yes, fuck it! The money. He offered me a sum I couldn't refuse." A long pause and then another shrug of the shoulders. "Every man has a price, you know. It's just the amount that varies." He gets up from the windowsill brusquely and starts pacing around the kitchen. "Don't you understand, the Russian would have had you go on with the Fights whether I agreed to train you or not. It was better that I did. How can you not see that?" He exclaims. "I trained you so well, better than anyone else could have. You understand? It was lucky for you that it was me and not somebody else. Don't you remember, you almost fucking died in that cage before I started training you." He takes a step toward me, but I back away from him.

"Damn it, girl, you yourself wanted me to train you! What difference does it really make that I got paid for it?"

Can it be possible that he doesn't see the difference? Oh, there are so many things I want to shout at him, but I contain myself. I pick up the check from the floor. "Seventy-five thousand dollars. Is that for the last fight you trained me for?"

He freezes in one spot and is silent for a while, avoiding my eyes. Then he turns his head, his motions slow yet determined, and looks me fully in the face. Something tells me that the words he is about to pronounce will hurt even more. I am not sure I want to hear them.

"No, that's for the next fight," he says.

A shudder runs through my insides, and the sinking feeling intensifies to such a degree that I actually have to place my hands on the back of a chair to steady myself. I breathe in and out deeply several times.

The next fight? There wasn't supposed to be any next fight. My deal with Sergey was for the five only, and I've done them. Yet they have already arranged for my future Dark Fights. They've decided between themselves that there is no way out of the cage for the Samurai Princess.

Yes, Drago trained me well, yes, he made me such a good fighter that I started to enjoy myself in the cage, hooked on the adrenaline and the high of the battle. My brother is right though—no matter how good a fighter you are, the risk of getting crippled or killed is ever-present as long as you are in the cage.

And the man who I thought loved me takes money to get me into that cage again and again.

Last night we went out to celebrate the end of the Dark Fights. We talked about taking a trip to some remote beach, where we could swim for hours as far away from the shore as we like and lifeguards would not whistle to us to come back. We ate and had a couple drinks and laughed, and Drago was in one of his affable moods where he barely criticizes the restaurant food and is almost civil to the waiters. Everything was wonderful in the restaurant, everything was wonderful during the ride home. While driving he noticed me look at him, smiled without turning his head, took my hand, and kissed it several times. Back in the apartment, he picked me up in his arms and carried me to the bedroom, and the night we spent together left me drained of all energy and overflowing with emotions.

And it was all a lie, a lie, a lie. I am nothing but a contract to him.

"Was fucking me a part of the deal too?" I ask and rush out of the apartment without waiting to hear the answer. I feel almost nauseous thinking about all the times we had sex, how I let him fuck me without a condom.

I press the button hoping the elevator will come as quickly as possible. I just want to get out of this building, away from the man in whom I put my absolute trust and whose betrayal is now causing such a painful reaction in me. The elevator doors open and, as I step inside and turn, I see Drago coming toward me fast. I press the "doors close" several times. The doors start shutting, but he presses the outside button, and they open again.

"Don't get in!" I press the button repeatedly. He places his foot in the way of the doors.

"Stop it, don't act like this," he says, looking at me out of his serious, almost severe eyes. I hold his gaze, and all of a sudden the corners of his eyes wrinkle up and such a familiar smile appears on his face. This is more than I can take. I try to push him back so that the doors would shut, but his stance is too strong and grounded.

"Listen," I say, "do you remember how long time ago I asked you if you are entirely good or bad? Do you remember what you answered?"

Well, I am not completely rotten, he'd said back then, and I can tell that he does remember now.

"What you did to me *was* a completely rotten thing to do to somebody. I fucking loved you and you lied to me and betrayed me!"

He cringes when I pronounce the L-word. It makes me think of an oyster squirming when you squeeze lemon juice on it. Suddenly I realize how useless all this is, the shouting, the accusations. If he loved me, he wouldn't have been able to go through with the work that Sergey had hired him to do. But he went through with it all right. And as an extra bonus, he got to fuck me. So no wonder my mentioning the L-word now makes him cringe. I thought it was impossible that if one person loves so much the other should not feel the same way. I was wrong. Not only is it possible, it is probably happening left and right in this fucked-up world.

"Listen, girl," he says. "You are too young and see everything in black and white. There are areas of life that are gray and cannot be easily defined or separated. Listen . . . the money for your next fight . . . I haven't yet agreed to accept it."

"But will you?" I ask quickly.

No answer. I wait for one, I wait for a long time, but it doesn't come.

"You know, Drago, you are just like those samurai you told me about—who were nothing but hired-hands and did everything their lords ordered them to do, as long as they got paid for their services."

A deep frown creases his forehead. "Stop this, girl! Just come back to the apartment."

"Fuck off." I push him again, as hard as I can, and the doors finally shut, and the elevator goes down.

CHAPTER 18

Waking up, my head feels extremely groggy and as if stuffed to the brim with cotton wool. The first thing I am able to comprehend is that I slept for over twenty hours, but I can't figure out where I am or how I got to be here. I look around and see some unfamiliar room. It is a very large L-shaped studio, fully furnished with comfortable and elegant pieces in dark blue and gray colors. There is a knocked-over vase on the table and a whole bunch of white tulips strewn around. I pick up the card. It is damaged by the water, but the words "Welcome, beauty. So glad to have you here" are still legible.

Staring at Sergey's note, my thoughts clear up.

I remember running out of the building on Roosevelt Island and seeing my brother on the bench by the church waiting for me. His silent, compassionate face and his very own gesture of knuckles gently rubbing against my forearm trying to comfort me. He volunteers to go up and get my things so that then we can go together to 82nd street and leave the whole Roosevelt Island life behind. Barely a few minutes after he is gone, Head Tattoo appears before me and invites me into the familiar metallic gray BMW waiting at the curb. I get in and the car drives off right away. I ask about Danny and my things, but Head Tattoo just tells me to relax and not worry about anything. I think the car is taking me to 82nd Street, but when I look out the window, I realize we are on the FDR going south. I look at Head Tattoo and he nods and shows a thumbs up. I do not ask any questions. A strange apathy takes hold of me, and I really don't seem to care where we are going.

The car drives up to the entrance of 2 Gild Street. Head Tattoo escorts me inside. We ride in an elevator to the nineteenth floor where he opens the door to one of the apartments. A huge bouquet of white tulips is the first thing I notice inside. Head Tattoo shows me around, opening the kitchen cupboards filled with plates and cups and stuff, the huge fridge stocked with fruit, juices, various snacks, the bathroom with the towels, the hair dryer, and bottles of shampoo, conditioner, and body lotion. He tells me this is my new home and asks if I like it and if I need anything else to make me more comfortable here. I sit down on the couch, rest my head on the soft cushions, and don't reply anything.

Head Tattoo takes out of his pocket a small plastic bag with several pills and explains he was instructed to give them to me. "These are just sleeping pills," he replies to my silent question. After he leaves, I hold a pill in my fingers for a long while, just looking at it, unable to gather my thoughts. I then swallow it, and a few seconds later a second one, washing them down with gulps from a bottle of Armagnac, another present from Sergey. Within about fifteen minutes my body starts feeling very light, almost weightless. I get up from the couch taking the bottle with me. I cannot walk straight and accidentally knock over the vase and stare zombie-like at Sergey's white tulips scattered across the table and the floor and the water dripping from the vase. I stumble across the room, having to make an effort to reach the bed. I take a few more long drinks of the Armagnac, and, as soon as I lie down, every shred of a thought disappears from my head and I fall fast into a dark, dreamless sleep.

And now here I am, waking up alone in this unfamiliar apartment at 2 Gild Street. I peer out the window at the surrounding high-rises of Lower Manhattan. I shiver, feeling a momentary chill run through me and thinking that it is definitely not a coincidence that I should end up in this place. Nothing in Sergey's web is accidental. Perhaps I'd be better off getting the hell out of here as fast as I can. I feel utterly lost and dispirited, though, and this apartment is so cozy and peaceful. The soothing colors, the comfortable furniture. Nothing here seems menacing or dangerous. Why run away? I am not a prisoner here, after all.

*****

After a while I realize I am so hungry I am almost shaking. There is stuff to eat in the fridge, but I want a real hot meal, so I get dressed and ride downstairs and walk under the archway, turn the corner, and open the door to Wolf Flannigan's. This pub is practically an extension of 2 Gild Street, but it does not occur to me to go anywhere else. The familiar bartender is behind the counter and he greets me as if he's seen me here only yesterday. As I glance toward the back room, I remember the subterranean route I took to my first Dark Fight. I immediately turn away and don't look in that direction anymore.

I sit at the counter and ask the bartender what's good today. He recommends broiled cod. I ask for the sides of salad and baked potato and he puts the order in right away. While I am waiting, he brings me some grilled calamari to snack on and says the appetizer is on him. We discuss what I should drink and after careful deliberation and some going back and forth decide on a mojito, easy on the sugar.

The pub gradually fills with people. Soon all the seats at the counter are taken. Men on both sides of me try to chat me up, but I don't respond, focused on my meal and only talking with the bartender. We discuss briefly why it is that real old-fashioned bars have mirrors on the back wall behind the counter. The explanation that seems most plausible to both of us is that this way the bartender can see what goes on and what trouble the customers are up to even when he is reaching for a bottle from a shelf or doing something else that requires him to face away. When other people join in the conversation, I lose interest and stop participating.

After the meal I take a walk to the South Street Seaport. I move my feet slowly, pausing every once in a while. Damn it. Without Drago everything just seems like a heavy cloud—a sticky, damp, cotton wool cloud, and I will have to be dragging myself through it for the rest of my life. What a bleak perspective.

What is it, this damn love, this inexplicable attraction to another human being, his skin, his voice, his smell, his mind? Why is it so intense and powerful? And it takes such a hold of you that when it's taken from you, you feel like you've been thrown into a bottomless bog? You struggle to stay afloat, but inch by inch your body submerges into the mud, and you are struggling for breath, being buried alive.

I feel such a heavy pain inside me that I wish I could vomit it and be rid of it.

One question tortures me the most—did he really not feel anything for me?

How is it possible? Drago, you were inside me, nothing separating us—nothing. We were as close as two human beings can possibly be, and yet you did not love me at all? No, that just cannot be. You did care for me, didn't you? Perhaps even loved me in your own way—it's just that you love money above all else.

I catch myself having a conversation with him. I must be pronouncing some words out loud, as I notice people giving me strange looks. That man had such a strong impact on me, that now everything inside me is permeated with him. "You fucking knew how much you meant to me, Drago!" I shout out in desperation, scaring a couple of tourists who jump aside and hurry away. "And your betrayal hurt more than the most brutal technique in the cage ever could."

"All these big useless words. 'Love.' 'Betrayal.' You are just torturing yourself with them, girl," his voice pronounces in my head. "Think of the gray areas in life."

Gray areas, yeah right, how fucking convenient.

I go out to the pier and sit at the very edge in one of those plastic chaise lounges they put out when the weather is good. I sit there for a long while thinking of him, of his voice, his different facial expressions, the types of smile that he has. That little smirk that often hovers on his lips and gives him a slightly smug appearance. And that wonderful, sincere smile that lights up his face sometimes when he looks at me. When he *used* to look at me. Damn it. Such heavy sadness fills my entire body. Ah, to run my fingers along his arm, to press my body into his, to smell him, to have his weight on top of me. But no, I will never go back to him. Whatever we had together is now completely corrupted, broken and unfixable. I think I loved him too much and got too badly burned.

I crack my knuckles and bite my lips until they start bleeding.

Back at the apartment at 2 Gild Street, I try to watch movies, but can't focus on the story line at all, and end up staring out the window for hours on end, and then I take a sleeping pill and go to bed. Next several days I repeat the same routine that starts with a lonely meal at the bar and ends with a sleeping pill. I can't say that the food at Wolf Flannigan's is especially good, but the cozy ambience and the bartender's friendly disposition makes up for the culinary shortcomings. A couple times Danny eats with me. I am worried how the presence of all the liquor might affect him and suggest we go somewhere else, but he insists we stay and only drinks ginger ale.

From my brother's hints over the years I have gotten a picture of 2 Gild Street being Sergey's little kingdom, where every night of the week wild parties take place, gambling goes on at all hours, and other illegal events such as porn movies shootings occur periodically. Now living in the building, I haven't seen any such activities yet. In the elevators I do encounter tons of people dressed for parties, but where they go after exiting the elevators I do not know. Other than Danny and the bartender I don't talk to anyone for quite a while.

*****

One evening, Head Tattoo comes into the apartment. Instead of his usual uniform of a white button-down shirt and black pants, he is wearing his training clothes.

"Let's go down to the gym," he says.

I ignore his suggestion. Training is the last thing I can imagine myself doing right now.

"Did you bring them?" I ask.

He takes a little bag with pills out of his pocket and throws it on the table.

I reach for it, take one out, and want to put it in my mouth. He stops my hand.

"Do you really want to go to bed at nine in the evening?"

I shrug my shoulders. I did not know what time it was, nor does it matter to me. I just want to take a sleeping pill and fall asleep, so that my tortured brain can have a few hours rest.

"Listen," Head Tattoo says. "Life is like a sieve. Many people come into it, and the insignificant assholes fall through. You understand? Because they are so small and insignificant."

I look at him somewhat surprised. I did not expect to hear such a philosophical statement from him. "Who said that?" I ask.

"I just did."

"OK." I am pretty sure he lifted that saying from somewhere. "And?"

"And . . ." He pauses, wrinkling his forehead and looking for words to express his important thought. Eloquence not being my tattooed friend's forte, the pause lasts quite a while. "And, the Balkan asshole fell right through," he finally pronounces. "So pull yourself together and come down to the gym. Training will do you good. Better than sleeping."

I have a sudden urge to ask him a bunch of questions. I bet he knows everything that transpired between Sergey and Drago, all their deals and arrangements with regards to me. Yet I contain myself and don't ask anything. It just does not matter anymore.

I look alternately at the sleeping pills and at Head Tattoo, unable to decide—go to bed or train?

"Come on," Head Tattoo insists, and I let myself be persuaded to change into my training clothes and take the elevator down to the gym.

I warm up, stretch for a long time, going through the motions on sort of an autopilot. Once we get to real training, I realize that I have absolutely zero energy or motivation. I am dragging my feet, am barely able to block attacks, and when I do a technique that Drago once showed me, I almost start crying. I don't want to train without Drago. That's just it. I can't seem to be able to make my body perform when my mind is so miserable.

Right in the middle of yet another failed technique, the door of the gym opens and Sergey comes in.

CHAPTER 19

The Russian is accompanied by the doctor who works for him, the same one who always treated my cuts and bruises and other minor injuries right after the Dark Fights and assessed if I needed to be taken to a hospital for further medical help. The two men sit on the bench and watch me and Head Tattoo work on some throws. My motions are sluggish and awkward. I fail to unbalance my training partner before attempting to throw him. At one point my knees give out and I sink down and stay down.

Sergey calls for me to approach him, and Head Tattoo gives me a hand and pulls me up from the floor. Without his help I really feel that I do not have enough energy even to get up. I take a few tentative steps toward the bench, collapse on it, and don't want to move ever again. Sergey offers me a bottle of water and places two pills in my hand. They will make me feel better, he says. Under normal circumstances I would start asking millions of questions, but right now nothing seems to matter much to me, and I swallow the pills without saying anything—just like that. I then lean my head against the wall and close my eyes. I do not know how much time passes, probably about fifteen minutes or so. I start feeling pretty strange, as if shaking on the inside. It comes on abruptly and intensifies fast, and soon I can't sit still and feel almost like jumping out of my own skin.

I get up from the bench and start pacing back and forth. Sergey motions to Head Tattoo to resume training and to attack me. He strikes several times in a rapid succession, and I move so fast that none of the strikes connect. I then grab hold of him and throw him down with a powerful *o-goshi* and finish with a *juji-gatame*—perpendicular arm bar. Two new training partners arrive, and Sergey tells them to join in the practice and to attack me.

A peculiar intense energy is almost splitting me apart from the inside, propelling me to perform all of the techniques with great strength and speed. When I'm doing an inner-thigh throw, I lift my leg too brusquely and injure my hamstring. The pain is very sharp, but I don't seem to care and continue training on what seems to be a pulled or maybe even partially torn hamstring. A strange need for destruction, violence, and aggression has taken over me, and I don't want to nor seem to be able to stop.

Then all of a sudden I start feeling nauseous, cannot control it, and throw up right in the middle of the gym.

Afterward I am exhausted like never before, and still nauseous. The doctor confers with Sergey and with his permission gives me another pill, assuring me it will take the nausea away and make me recover quickly after the intense training session. I take the pill and then rest for a while sitting on the bench. Sergey and the doctor get up to leave, and, as they walk away I catch a few words of their conversation, something about a very big Dark Fights night coming up.

Riding up in the elevator with Head Tattoo, I ask him about those words I have overheard, but he averts his eyes, wrinkles his forehead, and tells me he doesn't know anything.

*****

Back at the apartment, Ricardo the Stylist is going through my closet. After a careful inspection he declares I have absolutely nothing decent to wear and that, if it were not for him and the dresses he's brought, I would have to go to the party in my training clothes.

"The hell you talking about? What party?"

"The party! Tonight. The boss insists that you attend."

I want to tell Ricardo the stylist that I am not going to any party because I am nauseous and sick, but to my surprise I realize that the nausea is actually gone and I feel quite all right, physically. The doctor's pill really worked. Still, I am in no mood for parties. I will just stay here in the apartment and . . . hmm, do what exactly? Watch a movie maybe? Nah, they all bore me now. I got too used to watching movies with Drago, hearing his comments, asking him questions, and always getting precise and interesting responses, whether the topic being aliens and parallel universes, corporate espionage, or martial arts. I don't want to watch movies without him. So, what then? Go to bed alone with my sadness and try to fall asleep? I will have to take a sleeping pill. Hmm, maybe going to a party instead is not such a bad idea.

I take a shower and come out of the bathroom wearing only a pair of panties. As I put a compression bandage on my injured hamstring, Ricardo the stylist observes me with great attention and declares that I look out of shape.

"Possible." I shrug my shoulders. "Tonight is the first time I trained in quite a while. All I have been doing is eating and sleeping."

"It's all right. Perhaps you are not in a perfect shape for the cage, but you'll do quite well for a party. Ricardo the Stylist will make you look beautiful."

He helps me try on several dresses, and we settle on the steel-gray one with a very low-cut back. He gives me a pair of high-heeled sandals to go with the dress, then does my hair and applies a bit of makeup to accentuate my eyes. I look in the floor-length mirror and it shows a dressed up young woman with incredibly sad eyes. I can't take these sad eyes to a party, I think, and I'm about to take the dress off, but then change my mind again and leave the dress on. Maybe being in a crowd of people will do me good after all.

"Hey, Ricardo" I say while he is putting the finishing touches to my outfit, "you know everything that goes on around here. Have you heard about some important event coming up, some really big Dark Fights night or something?"

He freezes up for several long seconds, then gets back to adjusting a strap on my dress. "Nope, haven't heard anything like that."

*****

The party is two-leveled—in an apartment on one of the higher floors and on the rooftop of the building. I first take the elevator up to the rooftop. The music is blasting really loud. People are crowding around tables covered with food and the open bar. On the chaise lounges couples are lying down and drinking champagne. Everybody seems to be extraordinarily cheerful and there are bursts of laughter coming from every direction. It is extremely humid today and I start sweating even though I am only wearing the thin dress. I walk through the crowd and find an empty corner, where I stand leaning on a parapet and looking out to the city.

"Can I interest you in a glass of champagne," a voice with a strong German accent asks me from behind.

I turn and the owner of the voice is a tall, dirty-blond man with an athletic build, a polite smile, and clever eyes.

"Is it cold?"

"I will make sure it is. Don't move. I will be right back."

He comes back a few minutes later with a bottle of champagne in an ice bucket and two flutes. As soon as he hands me one I empty it in a long gulp. He refills it right away.

"It is very hot and humid out here," the German says. "I believe it is going to rain."

Oh good, small talk. Next we will be discussing NYC weather patterns. I turn and look out onto the city again. He leans on the parapet next to me and after a long pause starts telling me about himself, his work, places he likes to travel to. The champagne has gone straight to my head and I feel rather tipsy and I look at him with curiosity, studying his face, his words going in one ear and out of the other. I suppose he is a good-looking man. He definitely is. He misinterprets my fixed gaze and leans in and kisses me. I don't kiss him back, I don't even open my mouth. He pulls back, his eyes asking what's wrong, and all of a sudden I just start laughing.

"Are you all right?" he asks.

He really seems an understanding and nice-enough guy.

"Yes, thank you."

"Can I get you anything?"

I shake my head. "I don't think I am in the mood for company though."

"Got you. I'll be around, if you change your mind."

I stroll through the party, looking at people's faces, listening to shreds of their conversations. A number of men try to talk to me, but I do not pay attention to their advances and walk away. When the good-looking German kissed me, I did not feel attraction, I did not feel repulsion—I felt absolutely nothing, as if it were a brick wall touching my lips. And now looking at all these men, I do not see them as men, they might as well be lamp posts to me. There is only one man in the world and he has betrayed me.

This damn heavy sadness inside me. How do I get rid of it? I drink two more glasses of champagne, but do not feel any more cheerful. The only effect is that now I really have to pee. As I make my way slowly through the crowd toward the elevator, the first, weighty and fat drops of rain fall. When I exit the rooftop, it really starts raining and all the masses of people rush toward the elevators.

The party has moved inside, into the huge apartment. It takes me a while to find a bathroom and there is a long line of men and women in elegant and already crumpled clothes waiting to get in. So I go looking for a different one and walk into a bedroom. On the bed there is the German guy with two girls. The girls are completely naked except for a pair of stockings and a garter belt. I can't help but notice that the garter belt seems too tight and very uncomfortable for one of the girls, cutting into her flesh. Strange how your mind picks out such details.

The German guy notices me, pauses his activity, which at the moment consists of pushing the girls' breasts together and having them kiss each other, and asks if I would like to join them. "I am looking for a bathroom," I tell him. "There is one over there." He points to a door at the back wall and gets back to business with his two companions. Coming out of the bathroom, the scene on the bed has progressed. I now see the guy behind one of the girls who is on all fours, and he tells her to do the same things to the other girl that he is doing to her.

There are many rooms in the apartment and they are all filled with guests now. The lights are dimmed everywhere. Waiters glide around with an endless supply of drinks, and people are sitting on huge low couches and drinking and getting to know each other really well—well enough to get up from the couches and stroll together into one of the bedrooms and spend some time there and come out again and get to know other people really well.

I walk into a room, where several men and women are doing lines and they invite me, but I just stand there for a while observing them. I did not know cocaine was still in use these days, but I suppose this drug never goes out of style. The people in the room look contented and fulfilled, and there is a meaningful expression on their faces. I suppose they have found their own piece of truth for tonight.

I open doors to several bedrooms and the people inside either do not notice the intrusion or do not mind being watched. All possible sex variations are on display here. The one that perplexes me somewhat involves the presence of a rooster on a leash in a bed.

Wandering around the party I have a few more glasses of champagne. My mind starts playing tricks on me. On more than one occasion it seems to me I see Drago. It is not him, of course. Damn it, am I drunk? I do not feel drunk, just disoriented and very gloomy. I try to imagine what his face really looks like. I can visualize perfectly well every separate feature of it—the nose that has been broken a number of times but reset quite skillfully, the light brown eyes that can go from being warm to cold in a mere moment, the mouth that often has that little smirk as if he knew something other people did not, but can also do a true and wonderful smile, the wrinkles that appear in the corners of his eyes when the smile is real—yet the separate features do not add up to a whole picture. Ah, damn it, what would it take for me to rip these fragments of his face out of my memory forever? I bet there is not enough alcohol and drugs at this party to achieve that.

I encounter the charming German once more. This time he has a video camera in his hand. I remember he said something about being in the movie business. "Hello, beautiful girl with the sad eyes. Talk to me. Not to me. Talk to the camera. Tell the camera what you think makes people happy."

"A rooster on a leash in a bed makes some people happy," I say.

"And that's the ultimate philosophy." He laughs.

"Cheers." I raise my glass of champagne.

*****

I wander into the kitchen, and there, sitting at a table is Sergey with a few people. They are eating cheeseburgers and pickles and drinking vodka.

"*Privet*, Sasha, won't you join us," Sergey greets me.

Head Tattoo pulls up a chair for me and I sit down.

"Some vodka?"

"No, thank you."

"A cheeseburger then?"

"Yes." I suddenly feel very hungry and the cheeseburgers, on brioche buns with mayo and ketchup and pickles, look really good.

"Great. And how are you enjoying my party?"

I shrug my shoulders.

"I understand. This is not sufficiently exciting for you, is it? You crave something else, something that would get your blood really going, don't you? I know you too well, beauty. So now, I have an important question for you."

I am working on my cheeseburger at the moment and lift my eyes and look at him.

"Would you not like to do some more Dark Fights, Sasha?" he asks and holds my gaze for a few long moments.

I do not reply.

"My birthday is in two weeks," he says. "Do one fight as a birthday present for me."

"I've been hearing about some important event coming up. A big Dark Fights night. Is that what you are asking me to do?"

"What? No! What big Dark Fights night?" Sergey and the others exchange quick glances. "I have no idea what you mean. It's nothing like that. I am talking about my birthday and a small fighting bout for a select group of friends to watch and enjoy. What do you say?"

I finish the cheeseburger and get up from the table without answering the question.

"Come on, beauty. If you won't to do it for me, do it for yourself. You know you want to get back into the cage. You miss it. You enjoyed your last few fights, didn't you? I'll make sure you have even more fun in the cage this time around. I have something for you that will give you the best high of your life . . ."

What is he talking about now? What is it that he has for me? I want to ask, but he does not give me a chance to put in a word.

"You crave that amazing high, the adrenaline rush from stepping into the cage, don't you?" he goes on quickly. You know you want it again. What else have you got after all? Think about it, what else have you got?"

Is he right? He might just be. I really don't have anything else in my life anymore.

"So, beauty, how about it? Will you do the Birthday Fight?"

As I start walking away, I turn my head and give him a brief nod. I leave the kitchen hearing behind me Sergey's expressions of delight.

I go up to the rooftop again. It is pouring and there is no one here. I lean against the parapet and look at the walls of rain coming down hard onto the city. Within a few seconds I am completely drenched. My wet dress is clinging to my body, the water is cascading down my hair. I stand like this for a long time.

CHAPTER 20

Head Tattoo and I are sitting in the back seat of the BMW on our way to Sergey's birthday fight. Am I imagining it or is my usually calm and cool companion feeling rather nervous today? He is fidgeting, cracking his knuckles, starting to whistle and then breaking off suddenly, and throwing me strange looks every once in a while. What is up with him? At several moments I even catch him open his mouth as if to say something, but no words come out, and he just coughs into his fist and then remains silent. I have half a mind to ask him straight-out what is going on, but finally decide to just ignore him. I have a lot to worry about as is.

I have agreed to do the Birthday Fight, yet now am not sure if I'll be able to go through with it. I feel extremely weak and sluggish. Since that one training session two weeks ago I haven't really stepped into the gym, not having any energy or will to train yet not wishing to take those drugs that made me feel like wanting to jump out of my own skin. Instead of training I have been going to all types of parties Sergey invited me to, trying to dissolve my gloomy thoughts in drinks, music, and crowds of strangers, but never succeeding.

My muscles have lost their conditioning. My hamstring has not quite healed either. And worst of all, my body and my mind both simply refuse to shake off the half-lethargic state and wake up. Damn it, I really doubt that inside the cage I'll be able to perform at decent speed and energy levels. My opponent will be able to do what she wants with me.

The car drives up to the entrance of the nightclub in midtown that Sergey owns, and Head Tattoo walks me through the security. The main birthday celebration is taking place on the first floor, and there is a steady stream of people going in, but we take the stairs to the basement, where Baldy and Buzz Cut are manning the doors. I realize I am starting to feel somewhat nervous. I don't know what is waiting for me inside. I guess I never believed it when Sergey said tonight's fight was going to be a small low-key affair. As I am stepping in, I half expect to see something grandiose, a huge chamber filled to the brim with the usual bloodthirsty crowd.

To my surprise, the space is not large at all, with soft lighting, paintings on the walls, and wooden paneling. There are only a handful of couches and coffee tables, with no more than twenty or so people at them. It would look just like a comfortable and elegant living room if . . . well, if it were not for a fighting cage right in the middle of it.

Hmm, just as Sergey has promised, tonight's fight seems to be a small and intimate show for only a few of his friends. So, this is definitely not the big Dark Fights event that I have been hearing about. Still, I can't help but feel anxious. I know by now that nothing is ever exactly what it seems when it comes to the Russian and his schemes.

"The boss wants you to take these before the fight." Head Tattoo suddenly places a small plastic bag with two pills into my hand. "He says, you'll need them. You haven't been training much, if at all."

I shake my head. I don't want the drugs.

"Sorry," Head Tattoo says, an uncomfortable look on his face. "This is not a suggestion. It's an order. I am to make sure you take them."

So, there it is. I just knew that Sergey was up to something.

"Why? What the fuck is going on here?"

He does not reply, but I've already guessed that tonight is supposed to be a trial bout for me. This little show Sergey has arranged is to see how I fight on drugs.

"These are new. Pretty strong stuff." Head Tattoo nods toward the little bag in my hand. He wants to add something else but cuts himself off.

"Are you going to actually watch me take them and then have me open my mouth and check, like they do with psychiatric patients?" I ask. "Is that what Sergey has ordered you to do?"

He stares at me for a few moments, looking pretty embarrassed and unsure of how to proceed. I wouldn't be surprised if the Russian did, in fact, give such orders, or perhaps even tougher ones. In the end Head Tattoo mutters something unintelligible under his breath and moves away.

As I sit alone in the bathroom I twirl the bag with the pills in my fingers. Do I take them or not? If I am to step into the cage tonight, I must take them. There is no other way. If I don't, the condition I am in, I'll get destroyed, smashed on the canvas with a bad injury or worse. Do I take them or not? Do I take them or not? Ah, fuck it. I open the little plastic bag, throw the pills into my mouth, and wash them down with water from the tap.

When, some time later, Head Tattoo is leading me toward the cage, he looks at me questioningly. I nod.

*****

Stepping into the cage, I am already shaking on the inside and cannot stand still. The sensation is even stronger than what I felt the time I took the drugs during that training session. I clench and unclench my fists, jump around, do circular motions with my head, and stretch my neck and shoulder muscles in a sort of a jerky and erratic way. A violent uncontrollable desire to fight, to hit, to throw down and destroy comes over me. It's starting somewhere deep inside me and pushes out through my every pore. It is so intense and powerful, there is no way I can keep it in.

As soon as the referee calls "fight" I charge at my opponent—a very tall girl with pink hair and unnaturally bright violet-colored eyes—and throw a series of strikes. I easily avoid or block her attacks and land her a heavy blow on the sternum, throw her down, and follow up by brutal punches and downward elbow strikes to the head. I glance at the table where Sergey is sitting with a couple of guests. He looks very happy and nods his head at me and smiles a broad and satisfied smile.

The violet girl manages to clamber to her feet, but I immediately strike her on the temple. Disoriented, she raises her arm, trying to punch me. I grab her arm, hold onto it as if it were a tree branch, jump up and put one leg around her neck and the other behind her back and take her down onto the canvas in a spectacular and tough takedown. Driven by the desire for the aggression and destruction, I bring her down so hard, that I feel the strong impact in my own body. At this moment I am strangely aware of the fact that I'm really enjoying the brutal combat and finding its intensity fulfilling and pleasurable.

I have my opponent in my favorite *juji-gatame*—a perpendicular arm bar—hold her tight so that she does not have a single chance of escaping, and am about to end this fight by cranking her elbow joint, when suddenly I glance at Sergey's table again . . . and I release the *juji-gatame* hold, get up from the floor, and stand for a few moments just staring.

*****

There is a tall man standing at Sergey's table seemingly involved in a discussion or an argument with him. I can't see the man's face but somehow I'm sure it's Drago. I'm simply convinced that it cannot be anyone but him. I remain in one spot, having forgotten about the fight instantaneously, unable to avert my eyes from the man.

When the violet girl pounces on me from behind and attempts to put me in a *rear naked choke*, I am caught completely off guard. Once this type of choke is fully applied, it is practically impossible to get out of it. My speed and power still working in overdrive, I am able to hook my leg around hers, go down on my knee, turn my body brusquely, and throw her down. I then rush to get out of the cage, and the referee blocks my way. I punch the referee hard on the jaw and knock him out, and hurl myself over the top of the cage.

I feel the blood pulsating hard somewhere behind my ears and see colored spots before my eyes. In a kind of a frenzy I run up to the tall man and for some reason push him with both my hands in a not-very-martial move. He steps back, trips, tries to hold onto the table, almost overturning it and sending a bunch of glasses, bottles, and plates crashing to the floor. At that moment I realize that my drugged brain has played a cruel trick on me. It was just a hallucination. The man is not Drago. It is a complete stranger and he looks at me in dismay, his mouth pronouncing some words that I cannot seem to comprehend.

I am suddenly gasping for air and feel very nauseous. The drugs stop working and, just like that first time when I took them in the gym, I am now crashing, all the energy drained out of me. The new drugs being stronger, the crash is even worse now.

My legs crumble under me and I am about to fall down. Head Tattoo holds me up and helps me walk to the bathroom, opens the tap with cold water, wets a towel, and presses it to my face and the nape of my neck. He sits me on the bench, and I close my eyes, trying to control the nausea and to take strained shallow breaths, unable to breathe fully.

When I open my eyes again, it is Sergey and the doctor who are standing before me. Sergey takes my chin and lifts my head up. "Don't worry, beauty, I'm not angry with you," he says. "It's the drugs. We'll adjust the dosage for the next fight."

I have a very strong and almost uncontrollable desire to spit into his face, but I am somehow able to check myself. I just push his hand away, lower my head, and don't reply at all. I hear them having a discussion in hushed voices, and then the doctor hands me another pill that he says will make me feel better in no time. Sergey insists that after some rest I should come upstairs and join the big birthday party.

When Ricardo the Stylist comes in to help me get ready, I spot a pair of scissors among his things and, when he is not paying attention, grab it and am about to start cutting off my hair. I can't quite say why I want to do this. I suppose it is a gesture of desperation or rebellion of some sort.

Ricardo the Stylist screams out and stops my hand. I am still so weak I can't fight him. He takes the scissors from me, and, his eyes panic-stricken, begs me not to do a thing like this. The boss wants the Samurai Princess to have long hair, and it will be he, Ricardo the Stylist, who will suffer the consequences if anything should change in my appearance.

I don't argue. My moment of utter gloom and despair, or whatever it was, has now passed. The recovery pill is starting to work already and I am feeling better and my mood alters. I talk in a loud voice and laugh exaggeratedly. This abrupt change in mood is likely not a healthy thing either, but I prefer not to dwell on it.

Ricardo the Stylist puts me in a figure-hugging silvery dress and declares it looks stunning, beautiful, dazzling. All of a sudden I get very impatient and want to go upstairs. A desire to be in a crowd of people with music and alcohol comes over me. Before rushing out of the bathroom, I pick a very bright-red color lipstick and apply a thick layer to my lips.

*****

As I go up the stairs and into the main room, I see it's very crowded here. The English language is interspersed with a lot of Russian. The whole place is decorated in what I guess is supposed to be the prerevolutionary Russian style, with gilded furniture, replica Fabergé eggs, large candles, and even portraits of the last Tsar and his family. There is no stage, and a singer accompanied by a band is performing old Russian love songs seemingly right in the middle of the crowd. Waiters dressed as Cossacks are serving classic Russian sweet champagne and small blinis with a variety of fillings. A tray covered with blinis and black caviar appears, and people pounce on it so fast that it is empty within a minute.

A famous Russian opera singer, with a very heavy bust, tightly curled hair, and a kind pleasant face, is sitting at a table all by herself eating beef stroganoff and drinking vodka. I've heard rumors that she never starts singing unless she has had her plate of beef stroganoff and several vodkas. Once, as an experiment, she was served amaretto on the rocks. She was in a foul mood afterward and declined to perform.

I've met the singer at previous Sergey's parties, and she now waves to me to join her at her table. I have a vodka with her, but the sight of her eating beef stroganoff, putting chunks of meat into her mouth and chewing them vigorously, makes me a bit nauseous again, and I make up an excuse and leave the table.

A tray with champagne appears right by my side, and I drink two glasses straight away, one after the other. The alcohol probably doesn't mix too well with the earlier pill, for pretty quickly everything around me starts looking blurry and all the faces and voices blend into one loud, grimacing mass. As I take a few steps through the crowd, I realize I definitely cannot walk a straight line. Damn it, I'm a martial artist, aren't I? I should be able to be in control of my body. Ah, fuck it. Who cares! My unsteady swaying motions go well with the music, and I just need to have another drink to give in fully to the party ambience.

I reach for another glass of champagne, stumble, and somebody catches me by the elbow, and doesn't let me fall down. It's Head Tattoo again, and I am awfully glad to see him and I put my arms around his neck and kiss him on the cheek. I can discern a confused and slightly embarrassed expression on his face and start laughing. Head Tattoo doesn't let me drink more, declares I need some food in me right away, gets ahold of a fresh plate with caviar blinis, and makes me eat two.

He stays with me for a while, acting like a perfect gentleman, watching over me, and getting me to drink water and eat some more food. After making sure I am all right and can now stand more or less steady on my high heels, he lets me be, and I continue my way through the party alone, heading in the general direction of the opera singer's voice. She is now performing, accompanied by a pianist, and the music and her mesmerizing voice seem to transform this midtown nightclub into a true Russian imperial palace and give an air of authenticity to the gaudy and fake decorations.

Trying to get closer to the piano, I enter a particularly crowded area of the room, where bodies are in such close proximity you can smell each person's perfume, deodorant, cologne, or lack thereof. It seems to me that the singer's voice carries through and over the crowd, enveloping everything and everyone in a magical veil.

"Sasha," I suddenly hear a voice speak right into my ear, startling me. "Don't turn around," the voice says. "They are watching your every move."

CHAPTER 21

My first impulse is to turn and see who it is but something, perhaps the urgency and the gravity of the voice, stops me. I think I recognize the familiar intonations, but I don't trust my own senses right now. Perhaps I am hallucinating again. If it is the person I think it is, what could he possibly be doing here? Nah, it can't be him.

"Go toward the bar, turn left and then behind the column. There are no video cameras there," the voice dictates.

Full of doubts, I nevertheless do as the voice says, and a few seconds after I get to a sort of a niche behind the column, he appears next to me.

Liam.

It takes me a few moments to adjust my mind to his being here—a figure from my former and infinitely remote life emerging in the midst of my present. Can it really be him? Somehow it seems impossible to me that Liam should be right here, in these circumstances. But yes, it is him, and his inimitable dark eyes are burrowing into my mind as if trying to drill into my very core. We stand for a while just looking at each other. Liam's face is much thinner than I remember it, the cheekbones standing out more, the eye sockets deeper, the jawline even more pronounced than before. He is wearing his only suit and it does not fit him as well as it used to—the jacket is sitting somewhat loose on his torso. It is so strange, I feel as if it's been many years since I last saw Liam. He appears now out of a part of my life that I left completely behind and can never ever go back to.

"What are you doing here?" I ask.

"I'm working this event. Found out that the bearded bastard who said he was your uncle but is really a fucking gangster owns this club, so I got a bouncing gig here."

"What are you doing here?" I repeat my question.

He looks me straight in the eyes, and his gaze is so intense I almost cannot bear it.

"I came for you," he pronounces, emphasizing every word. "I should never have let you go in the first place, but I was angry and jealous. So fucking jealous." He pauses and swallows hard. I can see that he wants to tell me a lot and to convince me of something, but I know he is not used to giving speeches. He goes on, the words coming out faster now but a bit awkward. "I heard you were living with a guy . . . I now understand that when you really care for a woman you do everything to help her, even though . . . even though she's chosen another man. I understand that now, but before I just didn't know how to deal with the jealousy. I was an idiot. But now I am getting you out of here, this life, the Dark Fights, all of it."

He takes me by both arms and pulls me gently into him.

"You are coming back to the dojo with me," he says.

"Impossible. Sensei won't allow it. No." I pull back slightly and he lets go off my arms.

"We'll figure something out. The life you have now . . . it's not you. It's not who you are supposed to be. You've made a wrong choice and now you're so lost you can't even see it. You must listen to me for once. Chuck all this and come with me, Sasha."

His strong and urgent words manage to get through the muddled outer layer of my mind. I start to make sense of what he is saying. He could be right—perhaps somewhere down the road I did veer off the right course and am now lost. If I stay, I will keep sinking into this bottomless bog. If I go with him, I might make it to the surface again. But can I really do it, go with him, just like this?

He sees my hesitation and nods with reassurance and takes my hand. I put my fingers through his and hold tight. At that moment Buzz Cut and Baldy appear near us. I let go of Liam's hand. They look at us with suspicion. "The boss wants you," one of them says to me. "And *you* should be working the back door," he barks at Liam.

At this point I realize that the opera singing has stopped and there is now an interval in the entertainment. As I walk from behind the column, throwing one last glance at Liam, I can see that the crowd has dispersed somewhat, many of the guests now sitting at tables, on couches, and in armchairs, leaving the middle of the room empty. A gentleman in a tuxedo comes to the center of the dance floor and speaks into a microphone, going back and forth between English and Russian. He makes a toast and asks everyone to raise their glasses and drink to Sergey Petrovich's health, prosperity, happiness, and good fortune. He then announces that there is a special present for Sergey Petrovich—his favorite song.

The band—guitars and violins—starts playing, and several singers dressed as Russian gypsies sing. It is a romantic, deeply felt type of singing, going from very forlorn and dramatic to energetic and cheerful, and the rhythm changing from slow to fast. Sergey gets up from his seat, raises his glass, drinks from it, and throws it on the ground in a big Russian gesture. He then takes a few steps to the music moving his arms in the air, and glances around, as if looking for something or someone.

He spots me standing near the dance floor, walks right up to me, and extends his arm inviting me to dance. I shake my head and step back.

"Dance with me, beauty," he says. "Come on. It's my birthday."

He takes my hand and leads me to the dance floor. On a sort of an autopilot I first follow him, but then come to, free my hand in a brusque motion, and push him away. He tries to grab my arm again. I am a split second away from throwing him, when a fist appears as if out of nowhere, lands on the Russian's jaw and knocks him out. The lightning-speed fist belongs to Liam, and with Sergey cold on the floor, Liam and I stand for a moment or two just looking at each other.

The singing and the music halt. Everything is suddenly very quiet. I am vaguely aware of being in the center of a big room with lots of people, but for all I care I could be in the middle of a desert. I don't look at anything or anybody now. I stare right in front of me, into Liam's very dark eyes.

I don't know how long this strange state lasts. In actual time, perhaps no more than a second. The next moment, time resumes its normal speed, Buzz Cut and Baldy run up and pounce on Liam. Head Tattoo busies himself with reviving his boss.

Liam, Buzz Cut, and Baldy trade a number of blows that look rough but do not do much damage on either side. Buzz Cut then sneaks in a good punch and immediately attempts a head kick, but only connects with air. Liam lands a powerful shot on the chin of Buzz Cut, who wobbles, and Liam grabs him and throws him in a beautifully executed *ippon seoi nage*, a shoulder throw.

He then shoots for a double leg takedown of Baldy, who manages to react quickly and counter. Liam changes tactics and strikes him on the neck with a crushing open hand, and, while Baldy seems momentarily dazed, executes on him an extremely effective combination of an elbow lock and a throw.

A couple more bouncers join in the fight and at one point Liam charges in with great force but places his head too low, and within a split second his opponent gets him in a standing guillotine choke. The guy's hold seems pretty powerful and his body position is strong and centered, and for a moment I am scared there is no way Liam can get out of this choke. Yet perhaps I underestimate Liam's fighting skills and his strength. He escapes from the choke and the bout goes on.

Meanwhile Sergey comes to and yells, "Who the fuck let that crazy uchi-deshi in here?"

Head Tattoo tries to reply that Liam is one of the bouncers at this event, but Sergey just keeps shouting and cursing. He wants to know "who the fuck hired the crazy uchi-deshi" and when no answer comes forth, he continues cursing, interjecting Russian expletives into his speech.

With a brief hand gesture he orders more of his men to attack Liam. I want to jump in to help Liam, but Head Tattoo gets me in a powerful bear hug and holds me in place. I try to break his grip, but fail. I make an attempt to bend forward and sort of throw him over me—absolutely to no avail. I then dig my heel into a pressure point on the top of his foot. This pressure point is extremely powerful and the pain must be excruciating. Head Tattoo issues a loud agonizing growl but does not release his iron bear hug. "Stay still. You don't want to mix in that fight," he says to me.

For a while Liam puts on an excellent defense, causing serious damage to a number of the attackers, but, several men against one, they manage to overpower him in the end. He receives a few brutal punches and then they bring him down to the floor and continue landing him punches and kicks to his body and head.

I make another desperate attempt to get out of Head Tattoo's hold and, when that fails, shout to Sergey. He glances at me, deliberates for a moment, and then orders his men to stop and to stand Liam up. They obey the command and pick Liam up from the floor. Blood is streaming from a cut over his eyebrow and from his mouth. He still tries to resist but they have him in a tight lock, twisting his arms behind his back. Liam spits the blood to the floor.

"Sasha, come back to the dojo with me!" he calls and spits the blood out again.

"Get him out of here," Sergey orders, and his men start dragging Liam toward the exit.

"Sasha, you don't belong here. Come with me," Liam calls again.

I finally manage to break Head Tattoo's grip and get his arm in a standing *kimura* lock. All his strength and weight can do nothing against this painful arm lock. I then throw him and take a few hurried steps after Liam.

"Sasha, stop!" Sergey shouts. "Where are you going? Back to the dojo? They kicked you out. They don't want you. You stopped being an uchi-deshi the moment you stepped into the cage for the first time. There is no way back for you."

I pause, uncertain of what to do. I want to follow Liam, but Sergey words have a sudden and incredibly strong impact on me. *There is no way back for you* rings in my ears again and again. I can't help but succumb to the demoralizing effect of this phrase. I think of how I broke all the rules, went against the code of honor, and disobeyed Sensei. There is no place in the dojo for me anymore, for I am not a martial artist but just a fighter now. I feel strange, as if contaminated with something I cannot purify myself of, and so must not bring this contagion into the dojo. I remain standing in one spot, as if my feet are glued to the floor. No, I can't go back with Liam.

*****

I ask the driver not to take me straight to 2 Gild Street, but to ride around the city for a bit. My thoughts are in complete disarray and, as the car glides through the nighttime streets of Manhattan, a question emerges out of that chaos. What is my place now? Where do I belong? The answer is too painful to admit even to myself.

I thought I was an uchi-deshi and my life was at the dojo, but I lost that. I then thought that my present and my future were with Drago, but that was all shattered too. I pass my hand across my lips and stare at the dark-red streak of lipstick. I rub my lips in silent desperation and then smear the dark-red color onto my dress. I hunch over and wrap my arms tight around myself, trying to suppress the tears. *Ahhh*, a shout issues from deep inside me and I hit the seat with my fist several times.

By the time the car takes me to 2 Gild Street, the pain has mixed with a strange sort of cold bitterness and disillusionment that I haven't experienced before. Upstairs I pace around the apartment, not knowing what to do with myself and with my utterly gloomy and poisonous thoughts. I've heard that sometimes people just bang their heads against the wall, for no apparent reason. I guess, those people feel utterly lost and can't come up with a better outlet for their anguish.

At one point I find myself standing near a window wondering what it would feel like to drive my fist through the glass.

Later that night Head Tattoo comes up to the apartment with a box of blini and caviar from the party. He opens his mouth to say something but I interrupt him.

"Get changed and meet me in the gym," I tell him. "Oh, and bring some more of those drugs."

He looks at me, a silent question written all over his face. I nod emphatically. I've decided. I've made the choice. I am not quite sure if it somehow has been made for me or not, but right now this distinction doesn't seem to matter. I don't want to think about it too much, if at all. "Just bring them," I say again as I start putting on my training clothes—not a traditional martial arts *gi*, which I have not worn in ages, but a fighter's gear.

*****

Soon after Sergey's birthday party I do another Dark Fight. And after that one more, and then I do not want to stop. Sergey has doubled my prize purse for each win, but it's not of much importance to me at this stage.

I train endless hours at the gym at 2 Gild Street, which is now at my disposal twenty four-seven, get massages and cryotherapy to help my body recover after the overly intense training, and then the Dark Fights nights, the stepping into the cage, the putting everything I've got into each bout, and the ever-growing indifference to physical pain—mine or my opponents'.

With the intense training, my body returns to perfect fighting condition and keeps getting stronger. I also take whatever drugs Sergey's physician gives me and for the duration of a bout I abandon myself to the chemically enhanced exertion and violence. I now crave this feeling of emptying myself out completely. It seems to help rid me of the burden of sadness and anguish I carry inside. Afterward the crashing comes. The disillusionment, the desolation, and the bitterness return and weigh heavy on me, and I get the urge to get into the cage again and again. There does not seem to be a way out of it for me anymore. The circle closes, and with each spin I get colder and more brutal and have fewer and fewer qualms about inflicting severe injuries. In one of the fights, my opponent's arm gets broken in three places, but I do not dwell on things like this much, if at all. These days I try not to think about anything.

After the fights there are always parties, and if I am not too badly injured I always go. I don't want to be alone with my thoughts. I prefer the noise, loud music, crowds of people around, and meaningless inconsequential conversations. If I catch a glimpse of myself in a mirror, I see huge shadows under my eyes, lips dry and cracked, and protruding cheekbones. I apply tons of powder and a bright lipstick to make myself look less like a living corpse. And when I get back to my apartment in the early morning hours, I take a sleeping pill or two and fall into the dark oblivion, until Head Tattoo wakes me up to go training. The trek round the circle goes on and on, and the whole routine is carried out to the accompaniment of various drugs—the ones that boost my energy levels to the maximum and augment my power, strength, and speed, the ones that relieve the symptoms of the crashing afterward, the ones that help recover the sore muscles faster, and some other drugs that I don't even know or want to know what they are for. I don't ask any questions anymore except for one.

I keep hearing rumors about an upcoming event, a really big Dark Fights night, but every time I ask Sergey he avoids a direct answer. Perhaps he thinks I am not ready. The doctor is still experimenting with the optimum dosage of the drugs I take. Sergey says he wants to see the Samurai Princess "turn into a beast in the cage."

Strange, but I think I am actually looking forward to this important Dark Fights night. I guess there is nothing else in my life to look forward to.

In my lucid moments, it occurs to me that I am like a greyhound racing around a track, and Sergey is dangling the mysterious Dark Fights event in front of my nose as if it were a mechanical rabbit. I chase the unpleasant image away.

In these rare intervals when my mind works more or less clearly, I also think of Liam and wonder if perhaps I made a huge mistake of not going with him. These are not happy thoughts, and I prefer not to dwell on things and to have as few of these "lucid moments" as possible.

CHAPTER 22

They crave something absolutely spectacular and big, these people gathered here tonight. Something they have not seen before. You must deliver. A lot is at stake.

It is the night of the big Dark Fights event and Sergey's warning pops up in my head at the very height of the fight, when the crowd's clamor has become almost deafening. My opponent attempts a flying knee—a knee to the head blow, but I move too fast for the strike to connect. I plant my foot in her stomach and bring her down in a *tomoe nage* throw, slam her into the floor, get on top, and strike with my elbows and fists. For a few moments it seems to me that everything grows absolutely quiet and all I can hear are the thumping sounds of the blows.

The shaking on the inside is worse than on all the previous occasions. I don't know the drug dosage they gave me this time, but the feeling of wanting to jump out of my own skin does not abate with the intensity of the bout, and only grows stronger. The violent energy has fully taken over and I cannot stop striking. With my arms continuing to deliver the blows in an almost zombielike state, I glance around me. I see the white walls of the huge tent that has been set up on the rooftop of 2 Gild Street to prevent helicopters, drones, and people from other rooftops from looking in. I see countless figures crowding around the cage with their gaping mouths, whose shouts I cannot seem to hear.

All of a sudden an acute sense of danger shots through me. Out of the corner of my eye I notice something sparkle in my opponent's fingers.

She makes one quick move aiming right at my forehead. In a split-second motion I deflect her hand, and she cuts my shoulder instead of my face.

At this moment the roar of the crowd bursts into my head again, mixing with what seems like the equally loud noise of my pulse pumping somewhere behind my ears.

She must have hidden the tiny razor in the band of her shorts or her sports bra. I bet she was trying to cut me above my eyes so that the gushing blood would blind me. She is damn fast, but I do not give her a chance for a second attempt. I grab her wrist and twist it so hard I hear the sound of a bone breaking. She drops the razor.

We are back on our feet and the blood is streaming down my arm. There is no cutman cage-side to treat wounds, and the referee will not pause the fight anyway. I get her in a clinch and press my shoulder tight against her body trying to stop the bleeding this way.

I dig my fingers hard under her ribs in that brutal move that Drago taught me. I then drive my elbow into her sternum. She staggers on her feet and holds onto me, spitting blood into my face. I am just about to throw her again, when suddenly the cage door opens and several persons, Head Tattoo among them, hurry in. I don't understand what's going on as I look around and see the heavily packed audience start to move about haphazardly. The commotion intensifies inside the big white tent, and Head Tattoo gets me out of the cage and rushes me through the crowd toward the exit.

"What just happened up there?" I shout as we are riding down in the elevator. I am breathing rapidly and it's difficult for me to stand still. The shaking on the inside has still not gone away and I have not started to come down from the violent high the drugs produced. The dosage they gave me this time must have been huge.

"The police are in the building. Not because of the fight. Unrelated. But better to postpone the fight, just in case."

"Fuck that. Why did she have a razor? Did you know she would have a razor?" I grab Head Tattoo by the lapels of his jacket.

He remains cool and hands me a cloth to press against the cut on my shoulder.

"The doctor will look at it in a minute," he says.

"Fuck it." I throw the cloth on the floor.

We ride down to the garage, Head Tattoo puts me in the back seat of a car and leaves me alone for what probably are only a few minutes but seem like interminable hours to me. Finally the doors open and Sergey and the doctor get in.

"You had it all planned, didn't you? The razor? It was your idea, wasn't it?" I grab Sergey's shoulder and start shaking it, trying to shake the answer out of him. I don't think I am fully aware of what I am doing.

"Take these." The doctor hands me several pills. I hit his hand and the pills fly in different directions.

"She really needs to calm down," Sergey says and steps out again. Head Tattoo appears in his stead and suddenly gets me in a tight hold, pressing me against the back of the seat. The doctor has a syringe out already, and at the first opportune moment gives me a shot. Within seconds I start sinking into soft pleasurable waves, unable to think or care about anything.

CHAPTER 23

Several days later Danilo and I are sitting at Wolf Flannigan's. The bartender recommends salmon for dinner. Danny tries it and says it's really fresh and delicious, but I cannot seem to taste what I am putting in my mouth. My head feels as if it weighs a ton and my thoughts are all hazy and slow. I bet it's the drugs the doctor has been giving me since the last fight. The bartender brings me a mojito and I take a few sips. The summery concoction is not strong enough for my current condition, so I ask for vodka on the rocks instead. The vodka, however, also fails to revive me.

Danilo is drinking ginger ale and keeps glancing at my shoulder and shaking his head.

"That is a nasty cut," he says and strokes my arm with his knuckles. "Will leave a scar."

"No big deal. Doc said they'd be able to remove it with a laser later on."

"But it *is* a big deal, Sash. It is! She could have cut you much worse, on your face or something. Anything can happen in that cage. With no rules, who knows what your next opponent might try to pull. It's such a dirty business."

I try to find within me disgust, fear, apprehension, something, but I don't seem to be able to care. I am just numb. I do not feel like myself at all, as if I had been hollowed out and stuffed with some new material. Damn, what has the doctor been giving me?

"And what if the next time you are in the cage you can't control yourself and just kill your opponent? Have you thought of that?"

I remember what Hiroji once told me about the horror of killing someone. I don't want to dwell on any such possibility, though, and don't reply anything to my brother's urgent question.

"Listen," Danilo pronounces with great determination. "You must quit the Dark Fights. Let's just chuck everything here, tomorrow, and fly off to Amsterdam."

"Ah, again with your Amsterdam."

"Well, why not? Listen. We could live in Amsterdam, or we could also go and explore the Dutch countryside, all the small towns and villages and stuff. I don't care about casinos and all that anymore. We'd go to Delft. That's where that guy Vermeer, who painted *Girl with the Pearl Earring*, lived. We'll eat mussels and *pannekoeken*."

"What?"

"*Pannekoeken*. That's Dutch pancakes. They are super thin and can be sweet or savory."

Vermeer and *pannekoeken*. My brother has done quite a bit of research on the Netherlands. The idea of moving there has clearly gotten ahold of him pretty tightly. Hmm, but why shouldn't we go, if that is what he really wants? It's good to really want something. I wish *I* were able to really want something, but I seem to have lost that ability. Well, I'll do this for Danny. And the money shouldn't be a problem now either. I've made quite a bit of it winning in the cage fight after fight.

Perhaps I should stick around for the rescheduled big night Dark Fight though. It's worth the risk—the money from that one night would give Danny and me an additional year or two of quiet life in some small town in his beloved Netherlands. The new date for the event has not been set yet but it is to take place sometime soon and, if I win, Sergey has promised a really significant reward—fifty grand. He's a lying and manipulating bastard, but he has never cheated me out of prize money. And this time I will be on high alert for any tricks my opponent might pull. She won't be able to surprise me with her razor stunts or such.

"Well, Sash?" Danilo asks and strokes my arm with his knuckles again. There is almost a pleading expression in his eyes.

"You know what, we might just do it."

At this he smiles such a wonderful, happy smile that his face looks like a little boy's.

"Yay! So you will definitely quit the Dark Fights? And we'll move to Amsterdam together? Yay!"

I take a long drink of my vodka and finally start feeling a bit more alive. I cannot quite tell if it is the vodka or Danilo's earnest enthusiasm that has revived me somewhat.

The bartender comes over from the other end of the counter where he's been serving side cars to a group of regulars, and all of a sudden he just freezes with an empty tray in his hands, looking somewhere behind me. His face gains a tense and grave expression. I glance in the mirror on the back wall, and, among the rows of bottles see the reflection of Sergey standing a few feet back of us. Fuck. How long has he been standing there? Did he hear us? I bet he did. Danilo and I were not exactly whispering.

*****

Sergey comes up and leans on the bar counter and looks at me and my brother for some time without saying anything.

"*Privet.*" He slaps my brother on the back. "Why don't you and I go and sit at that table over there and have a drink together and talk some things over. Your sister wouldn't mind waiting here for a bit, would she? Our friend the bartender will keep her company." And he motions to the bartender to get me another drink.

Danilo looks at me, doubt and apprehension in his eyes. I put my hand on his arm.

"No, Sergey. Danilo will stay right here. Anything you want to say to him, say it in front of me."

Sergey is quiet again for a while, observing us, his eyes shifting from my face to my brother's.

"Well, all right," he finally says. "I'd like to caution your brother to stay the hell out of your business and not give you any stupid advice about quitting the Dark Fights. Too much is at stake here. He needs to stop throwing careless words around or he might learn the lesson the hard way." The tone of Sergey's voice leaves no doubt as to the seriousness of his statement.

"Are you threatening us?" I ask.

"No, just giving your brother a friendly advice." He slaps Danilo hard on the back again. "And if it's the *pannekoeken* that he craves so much, we will find a restaurant here in New York that serves true Dutch *pannekoeken*. You can find anything your heart desires in this town. And if, for some reason, there are no *pannekoeken* available here, I will fly in a chef from the Netherlands. There is nothing that I cannot do. There is nothing that I would not do. You hear me?"

What the hell. There is nothing that he cannot do? There is nothing that he would not do? Is he still talking about the *pannekoeken*?

"So, I will leave you two now." Sergey starts walking away but then pauses and turns toward me. "You are to step into the cage again very soon, beauty. The Big Night event awaits," he pronounces in a quiet but weighty voice. "You love the Dark Fights. You crave that high that only a Dark Fight can give you. And remember, you don't have anything else outside the Dark Fights."

"That is not true!" Danny shouts. He has been silent this whole time, but I could see fire building up in him and hoped he would contain himself, but now he just snaps. "She's got life outside of the Dark Fights. She's got me."

"Well, something can be done about that, no? Ha-ha-ha." Sergey laughs as if he had made a good joke. "We understand each other, my friends, don't we?"

"Not in the least. We do *not* understand each other," Danilo says. "First you get me into the Dark Fights just so that you can get to my sister later on. And now you have her entrapped and would not let her out. But I will not just sit and do nothing about it. I will convince her to quit. I will!"

Sergey watches him for what seems like a long time, his gaze intense and heavy. He then nods and walks to the door.

Danilo and I exchange a look. He opens his mouth as if to say something, but changes his mind and remains quiet. For a few minutes we sit silent and motionless, both deep in thought. After a while he asks the bartender to give him a whiskey.

"Jameson?"

"Hmm, nah, Macallan."

"You got it."

"Oh, Danny, no, please," I say. "You've been doing so well. Please."

"It's Ok. Just one drink. I really need it now."

The whiskey arrives and Danilo picks up the glass and holds it close to his mouth for a few seconds. He then slowly puts it back on the counter and pushes it away from him.

"There is never just one drink," he says.

"Danny," I say, take his hand and squeeze it.

I am so proud of him. My brother, who in the past had never been the strongest and most disciplined of men and could never stick to his decisions and keep his word, now seems quite different. I think the change started that morning when Drago woke him up brusquely, dunked his face into the sink filled with freezing water, grabbed him by the collar, dragged him out of the apartment, and drove him to a rehab on Long Island. Drago stayed with him for a few days, and I never asked either of them what exactly happened there. I have a suspicion that that man really helped my brother, and that the rough, forceful manner in which he did it worked when nothing else would have. Drago might have shattered something in me, but he did save my brother. A part of me . . . some part that doesn't feel betrayed and hurt, is grateful to him.

*****

A phone call wakes me up in the middle of the night. A man's voice introduces himself as Officer Lau and verifies that he is speaking to Danilo's sister.

"I am sorry to inform you that your brother was in a hit-and-run and is now at Parkside East Hospital."

At first I cannot quite comprehend the meaning of his words.

"Hit-and-run? I don't understand. My brother does not drive."

"I am sorry I was not clear. Your brother was the one who got hit."

At this I jump up from the bed and start pulling on clothes as I continue talking to Officer Lau.

"How is he? Is he OK?"

"He is in surgery now."

"I'll be right there!" I shout into the phone and rush out of the apartment.

There is a cab at the curb of 2 Gild Street, and a group of party goers are about to step in it. I push them all aside and get in and shut the door right in front of the nose of an angry yelling face.

"Parkside East Hospital," I tell the driver. "Please drive as fast as you can. Please."

"I got you," the cabbie replies. "We'll take the FDR and will be there in fifteen minutes."

*****

Running into the hospital through the main entrance, I tell the man at the desk, "Surgery. Trauma surgery."

"Thirteenth floor. Elevator to your left," he replies instantaneously and prints out a pass for me.

My hands are shaking, and I can't seem to scan the pass correctly to go through the turnstile. A security guard helps me.

On the thirteenth floor I see a police officer in a hallway.

"Officer Lau?"

"Yes."

"I am Danilo's sister. Is he still in surgery?"

"Yes. It will take a while."

"But how is he?"

"When I arrived at the scene, your brother was lying unconscious on Madison, close to the curb. He was taken to Parkside East right away and went straight into surgery."

"Do you know what happened?"

"A doorman from a nearby hotel said he saw your brother come out of the Brave Argonauts bar and start crossing Madison, when a car, driving at full speed hit him and drove off. I am sorry, that is all the information I have right now."

The words "unconscious" and "driving at full speed" drill into my mind and I lean against the wall and look at officer Lau and want to ask him more questions but feel my jaw and my lips trembling and know the words will not come out.

"Would you like some water?" he asks.

I shake my head.

"You'd better sit down. Please, the waiting room is right through here."

*****

I sit in the waiting room for several hours. A few times I get up and walk around a bit and pause by the window and stand there for a while, pressing my forehead to the glass. I then go back to my seat. There is nobody else in the room and I can choose any chair I want, but I always return to the same one I sat in first.

Time loses all its regular properties and starts playing tricks on me. There are moments during my waiting, when I feel that one minute lasts and lasts for hours, but then later on a whole hour seems to pass in a mere second.

There is already light outside when two doctors come in, and I stand up and they ask if I am Danilo's sister.

I look them straight in the eyes and right then, at that exact moment, my world cracks. It just fractures in two parts, the before and the after, with rugged sharp edges that can never be attached again. I look away, glance around the room, cannot find anything to fix my eyes on, then look down and see one of the doctors' shoelaces are untied.

I stare at the untied shoelaces the whole time the doctors are talking to me.

"We are very sorry. A team of doctors tried to save your brother's life, but his injuries were too severe and unfortunately we could not save him. He had a traumatic head injury, hemorrhaging in the brain, and a chest injury with both lungs collapsed. During the surgery he went into a cardio-pulmonary arrest, and we could not resuscitate him. We are very sorry."

"Was he ever conscious?"

"Your brother lost consciousness at the moment of the accident and never regained it."

I hope he didn't feel any pain. I hope he didn't lie there on the street suffering, the pain invading his body until he was nothing but the pain itself. Somehow my mind fixates on this one idea and doesn't let go. My brother, my Danny in pain, unbearable, all-consuming pain. No, no, that cannot be. He must have been spared that. He must have.

"You may see him a little later if you like," one of the doctors says. "A nurse will take you. Again, we are very sorry for your loss."

"Doctor," I call when they start walking away. They both stop and turn. I point to the untied shoelaces.

A nurse comes to take me to see Danilo. In the hallway I see officer Lau talking to the two doctors. The nurse leads me to the door of what she calls a "recovery room." I stare at her in disbelief.

"A recovery room? This must be a mistake."

"Oh, I'm sorry. That's just a term we use, just a name. I am sorry."

Before opening the door she hesitates for a moment.

"Miss, I must warn you . . . your brother . . . we were not allowed to remove any of the tubes, IV lines, catheters. They are all still in. I'm sorry, it's a protocol, for the medical examiner, you see. I am so sorry."

"Medical examiner?"

"Yes, the autopsy. The police have opened a criminal investigation. I'm sorry."

We walk into the room and she switches the lights on, but they clash with the light coming in from the window and she switches them off. There are several stretchers in the "recovery room" and my brother is lying on the one closest to the door. I look only at his face. I try to convince myself that it is my brother's face. That it is still him. That this mouth, this nose, these eyes are still my brother. Yet the longer I remain in this room staring at the face, the stronger I feel that it has nothing to do with my Danilo. It is just not him anymore. My brother is not here with me, not in this room, not anywhere. Danny. My Danny.

CHAPTER 24

I don't know what day of the week it is, nor what the date is. Night and day make no difference to me. The blinds are closed and the thick blackout curtains are drawn. I do not leave the apartment, except to go to the precinct once or twice, and am alone the rest of the time. Seeing or talking to people is absolutely unbearable to me now. My phone rings every once in a while, but I only answer Officer Lau's calls.

The pre-operation bloodwork revealed, and the postmortem confirmed, that Danilo had a high alcohol content in his blood. Cameras from the street showed he stepped off the curb on a red light. Officer Lau assures me they are, of course, doing everything to find the car and the driver. He also mentions the word "accident" several times.

My mind clutches onto that word. An accident. Damn it. I remember the way Sergey looked at my brother at Wolf Flannigan's. That steely, hard gaze. "There is nothing that I cannot do. There is nothing that I would not do," he said.

High alcohol content in Danny's blood—that alone is extremely suspicious to me. He had stopped drinking and was being really strong about it. Somehow they got to him. And that unidentified car, I don't think it was just a random car. No, I do not believe it was an accident, but I do not share my thoughts with Officer Lau nor do I mention Sergey's name at all. I do not see the point.

I have a strong suspicion that in Sergey's empire such an "accident" is a common occurrence and is carried out with great mastery, without leaving traces or lose ends. The police are looking for the car and the driver. Yeah. Something tells me they will not find them. The thread of the investigation will break and will never ever lead to Sergey. A drunk man crosses the street on red light and gets run over. The criminal investigation will be closed eventually.

*****

Danilo is buried on what is called a "family plot" at the cemetery. Grandpa bought it when our parents died. Now my whole family is laid to rest in that plot. I am the only one remaining above ground.

After the burial service, which I requested to be short and simple, I throw the first handful of dirt on his coffin. Some of Danilo's friends know the tradition and follow suit. Others don't seem to understand what is going on, exchange glances, but after some hesitation proceed, throwing dirt into the grave too. I don't stay to watch and start walking away. The bartender from Wolf Flannigan's wants to keep me company, but I shake my head silently and he falls back.

Near the cemetery exit, Sergey comes up to me, four of his men at his side, and expresses his deepest condolences and says he is here for me, for whatever I need. I listen to his little speech standing very still, my eyes fixed on a spot on his neck with a pressure point where it would be best to strike before getting him into a neck-break. I do not reply anything to his words, but I lock my gaze on his for a few intense moments, and I suppose he reads something very definite in my eyes that makes him avert his. He walks away and I stand alone for a long while, watching him disappear in the distance, his bodyguards following close behind.

No, the funeral is not the time or the place. I will get him, though. I do not know how or when. I do not have an exact plan. Back at 2 Gild Street, I go up to his apartment. One of his bodyguards opens the door and says Sergey Petrovich is not available. I ask to speak to Head Tattoo. I am made to wait out in the hallway until he appears. I tell him I want to see his boss. He shakes his head and avoids looking me in the eye. "I'm sorry," he mutters under his breath and wants to say something else, but

I do not listen and walk away. I try to gather my thoughts and plan my actions out, but I can't think clearly. At another time I go up to a rooftop party, half expecting not to be let in. To my surprise they do let me in, and I wander in my old jeans and a T-shirt among the elegantly dressed people, physically in their midst, but feeling as if I were on a different planet. I spend quite a while looking for him, but Sergey is not at the party.

How long will he be avoiding me? I guess I need to wait it out, till things settle down, and Sergey is convinced I do not blame him for my brother's death. But how long will I have to wait? I don't know if I have the necessary patience.

I suddenly remember that the interrupted Big Night Dark Fight is to resume a few days from now. I am scheduled to fight. Sergey will be there, for sure. I have not quite formulated in my head what I will do when I get access to him. He will be on high guard, surrounded by his men, not trusting me right now. But one thing I know with certainty—it is simply impossible that I will let Danilo's killer go unpunished. Danny dead and Sergey alive and well? No. It seems to me that something would be terribly wrong with this world if my brother's death were not avenged.

My thoughts, poisoned by the pain, hatred and rage keep running in a circle, a never-ending circle that drains me of all energy and leaves my mind exhausted and limp. To stop myself from thinking for a bit I take a sleeping pill and wash it down with alcohol. It gives me a few hours of deep, dreamless sleep, and then I wake up with a heavy head and the thoughts rush in again, continuing their circle.

I feel cold all the time. It started at the burial when I was watching the casket being lowered into the ground and thinking that the procedure, the ceremony, had nothing at all to do with me or with my brother. The object in the casket, the body with Danilo's limbs, his face, his hair, his skin . . . was not my Danny and was far removed from everything that my brother had been.

It was a hundred degrees outside and I suddenly started shivering from cold. And now, days later, I am still shivering and cannot get warm.

*****

I am lying in bed under a heavy blanket when I hear the intercom ring. I make an effort and get out of bed, and a doorman informs me that there is food delivery for me from Chauve-Souris Café. My first impulse is to tell him it is a mistake. I have not ordered any food. Then the name Chauve-Souris Café catches my attention. It is the place across the street from the dojo. Strange. I tell the doorman to send the delivery person up.

I open the door and the man standing before me removes his cap, which was pulled extremely low onto his face.

"Liam," I whisper. I don't know why I am whispering. "Liam."

He steps into the apartment, I close the door behind him, and we stand for a few minutes just looking at each other. I now see in his eyes the same tenderness and affection that I thought I noticed a couple times while living at the dojo but was sure I was mistaken. I know I am not mistaken now. He holds a large paper bag in his hands. He puts it on the floor, comes up close to me, and wraps his arms around me.

In his arms, I feel the steel ring that has been sitting around my head and pressing on it start to let go. All of a sudden I am crying. I have not cried at all since Danilo's death. Not at the hospital, not at the funeral, not alone in my apartment. I just have not been able to. And now, holding on to Liam, I cannot stop crying for a long time, the heaviness that has built up inside pouring out of me with these tears.

"Liam . . . my brother is dead, my Danny is dead," I pronounce in between the sobs. This is also the first time I have said it out loud.

"Sasha," he whispers into my ear and strokes my hair gently. "Baby. I am so sorry I was not with you. I am so sorry you had to go through that alone. But from now on I will always be with you. You will never have to be alone again."

He leads me to the armchair, sits me on his lap, and rocks me like a baby, all the while stroking my hair and whispering to me. After some time I stop crying but still continue sitting on his lap, my cheek pressed against the wet spot on his shirt. I start having hiccups and Liam gets me a glass of water, which I drink in small sips until the hiccups go away. We then move to the couch, and I curl up against him, and he places his arm around me, holding me tight. He tells me that he only learned about Danilo's death earlier today and immediately tried to see me, but the doormen would not let him up, and so he had to resort to this masquerade of food delivery.

Yep, I've always suspected that the doormen at 2 Gild Street are all on Sergey's payroll, and they must have received strict orders from him concerning Liam. For a moment I hesitate whether to tell Liam all of my thoughts about Sergey and Danilo's death and my plan of actions, but I decide against it. I don't want to get him involved. This is something I will have to do on my own.

I suddenly feel Liam's body tense up and see him turn his head and squint his eyes looking toward the other end of the room. With a brusque motion he gets up from the couch, walks across and stops by the bar counter that separates the kitchen from the living room. There, in plain view are various bottles and small plastic bags with pills. I am actually surprised he has not noticed them before. Now he picks several up, examines them, and then turns toward me. There is anger mixed with fear in his face.

"You are done with all this shit. You hear me?"

"Liam," I start saying.

"No!" he interrupts me. "This shit is over."

He collects all the bottles and plastic bags from the counter, walks with them to the bathroom, and after a while I can hear the toilet flush. He comes back and sits on the coffee table facing me.

"Ok, listen to me carefully." he says. "You cannot stay here. If Sensei does not accept you as an uchi-deshi again, I will quit my uchi-deshi position and we will find a place to live together."

I shake my head and tell him that he must not give up being uchi-deshi and move out of the dojo. He still has many years of training until Sensei allows him to open his own dojo.

"You cannot give up on your dream because of me. I won't let you."

"Well, it *has* always been my dream, but dreams can change, can't they? My dream is to be with you."

He sits back on the couch next to me. I put my head on his shoulder and he kisses my hair and holds me tight against him. We sit like this for some time without saying anything.

"You're hungry, aren't you?" Liam says when my stomach makes a rumbling noise. "Let's eat. I really brought some stuff from the Chauve-Souris. Here, take a look." He gets the bag he left by the door and unpacks several sandwiches, two salads, and several pieces of rugelach for dessert. "Fuck. I forgot to get anything to drink."

I tell him there is plenty to drink here and he can open a bottle of wine if he likes. He opens a bottle of Chablis and fills two glasses.

"You know," I say and put my sandwich aside. "Let's drink to my brother."

"Yes. To Danilo, may he rest in peace." Liam wants to touch his glass to mine, but I move my hand away quickly.

"Oh no, according to the Russian tradition, you don't touch glasses when drinking to those passed away."

"I am sorry, Sasha. I did not know. But how come you are so Russian all of a sudden?"

"I am not really. Just today, I guess."

After the meal I start feeling sleepy.

"Let's get you to bed," Liam says when he notices me yawn.

"I won't be able to fall asleep though. Not without a sleeping pill, and there are no more left. You've flushed them down the toilet along with the other ones."

"You don't need any stupid sleeping pills. Come on, you'll see, you'll fall asleep just fine."

I brush my teeth, undress, and get under the blanket in my panties and a tank top. In the meanwhile Liam pulls aside the heavy curtains and opens the blinds and one of the windows saying a bit of fresh air will do me good. He then sits on the side of the bed and tells me to close my eyes and starts stroking my hair. Later on I ask him to lie down next to me. He takes off his jeans and shirt and lies down on his back and I put my head on his chest. It is so nice and cozy lying like this, but all off a sudden I feel the tears come up again and cannot stop them. Liam holds me tight and whispers to me and strokes my hair until I calm down. I eventually doze off, but then wake up with a start and he whispers to me again. Several times throughout the night I wake up, and Liam isn't sleeping, just lying here watching over me. He strokes my hair and my arms gently and comfortingly, and his touch makes me feel safe and protected. I relax and fall asleep.

CHAPTER 25

When I wake up again it's still dark outside. I have a strange feeling that this night has stretched beyond its allotted timeframe. I don't want to sleep anymore. I get up to go to the bathroom and on my way back pick up the unfinished bottle of wine and sit on the side of the bed drinking straight from the bottle. I shiver.

"Are you cold?" Liam asks

"I'm always cold these days."

He motions for me to get back in bed. I lie down and he pulls me in very close to him and holds me in his arms. We stay like this for some time. It feels different from before though. Now, lying together, every muscle, every nerve in our bodies seem to be tensed to the extreme, and eventually I am the one who initiates it. I run my fingers through his chest hair and touch his shoulder with my lips. I feel him tremble, yet he does not do anything just yet. He waits.

He is very hard already but still remains perfectly motionless, as if he were afraid to scare me away. I press my fingers into his arm muscles, move my lips across his two-day stubble, and find his mouth. I do not kiss him, just touch my lips to his. At this a big shiver runs across his body and he opens his mouth and starts kissing me but suddenly pauses.

"Baby," he whispers. "You know how I feel about you. I always have." He waits for a few seconds, perhaps expecting an answer, and then kisses me again, first gently and softly as if my mouth were some precious fragile object, then with an increasing and almost uncontrollable intensity. He lays me on my back and kisses my neck, my shoulders. He pushes aside the fabric of my tank top and kisses my breasts for a long time. I want him inside me now, but he does not seem to want to rush. He passes his hands all over my body, removing first my top and then slowly pulls down my panties, all the while kissing my stomach, hips, my thighs. He rolls me over and kisses my back, my ass, my legs. Then I feel him move away.

I don't know what's going on and I turn around and see him kneeling down in *seiza* position at the bottom of the bed, just looking at me. I sit up and move in close and touch his face, his shoulders, his arms. I kiss him hard on the mouth and then lie back down pulling him on top of me. He pushes inside me with a motion that is a bit awkward and too brusque, and I wince and let out a small cry. He stays still for a few moments to make sure I am all right and then moves slowly for a while. At one point I think I hear him say something, but I can't make out the words. He repeats and I realize he is asking me to open my eyes. I open them and we are peering into each other's eyes with such strange intensity as if we were trying to find answers to all questions that have ever existed in the world.

His motions become stronger and I close my eyes again, stretch my arms above my head, and clutch the sheet and then the edge of the bed. When I feel the onset of the orgasm approaching, I grab Liam's shoulders and hold onto them as hard as I can and wrap my legs around his hips, tensing up my pelvic muscles to the utmost.

After I come, for a few minutes I am lying motionless, my body limp and as if completely weightless. I can feel Liam kissing my face and my mouth but do not have the energy to kiss him back. When I more or less recover and become responsive again, he keeps going, picking up the rhythm, lifting himself up on his arms to be able to move with more force. He pulls out and I want to see him come and watch his face when he does. I do not get to see anything, because he falls on top of me and presses himself tight against my belly, and I can feel his contractions as he comes.

I hold my arms around him with such strength, as if I never want to let him go, and suddenly I start crying again. I am crying silently, tears just pouring out of my eyes. I have no idea why I am crying, and I am glad Liam is too exhausted right now to notice anything. We stay glued together for a long while, his head on my chest, the full weight of his strong muscular body on me. It is strange how when the sex is over, you suddenly realize that your lover's body is almost crushing you, yet during the sex you do not seem to mind at all and actually enjoy it. I put my hands on Liam's head and press it harder to my chest and all the while just can't stop crying.

By the time we separate our bodies, my tears have dried up.

Liam gets up and finds a box of tissues and cleans himself standing near the bed looking at me. I ask for some tissues too, but instead of giving them to me he leans down and cleans me himself, gently and thoroughly. He then kisses my lips, the tip of my nose, my eyes, and my hair.

*****

"I love your face, it's so beautiful," Liam whispers as he traces its contours with his fingers. We are lying down facing each other. He touches a small scar right under my lower lip and kisses it, then examines another barely visible one near my right eyebrow, and kisses it too. I shiver inwardly, remembering the razor girl and what happened or almost happened the last time I stepped into the cage. Well, I think, I'm definitely lucky I managed to go through the Dark Fights without acquiring any bigger scars on my face. I've seen fighters in the cage with pretty nasty looking scars and their noses and ears permanently misshapen. Yeah, I definitely appreciate the fact that my face is intact.

"What about my body?" I ask.

"Let's see." He smiles and pulls away the covers.

He then puts on a very serious look and proceeds to inspect my body intently. He furrows his forehead and knits his eyebrows but there are visible glints of delight in his eyes. When he encounters a few scars, his expression changes to genuine sadness. Well, it could have been much worse. Fortunately, most of the cuts and breaks healed cleanly without leaving a visible trace, if you don't count slightly misshapen toes and a couple of odd-looking knuckles on my fingers. I suppose on the outside my body is in a good enough shape, and the problems with my knee, my elbows, my shoulder, and a few other old injuries are scarcely noticeable when I am lying naked in bed.

Liam continues his detailed inspection for a while, but the game stops abruptly when he gets to the scar on my side. He does not say anything but just locks his eyes on mine and shakes his head. This scar is not from a Dark Fight. It is from the *tanto* cut during my second-degree black belt examination.

"Liam," I say. "I know it was that crazy Martine who switched the wooden *tanto* for a real one. And she was the one who threw me down the stairs. I can't believe I could ever think it was you. I am sorry."

"I'm sorry I failed to protect you and . . . well"—he sighs and lies down on his back and stares at the ceiling—"I gave you a hard time at the dojo myself."

"Well, yeah. Why did you?"

"Don't know, baby. I'm not good at handling feelings because . . . well, I never told this to anyone, not sure it's a good idea to tell you."

"Tell me."

"It was years ago . . ." He pauses and glances at me.

He seems very nervous and I can tell this is really difficult for him, so I stroke his arm and take his hand and hold it the whole time he is talking.

"I was already training a lot but wasn't an uchi-deshi yet. I'd just moved to the city and I met this girl. It was the first time I was really crazy about anyone. I was sure she felt the same way about me too."

"She liked to go clubbing and stuff. I didn't care for that, but I went too, for her. One time we were supposed to meet in a club, but I couldn't find her there. Someone told me she was in one of the back rooms. So I went in and saw her with a guy. He had her pinned under him on a couch. I went mad, absolutely mad, enraged. I thought he was raping her. I attacked him and beat the shit out of him. I would have killed him. I don't remember how or who pulled me away. I was just blind with rage.

Turned out he was not raping her at all. I got it all wrong. She admitted she was fucking other guys behind my back."

He is silent for a few long moments.

"I was charged with assault, which in New York is pretty serious," he then says. "With the extenuating circumstances though, I was given a lenient sentence and only served a year of actual time, and when I came out Sensei took me in. My first two years as an uchi-deshi I didn't set foot outside the dojo, just didn't want to see or deal with the fucked-up world outside. I also promised myself never to fall for another woman ever again, and I was doing all right, till I met you. After that one night we had, you changed your mind, and I was stupid and angry, and very jealous and tried to convince myself that I hated you. I would look at you and realize just how much I wanted to hold you and kiss you. And then I would get even angrier with myself, for not being able to stick to my promise. And I took it out on you."

Liam breathes deeply and looks at me. "Do you think I'm totally messed up?"

I don't answer but move my face close to his and kiss him on the lips with all the tenderness I feel inside. I put my head on his chest and he wraps his arms around me, and we stay like this for a long while.

"You know, I was not quite finished with the full-body examination," Liam then says. Without even looking at him I can hear the smile in his voice. He goes back to inspecting me, pretending to look for scars. He uses his mouth and tongue, focusing on my breasts, not relinquishing my nipples for a long time, and then moving further on. After a while he kisses me on the lips and I kiss him back, but this time the tenderness is replaced by something much stronger and more urgent. I kiss him hard and deep and bite his lower lip as I feel him go inside me.

*****

Afterward we fall asleep and when we wake up it is almost noon. Liam is very hungry and wants us to get dressed and go out and have a big break-fast or lunch. I am not sure I want to go, but I don't feel like disappointing him. He says we'll ride down together and walk straight past the doorman. He doesn't care if our being together is reported to Sergey. But I have other thoughts on the matter. I don't want to set Sergey off and have him send his men to deal with Liam. So I convince him to pull his cap low over his face again and go out first. I meet him some ten minutes later around the corner. As we walk on the street Liam holds my hand. It feels strange and unusual, but I do not take my hand away. We go to a nearby diner. It is supposed to be one of the oldest and most famous diners in Manhattan, and maybe for this reason it is pretty packed and we have to wait a while before we can get a booth. I order a tuna melt and Liam has a turkey club and we drink black coffee with our meal.

"So, I think we'll go to Fulton Station now." Liam says after we are done eating. "We'll take a train there and go straight to the dojo and talk to Sensei. Sounds good?"

I don't answer for a long while, drinking my coffee, looking into the cup. "Babe?"

"You go to the dojo. I cannot come with you."

"What are you talking about? I thought we decided everything last night."

"I am sorry."

"Baby, what's going on?"

"I cannot return to the dojo. I have things to take care of."

"What things?"

I get up from the couch on my side of the booth and go over to Liam's. I put my arms around him and kiss him on the mouth.

"I have to go now," I say then. "Please, don't follow me. Goodbye."

Walking out of the diner and passing by the window I see him looking at me. I turn away and hasten my step, blinking in rapid succession so as not to cry. I cannot cry anymore. I cried enough last night and it should stay in that night. All of it should stay in that night. I need to push down and block away whatever emotions and feelings Liam has brought out in me and get back to my pain, anger, and cold hatred.

CHAPTER 26

I am alone in my apartment at 2 Gild Street. Anxious and restless, I am pacing the room. Waiting. Waiting.

I took a shower hours ago but am still wearing the towel. As the nerves get the better of me, I tear the towel off and fling it on the floor. I catch my reflection in the floor-length mirror. In the semidarkness of the room, I can't see the details, just the overall silhouette of a very fit young woman with a vague oval of the face, big eyes exaggerated by the play of shadows, and long hair, which they have not allowed her to cut short lest the image of the "Samurai Princess" be ruined. Suddenly it occurs to me that I don't recognize this person at all and throw the towel over the mirror so as not to see her.

I resume walking around the apartment, then press my face to a window, and look at the lights of the city. Waiting. Waiting. It's getting close to midnight. I braid my hair and put on my shorts and a sports bra with the securely inserted breast guards.

Finally the doorbell rings and Head Tattoo comes in.

"Ready?" he asks. "Put on a hoodie or something. Does not matter what. We are not going far."

We take the freight elevator down to the basement and walk along a wide hallway with a low ceiling. I am not sure if we are still under 2 Gild Street or have crossed into another building. As we walk, Head Tattoo takes a small plastic bag with pills out of his pocket and offers it to me. I do not take it. He gives me a quick, curious look but does not say anything. We reach a steel door and Head Tattoo talks into his lapel mic. An unknown gentleman opens the door and lets us in. Baldy and Buzz Cut are not around. I guess the protocol has been changed. Well, at least Head Tattoo is still here.

It is the same space where my first Dark Fight was held. There is that cage in the middle of the chamber, elevated a few feet above the floor, and the same elegantly dressed mass of people walking and sitting around in low, oversized couches, eating, drinking, talking, and not paying much attention to the cage just yet.

As soon as the "Samurai Princess" is announced, most of the guests leave their comfortable seats and gather around the cage. The crowd grows denser with each second. The fight hasn't even started yet, and they are already yelling "Samurai Princess" and cheering, and the overall level of excitement is the highest I have ever seen cage-side before a bout. I guess the audience is pumped up by what they saw in the cage not so long ago during the interrupted Big Night and anticipates a continuation of that brutal spectacle.

I expect the Razor Girl to step into the cage again and am greatly surprised when I realize she is not the one I am fighting tonight. My opponent turns out to be that same Formidable Freya whom I fought in my very first Dark Fight event. I remember her well. She has excellent technique combined with great strength and speed.

After the announcer calls "Fight!" Formidable Freya and I walk around the cage for a few seconds measuring each other up, just like we did the first time we met. Tonight, however, I do not wait for her to attack first. I charge in with a series of strikes and then move in past her defense and throw her down with an *uchi-mata*—an inner thigh throw, and on the ground go for the *kimura* lock. She gets out of the *kimura* before I can fully apply it, and after a while we are up again. Formidable Freya attempts a throw, we are locked in a tight struggle for a few moments, and it seems she might indeed throw me down, but I manage to cartwheel out of it.

Without the drugs that I have gotten so used to, I don't know how long I can sustain my energy level, force, and speed in this fight. I also get distracted searching the crowd for the bearded face. One of Freya's powerful strikes connects with my head. I feel disoriented and she throws me down, pounds me with fist and elbow strikes, and then gets me in an arm triangle choke.

My head turned at an awkward angle, I suddenly see Sergey cage-side. At that moment something goes off inside me, and the anger and desire for revenge rise and fill everything in me and work almost like the drugs. With the rapid surge of the brutal energy, I get out of Freya's arm triangle, and we fight on the ground.

I lock my eyes on Sergey and my fury reaches its maximum. It is directed at the bearded Russian, but I am taking it out on my fighting opponent. I get her in a rear-naked choke, almost hallucinating that it is Sergey's neck that I have between my arms. My opponent is trying to escape, but I apply all the force I have in me. The audience absolutely loves it and goes wild cheering me on.

Freya does not tap out. The blood flow to her brain through the carotid arteries is restricted and within a few seconds she passes out, her limbs going limp. I still do not release the choke, and the referee does not stop me. A few more seconds and I will have choked her to death, and yet I cannot seem to let go.

*****

"No! Don't! Sasha, stop!" A voice shouts so loud that it is heard above the roar of the crowd.

It is Liam's voice, and hearing it wakes me up from my trancelike state and brings me to my senses.

I release the choke, hoping it is not too late. What if it *is* too late? No, no, it simply cannot be. I get on my knees beside Freya and try to feel the pulse on her neck. I then put her head on my lap and stay in this position for a while.

Damn it. What have I done? What am I? A martial artist or a killer? It becomes clear to me that what I've been doing in this cage tonight and what I did on the previous occasions is not martial arts anymore.

After a while Freya comes to. I feel such an enormous relief and even joy as if it were a person close to me who has been brought back to life. It is so strange but right now I cannot help but view Formidable Freya, this unknown woman with whom only a few minutes ago I was locked in a brutal fight, as somebody close and dear to me.

Still on my knees, I bow to her.

This is something I have never done in the cage before. No one ever does this in the cage. With a traditional martial arts bow I acknowledge her, not as a fighting opponent, not as my enemy, but as a fellow martial artist.

*****

The audience does not understand what is going on and grows unusually quiet. I walk to the cage door and Liam helps me get out. The crowd starts booing, first tentatively, and then louder and louder, until everyone in this elegantly dressed beautiful mass of people is shouting and booing and trying to block our way. Liam lets go of my hand, struggling to clear a path for us.

Momentarily I am separated from him, and the space between us fills with people. Someone grabs me aggressively by the forearm and in an instinctive reaction I do a z-lock. I apply too much sudden force and the person's wrist breaks.

"Get back into the cage!" Sergey shouts at me, grimacing in pain and holding his injured wrist with his good hand. "Get back into the cage right now and finish the damn fight."

"Fuck off, Sergey-fucking-Petrovich. I'm done with the Dark Fights."

"That is not for you to decide. You belong to me and I will not let you quit!"

"Is that why Danilo had to die?" I ask a question for which no answer is needed at the same time as I strike Sergey on the side of his neck.

I then get his neck in the bend of my arm, torqueing his head and pressing it tight against my body. It will take me a split second to break his neck now. I just need to tighten my grip a bit and apply some pressure. That is all. Very easy. The situation is perfect. There is pretty much chaos in the room now. His bodyguards are nowhere to be seen. In a mere moment I could finish Sergey off and no one would even notice what happened.

Damn it. I do, I really do want to take revenge for my brother's death, but I just cannot seem to be able to bring myself to kill. No, I will not be a killer.

I release my grip.

He can just walk away now. But no, the idiot makes the same mistake he made a while back at the dojo, when he tried to punch me and I really felt like breaking his elbow but controlled myself. Beside himself with rage, he actually tries to punch me again. I block and get him in a standing *ude-garami*, immobilizing his shoulder and his elbow. "*Svolochi*, fucking bastards, you and that *sukin syn* Danilo," he shouts out in Russian and in English, cursing me and my brother. As soon as his mouth pronounces my brother's name I make the final move. Yes, I might have decided to spare his life, but at least he will not get out of this unscathed. He is completely trapped in the lock, and a small motion is all it takes for me—Sergey shrieks out in pain, as the bones in his arm break.

I push him away from me, and the crowd absorbs him.

*****

I should start moving immediately, try to get out of here, but somehow my feet refuse to take a step. I remain motionless, as if glued to one spot. I have an unsettling sensation of standing all alone, disoriented and lost in the midst of this multitude of people, their angry gestures, and shouts.

Then, out of all this chaos Liam's eyes appear and his gaze holds mine and does not let go. The next moment he is by my side again. Head Tattoo appears as well. A quick thought crosses my mind that perhaps he has been around this whole time and deliberately chosen not to help his boss.

I want to make a dash for the same door Head Tattoo and I came in through earlier tonight, but he now takes us to a different exit, on the opposite side of the chamber. The three of us then hurry along the hallway until we reach a metal door, which Head Tattoo unlocks. Behind it there is the narrow cement-floored hallway that I have already seen before.

"You know where it leads," he says to me.

I nod.

"Later." He turns around.

"Thank you," I call after him.

He shows a thumbs up without looking back.

Liam and I walk along the narrow hallway till we get to a staircase. We go up and there is another door, and it is locked. Liam starts banging on it. I bang too and shout, "Hey, open up, open up!" I doubt anybody will hear us though. Liam tries to break the door down with his shoulder but, standing on the staircase, he can't get a solid stance or enough leverage to do it. He goes down a couple steps looking for a possible position for a high kick.

All of a sudden the door opens and the Wolf Flannigan's bartender is staring at us. He comprehends the situation right away and lets us into the pub's back room.

"You guys all right? Want a drink or something?" he asks.

"Thank you. Another time," I say, and he and I exchange quick meaningful nods.

*****

Coming out of the pub I feel very cold. It is warm and humid outside and yet I am shaking all over. Liam puts his arms around me and holds me tight. He wants to get a cab, but I prefer to walk for a bit to clear my head and calm down. I wouldn't even know where I would want the cabbie to drive.

Where do I go from here?

We walk toward South Street Seaport, go out onto the Pier, and lie down together in a plastic chaise longue looking out to the dark water. I press in closer to Liam and put my head on his chest.

"How did you find the location of the fight and how did you get in?" I ask him.

"Your tattooed friend."

"Ah."

After that we are both quiet for a long while. I realize how tired I am, absolutely exhausted, and I don't believe I would ever have enough strength to get up from this chaise. I have a strange feeling that I am to stay at this Pier forever, that I have reached a dead end.

"Baby, listen," Liam says and his words break the silence that has already started to seem like an eternity to me. "I have a message from Sensei for you. He says you can come back. Will you do it?"

I think this over. Liam does not rush me. I consider my answer and all its implications with great care. Once I've made up my mind I know immediately that it is the only right decision for me.

"Yes. I want to come back to the dojo and be an uchi-deshi again. Yes."

He does not say anything and just kisses me on the mouth and then on the tip of my nose. Suddenly the edge of this Pier does not seem like the end of the road for me anymore. I realize I am smiling. It feels strange. My facial muscles must have grown unaccustomed to this expression. I believe this is the first time I've smiled in a long while.

*****

It is almost six in the morning and I get up after a few hours of sleep. I must hurry as it is time to open the dojo for the first class of the day. My immediate thought is that I have nothing to wear for training.

There is a knock on the door, and right away I have a chilling sensation in my stomach. In the past, a knock on this door often brought bad news or trouble. I open it, bracing myself for whatever might come. There is nobody outside, but on the doorknob I see a hanger with a *gi* and a black belt. Liam. I smile as I put on the traditional martial arts uniform—the pants and the jacket.

I pick up the black belt and hold it in my hands for a few long moments. No, I can't bring myself to wear it. It wouldn't be right. I feel with every ounce of by being that it just won't be the proper thing to do. I fold the black belt carefully and put it down.

I search in the closet, and at the back of the bottom shelf I find my old white belt, which I left behind when moving out of the dojo. The belt is not exactly white anymore, because I had worn it for so many years and never washed it. Martial artists are not supposed to wash their white belts—according to an ancient tradition, with time and hard training your white belt gets darker and darker until it turns black. That's what the black belts' color symbolizes. And so I pick up my old "white" belt and tie it around my hips.

I go downstairs and, when Sensei comes down, I bow and stand quiet before him. I am very nervous and not really sure what to expect. I disobeyed Sensei, betrayed his trust, and disgraced myself as a martial artist. Even though my initial motives were pure and honorable and all I wanted was to save my brother, along the way I forgot who and what I was and went against everything Sensei'd taught me. Can he really take me back to be his disciple again?

Sensei looks me over, resting his eyes on the white belt for a moment. He does not comment on it. He understands perfectly well that I have decided to remove my black belt as a sign of repentance and start my training from the beginning.

"You are here," he says, his face very serious, almost severe, the corners of his mouth drawn down, "but are you truly here? Are your heart and mind open to the ways of the true Martial Arts or do the Dark Fights still have a hold on you?"

"I am here, Sensei, truly and completely."

"We'll see." He moves his head slightly and I cannot tell if it's a nod or a sign of doubt.

"Well, get back on the mat then," Sensei orders, his expression still very stern, but this time I am pretty sure I notice the corners of his mouth go up in a barely perceptible smile.

"Yes, Sensei," I reply and bow.

Stepping onto the mat, my first impulse is to go to the front row, where, according to the dojo tradition, black belts sit in *seiza* at the beginning of the class. I realize my mistake however and hurry to one of the last rows and take my position among fellow white belts.

As the practice begins and Sensei demonstrates the first technique, all the anxiety and uneasiness leave me. Sensei's focused and almost stern expression—at times lit up by a quick smile—and the large number of martial artists so eager to receive a word or gesture of instruction from him, the old mats, the squeaky narrow stairs, the faded red couch upstairs, Amadeus the Homeless Guy just outside—every detail fits into an intricate mosaic that I have the privilege to call my home again.

Now is the time to choose our training partners. Across the mat Liam's dark eyes find mine. I bow to him and he returns the bow. We train together, keeping up a fast pace, and barely ten minutes in we are covered in sweat. Toward the end of the class our gis are soaked through and like years ago, when I'd just started at the dojo and we trained together to exhaustion, everything inside me feels at peace with everything else.

After the final technique we bow to each other.

ACKNOWLEDGMENTS

Enormous THANK-YOUS to—

Richard Curtis, who is simply the best and coolest agent and "corner-man" a writer could wish for.

Yamada Sensei, to whom I bow in gratitude, respect, and admiration.

Mike Abrams, whose instruction and friendship mean the world to me.

Greg Gutman, whose dojo I walked into one day not believing that miracles could still happen.

My amazing instructors, training partners, and friends.

The wonderful, dedicated, and cool people at Blackstone Publishing.

M, who proudly holds the title of "the most horrible man in the world" :)) and who once told me to "sit my butt down and just write." It worked . . .

The City of New York, my love for whom permeates every page of this book and who knows how to love back with a tough, gloomy, moody yet enchanting and captivating kind of love.